Captain Cooked

Hawaiian Mystery of Romance, Revenge...
and Recipes

T0164227

Special 10th Anniversary Edition

S.P. Grogan

Captain Cooked

Hawaiian Mystery of Romance, Revenge...
and Recipes

Addison & Highsmith

Addison & Highsmith Publishers
Las Vegas ◊ Chicago ◊ Palm Beach

Published in the United States of America by
Histria Books, a division of Histria LLC
7181 N. Hualapai Way
Las Vegas, NV 89166 USA
HistriaBooks.com

Addison & Highsmith is an imprint of Histria Books. Titles published under the imprints of Histria Books are distributed worldwide exclusively by the Casemate Group.

Library of Congress Control Number: 2020945311

ISBN 978-1-59211-065-0 (hardcover)
ISBN 978-1-59211-112-1 (softbound)

Contents

He could not believe his good fortune, or so he thought. The hunger he carried with him since morning gurgled and cried out for all that was spread before him on the table. With a handful scoop he popped a half dozen fresh shrimp, the cold taste soothing his mouth. He gathered up abalone sashimi and plopped it on top of a crisp won ton for his personal sushi. Woozy, he shook his head, as he swallowed, still famished. Chicken wings marinated in soy and sherry sauces were sucked in slurps, with the greasy bones thrown to the ground. Tasting through every dish on the table, he grabbed with both hands, alternating, stuffing his face. His head burned with the temperature he carried all week. Food was medicine. The more consumed, he believed, the quicker he would heal. Then, he saw the koa calabash bowl, the food filled within; this special treat must be for him. Memories of childhood flooded his mind and brought a smile to his face. He sensed a presence. Around the table, he imagined his parents, brothers and sisters, the warmth of family. His mother handed him the bowl, and said, "Eat and enjoy, my son, this is special for you. Aloha wau ia 'oe, e ka'u kei-ki." Someone, a stranger, shouted, "Hey, if you don't mind…"

He heard no more. Death had come to the buffet.

Dedicated to: my father, Doyle T. Grogan (1912-2010)
Stationed in Hawai'i during World War II; he always
remembered the islands with fond memories.
He still is missed.

Our thanks to the many people of Hawai'i who made every visit enjoyable
and the hospitality memorable.
Mahalo nui loa.

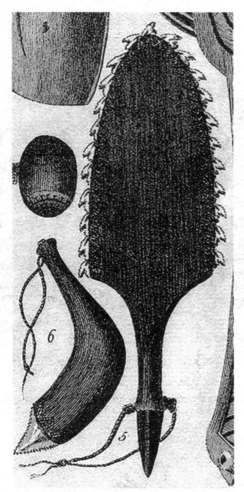

#5 Lei-'O-Manō, shark teeth war club
[page from the first folio issue– 1784—for the
Official Account of the Third Voyage of Captain Cook
– in the author's collection]

Probably the only place on Earth where graffiti is accepted as sacred. . .

Chapter 1
Paradise Waypoint

A chalkboard weather report posted at the entry gate announced the atmospheric conditions on my arrival: "78° feels 85° – 65% humidity— scattered clouds—Fair is foul, foul is fair." Considering what I am here to do, I would have said: 'Fare is fowl, the fowl is fair.'

I hover at the carousel at the Kona International Airport on the Big Island of Hawai'i. My luggage and camera equipment from my L.A. flight should momentarily come spitting out from behind hidden doors. At the same time my father's plane from Chicago is arriving, exact to the schedule we planned. RA Flight 19165. Father and daughter to be teamed up for a business adventure, a first.

I adjust to the constant breeze of Pacific heat, my blouse soaked in rivulet perspiration beads. Around me, a sea of tourists ebb and flow gathering up arriving luggage. A people watcher by nature, like my father, but where he might have seen nuances in facial expressions, or interpret hand gestures as more sinister to defining character, I offer silent snickers at ill-shaped bodies and sloppy fashion choices.

It is here, at this moment within the crowd, I make a serious error in my harmless voyeur exercise, accepting the general view and ignoring understated detail. Looking back on my later experiences with the hotel chauffer and the Beautiful People, damn, how extraordinarily lame I acted on both counts, totally off base, out of whack, to the timeless adage, revised in this case, you cannot judge a cookbook by its cover.

Take the Beautiful People, for example. My eyes are drawn to a boisterous group at the luggage carousel across from mine. They grab at arriving suitcases. Youthful, in my age range. A party in motion, laughing, teasing. Onto a baggage cart, they inventory golf clubs, tennis rackets, and scuba gear. Even tech com their vacation with two of them fiddling with what look like miniature walkie-talkies. My eyes strain to read their casual attire T-shirts to define their bumper sticker mind-set. One shirt reads, "San Quentin Law Library." Another T-shirt marquee: 'Careful, or you'll end up in my novel'. One shirt phrasing, I assumed, to quantify his intelligence, speaks in some numeric gibberish: "Waypoint to Fun is N 36°04.976" and more numbers I couldn't see. Whatever that means? And then an "Or..." with an arrow pointing towards his belt line and suggestively, below. I get that part.

There, in their midst stands their leader, definitely head stallion issuing commands and hand signals, directing the melee, seeking order from the jocular chaos. In that rarity of character he seems to lead by personality, good-natured in his cajoling. His face unshaven fuzz topped by a mop of hair hardly blowing in this stovetop wind; nor do I see sweat to his brow. For several long seconds, our eyes bounce together before his buddies drag him back to his responsibilities.

The leader's T-shirt, on a washboard stomach, I presumed, read: "Honest Rogue for Hire" and then squinted to see below that: "Solves Impossible Dreams." As if.

Unaware of my presence, of my existence, I snapped quick, candid photos of them. These people were in that mirthful world I somehow kept missing. The women were drop-dead gorgeous, blemish free, the men like their leader, swarthy handsome. The women wouldn't be lacking for male attention, the ratio being three perfect women to seven men. One of the women, a blonde of course, resembled a gym-sculpted, tanned, beach volleyball star. Her healthy mountainous chest might draw men, like bees to flowers, but the back of her shirt qualified who might stay and gather nectar. It read: "Ready for Moi? XXX Sports is my Foreplay." The salty taste in my mouth was the drool of envy.

A young man approached me, invaded my space. Definitely a local. Black shorn hair, thick to his neck, but looking salon cut. Asian-Polynesian features, spiffed out in his ironed aloha shirt, sporting a grin, and bearing the gold nametag of Michael K. I assumed he is the official hotel greeter from the Ho'oilina Kai Grand Hotel Resort. Around my neck he draped the customary welcoming lei of purple-white orchids. Both cheeks, received not pecks, but kisses beyond the customary norm, warm and lingering, and he looked deep into my eyes but said curtly, "From your Father. I'll help with your luggage."

Talk about let down. Hardly the greeting one expects to launch this week-long island sojourn, suggestive by tourist brochures of succulent food and expectant starry, starry nights looking down on wave caressed sands. Perhaps, for me, who knows, does one dare say, "romance?" These days my famished love life is served with an empty plate of desire, garnished with a single crumb of hope. This trip to Hawai'i wouldn't it be nice to be a member of that Beautiful People crowd, not relegated to a driver of the hotel shuttle?

I spot my father, Jeffrey Dayne, foodie TV star. Of course, he is with a woman, better defined as an autograph seeker, a fan, almost always a woman. She is probably Chatty Kathying on about Jeffrey's second and latest cooking travel book, somewhere listed and rising on the New York Times and Amazon bestseller lists. *Insatiable: Further States of Epicurean Delights*. She probably squirmed a seat next to his on the plane ride over. The public, all the women fans, know he is a recent widower. Vulnerable. I rudely intrude between them with exaggerated hugs for my father, and steer him away. Not this trip, honey. Or anytime soon.

I should feel sorry for Michael K., our van driver and hotel escort. I had given him my claim stubs for the luggage. Showing his strength, which seems muscular under his hotel uniform shirt, he is grunting along a push cart loaded with my father's luggage and all my cased and boxed paraphernalia, the cameras and production equipment for the television show we are going to tape on island.

This is Jeffrey Dayne's thirty minute, popular cooking program on the Food Television Channel, "Insatiable Delights." As we head out of the airport in the Ho'oilina Kai van, Michael K. asked if we were doing a documentary film of the island.

"A television show," I replied, enjoying an air of smugness. Why not, we were V.I.P. Like usual, my father corrected, or would one say, he enhanced my conversation.

To our driver, Jeffrey added, "A television program about the best delights in Hawaiian food."

"Oh, you are those Daynes, for the Lū'au Challenge." From the backseat, we both nodded. With restraint, I held back my snooty witty retort: Were there any other great Daynes?

I stared out the window considering the landscape where we would spend the next week. Vehicles went bumper-to-bumper heading into the town of Kailua-Kona. In paradise the march of civilization seemed to slow crawl. At least the van is going the opposite direction. The highway cut through black lava fields, moonlike desolate except for the roadside messages laid out in white coral rock. Probably the only place on earth where graffiti is accepted as near sacred, a taboo if messed with. White rocks, long dead coral, show designs of everything from hearts to sharks, and a variety of names, J ♥ Chachi types, a reality check from those since departed from too-short vacations. *Ikaika wuz here* — *IMUA KS!* — *Griswolds Rock*. Even sad highway memorials: *RIP Cobra*. My Dad is scanning today's local paper, reading an article about the upcoming lūʻau competition at which he will be a celebrity food judge. I glance at the newspaper's back side, seeing headlines suggesting less pristine paradise and more urban intrusions: increased traffic accidents call for a highway lane expansion; renewing permits filed for inter-island ferries, and, local controversy, at a place called Black Sand Beach Estates, I read where the cabana expansion to the bluff home owned by a South American millionaire will disturb the nesting grounds of the ne-ne, the endangered Hawaiian goose and state bird, thereby frothing up anger among the enviro bird huggers. Who cares? I am going to ignore everyone else's problems. Just keep crowds away from any beach I occupy, whether white, black, or puce sand.

My attention goes back to the roadway. I see "watch for wild donkey" signs, but see no braying critters. Long-distance bicyclists, straining leg muscles, churn out the miles. Not my sport. Out on the ocean, barely visible, are occasional white wispy spouts to signal migratory whales. As they so advertise, this place better be the harbinger of tranquil paradise. I am determined to have a fun week.

Chapter 2
Barbarians at the Gate

Not to be.

Waving flags and placards greet us as we approached the Ho'oilina Kai Grand Hotel Resort. Not the welcome wagon delegation. Protestors, like angry wasps from a disturbed hive, chant their slogans and spit stinging barbs toward us, closing in on the van from both sides, blocking our entrance to the hotel grounds.

"This is not a mere casual protest demonstration," noted my father. "There seem to be separate groups objecting to our presence. Can you explain the significance, Michael?" Jeffrey Dayne, my father (not 'Jeff,' but Jeffrey) has this pragmatic insight to distinguish tree varieties within a forest, moldy leaves within healthy branches. As usual, he was right on. Where a moment before I saw only a hodgepodge of rabble protestors surrounding the van, on closer inspection, there were groupings within the mob, organized and even color-coordinated.

Looking into the shuttle van's rear view mirror, my eyes locked with Michael's, our hotel escort and chauffer. Did I see embarrassment in his eyes? Or was he merely examining me, seeing less the woman, more the paying guest?

"Am I not correct?" pressed my father.

"Those mostly in green shirts are part of the Kingdom Restoration Society."

"Ah, yes, I see flags for each group. Very tribal," said my father. "The Society has a version of the Union Jack state flag, but it's turned upside down."

"Originally, the Monarchy Flag from 1814. Upside down is a signal for distress, as in political 'distress.'"

"I read where there are those who demand the United States cede Hawai'i back to the previous government, the monarchy, the Hawaiian royal family."

Michael confirmed the green shirts' identity.

"They were successful in lobbying local political leaders to pressure Congress in 1993 to pass the Apology Resolution admitting the United States illegally deposed the rightful monarchy. An unlawful coup. The Society's goal is to restore the old culture and traditions by restoring a full blooded Hawaiian as king." He looked at me. "Or queen." I noted animation in Michael's voice and suspected he supported their beliefs. After all, his bronze features spoke Pacific Rim bloodlines, a rounding-face with Hawaiian lineage, yet highlighted with those Asian eyes. A grown man, but young, his face though smooth held face-lines that suggested some outdoor weathering. Michael edged the van through the crowd. His caution, I realized, was intent for their safety as much as ours, but then he probably knew these people would not haul us from our vehicle and lynch us to the nearest palm tree. I could hear their chants of protest. They were in sing-song Hawaiian and shouts of onipa'a — probably their version of "We Shall Overcome." Their placards were in Hawaiian except for two or three handheld signs critical of the Ho'oilina Kai Resort, the most intelligent one of those reading, "Stop the Desecration." The word misspelled. All their colorful green shirts were either in Hawaiian flora art, several with the pre-1893 island national flag, or silk screen photos of former kings and queens of the island.

All this said, to get to the point, I prepped for this trip, learning the history of the islands. So, I knew the silk-screened visages plastered over protestor shirts, pudged or bamboo bodies, were those of Queen Lili'uokalani forced into abdication in 1893 by a cabal of local plantation owners and businessmen backed by U.S. military troops. And, King Kamehameha, founder of a unified Hawai'i by conquering the other island kingdoms. Score points for me.

"That one elder in the crowd seems to be staring at you, Michael, rather than us." Jeffrey and his observations. This old man's glare ate through our van. His face bore chiseled creases, and yes, his glare focused at Michael. Less anger, I thought, perhaps more a sad frown, like disappointment, than vitriolic. His back humped and bent to his age, his white hair whipped in the wind. He carried no sign, yelled no epithets. I immediately sensed people in the demonstration would defer to him as a leader.

Michael had not immediately answered my father. That embarrassment again, momentary silence from our driver until he realized by our questioning stares we both sought a response.

"That's my uncle, Joe Pa'ao, but everyone calls him Joe Coffee. Has Kona coffee acreage near Kealakekua. He's very old school. A purist. Believes all things on Hawai'i must be as it was one week after the first Polynesians arrived 1,900 years ago, and one week before Captain Cook aboard the ship Resolution saw the outline of Kaua'i in 1778."

"Doesn't he approve of your working at Ho'oilina Kai?" My father seemed more intent on Michael than soaking in the assorted riff-raff tussling outside. It was the investigative legal beagle still in him. Before becoming a famed culinary TV star, my father had started his career as a lawyer, later a public defender in Chicago, skilled at dissecting witnesses for their core truths. More about that later.

I could see Michael's grip on the steering wheel tighten. "My uncle did not appreciate my going mainland, off to Nevada to the UNLV Hotel School. He felt I would lose my ethnic heritage, assimilate to the iPhone culture. But if you want to succeed on island, the best jobs are upscale resorts."

Jeffrey sliced further, the verbal sensitive surgeon with scalpel. No pain, no gain. "And, especially working at the Ho'oilina Kai?"

"Would you like it if a bulldozer went to your family cemetery and scraped up your grandparents' bones?" Icy silence filled the van. Hired staff should not be offensive to guests. I did my best to recapture the status quo of civility between driver and passengers.

"And those other groups? The orange shirts look younger than the green shirts, the white shirts more clean-cut. They all seem to be Hawaiian except the white shirts who have a few protestors who are…" Caught off guard at his abrupt rudeness, I wanted to find the politically correct word to use, so I said, "Anglo."

Michael glanced my direction, resumed his ease and laughed, not so much at me, as realizing his own spouting diatribe. Okay, he gained my re-appraisal. Accepting that his college years at hotel school had taught him speech and manners, he did exhibit, which I had not caught earlier, a maturity more so than other goofball guys my age. Our age, mid-twenties.

"Those 'Anglos,' I rather call them haole trust-fund babies. They're rampant up on this part of the island, living in the best neighborhoods of beach front properties. They all seem to need a cause, and the problems we poor islanders face give them justification to join the cause of the moment." Michael seemed to internalize his frustrations, probably screaming for a speaker's podium, for a sympathetic listener. My father kindly assented with a "go on."

"Hawaiians," said Michael, almost in a relieved sigh, "are as dysfunctional as Republicans and Democrats saying they are parties of unity. For two or three causes we have about one hundred different political organizations. The green shirts are run by a friend of mine, Larry Tutapu. They're called People's Party of Free Hawai'i. They believe that the monarchy, King Kamehameha and his court, stole all the land from the High Chiefs who in turn were guardians in trust of the people's land Konohiki. Some still believe the King never conquered them. On Kaua'i, King Kaumuali'i might have paid tribute to Kamehameha, but was never forcibly conquered. Hence, for the green shirts, the people own the land, not the state or wannabe royalty. Tutapu and his group splintered off from the Monarchy Society about five years ago. They try to be more youth-based hip revolutionary, picking up followers who have no moral foundation of their own. They pattern themselves after Jamaican rap posses, dress the part, get into local band culture where they can find angry lyrics to chant."

Wow. I thought to myself, this guy is too uptight.

"And the white shirts?" I could see their banners, well printed catchy phrases, "Equal Rights," "Improve Hawaiian Lives." White shirts were not IBM-styled button downs, more free flowing cotton shirts. One tee shirt had Donald Trump's photo, the caption stating, "Ho'oilina Kai — You're fired!"

"That's the 'Committee for Economic Independence.' A bunch of opportunists. Their fondest dream is to bypass the laws of the Hawaiian Homeland Commission and seek inclusion in the Indian Gaming Regulatory Act. The purists like my uncle don't want to be Indians."

The van reached the guard gate, which seem to be manned to the teeth with security people; none armed if one ignored the side holsters of mace and billy clubs. They waved us through, recognizing the hotel van's cargo as guests of honor.

"I get it," said Jeffrey. "The white shirts are for casinos." Michael nodded his head in affirmation and gave my father further study. Jeffrey surprised many people, a learned man who read beyond cookbooks. He was my ideal, which I would never tell him, of what today's Renaissance Man should be. The mold, when he arrived on the scene, had been broken. I would never find my own passionate life mate with those characteristics and so my dating life lacked, my standards set too high for serious relationships. My physical needs, liked getting screwed with tingling satisfaction, whatever century that last occurred, had been one-nighters riddled with morning repulsion, at myself.

Back on subject, I gave my father a blank face.

"Madison, if the Hawaiians," he explained, "gain inclusion into this IGRA, the main attribute being 'quasi sovereignty,' their status would be similar to the federal government having to deal with a foreign nation. As now with Native Americans and their reservations."

"My uncle and his people believe history shows Hawai'i has always been a sovereign nation. The U.S. government with warships and bayonets ignored international law."

My father continued. "If native Hawaiians achieve sovereign recognition, they gain the right to negotiate for casinos on the island. I am guessing the white shirts are secretly well-funded by large mainland casino interests."

Michael affirmed. "Ten times more cash in their Political Action Committee than the other two groups combined who live hand-to-mouth. This committee of future pit bosses would do a disservice to Hawaiian culture, commercializing it beyond the current perception of tourist tacky."

Michael went silent. Maybe he said too much, spoke out of turn, to his job limitations. Definitely, he looked good smoldering. I found his character interesting, but he was not my type.

Chapter 3
Hoʻoilina

We drove through the manicured grounds of the Hoʻoilina Kai Grand Hotel Resort, newly opened, and on its inaugural shake-out first month. From my vantage, I immediately sensed this playground for the wealthy and those with zero balances on their credit cards was barely completed. Lumbering earth-moving equipment everywhere chugged rampant. Dump trucks hauled out excess lava rock, while graders and rollers were crushing the remaining lava stone piles (the hotel website had said this whole area was a recent lava field, only two hundred years old, still without topsoil). The project, I had read, was to build terraced pads for future housing, homes that I suspect would price list over $2 million for a townhouse starter. Closer to the main hotel sounds of hammers and saws rose from clusters of wood framing on uncompleted villas.

The golf course, in play, was immaculate, the greens smooth as if groomed by razor and the fairways meandered gracefully on rolling hills throughout the property. The clubhouse and main hotel toward the beach were in full operation. We pulled into the porte-cochere. A breezy banner announced "Tenth Annual Lūʻau Challenge," and a subtext poster highlighted "Hoʻoilina Kai Welcomes Jeffrey Dayne and the Insatiable Delights TV Show." The lūʻau competition was a day off and so my silent cry: "Where's the beach?" Not achieved easily as we must make an entrance befitting a foodie star. Jeffrey is going to be the primary celebrity judge for the lūʻau food competition, which, in my associate producer capacity, I will Hi Def digitize. As in the past travel food shows, he will work with the hotel and various restaurants to jointly prepare meals. Give the locals a national P.R. plug through his television show.

Introductions were made. Greeting us at the front steps was the Resort's General Manager, Mr. Mahon Cahill. With him was his head of Public Relations and Marketing, Desideria Cardoza. My antenna popped up full alert. Ms. Cardoza wore no wedding band. Stunning, thin and beautiful, late thirties, my guess. Her eyes, eye lashes, brows, all like her hair, raven black in coloring. And she said those words beguiling to any author and TV star, "Oh, Mr. Dayne. Can I call you, Jeffrey? I have both your cookbooks; I've seen your show. We are so lucky to have you staying with us. Call me Desi." Anyone could read 'Desi' on her name tag. She might as well have flung herself into his arms yelling, "Take me, you brute." I can translate feminine body language quite well, especially flaunting aimed at my father.

Mr. Cahill, impeccable in retro Hawaiian shirt and white slacks, spoke with an English accent. I could see a past life in the ladies department at London's Harrods. As he escorted his guests into the lobby he effused sweet syrup explaining the resort services at our disposal.

The hotel lobby smelled of interior designer money spent without budget. Dark cherry and teak woods balanced and edged against white walls; the open promenades, arched bridges over lilypad koi pools, song birds in white cages, and artsy floral arrangements of Birds of Paradise, red and pink ginger, giant mums and hydrangeas. Delicate orchids were scattered in nooks and crannies in oriental cloisonné bowls. At the front desk we were offered moist heated towels, mint scented, to wipe our hands. From the long plane trip, I wanted to wipe my underarms, but I refrained.

"Everything has been taken care of," extolled Mr. Cahill, actually finger-snapping, ordering bellmen to deliver our luggage and my camera equipment to our respective guest suites. As we headed toward the elevators I saw the 'box,' a simple white file folder carton, taped shut, heavy in contents. I know it carried cookbooks culled from my mother's collection. Jeffrey maintained the cookbooks in their house, now his, as sacrosanct. I expect these books would be on Hawaiian cuisine, a mixture of historic with those more recently off the presses. These editions would act as reference and he'd spend as much time studying and cooking as he ever would be at play outside.

Manager Cahill deferred to his Public Relations executive that all pre-arrival requests were in place. Miss Hotty Pants wore a pink silk blouse, a navy blue skirt with matching jacket and embroidered hotel badge crest, perhaps the simple staff wardrobe, but on her the clothes draped in nonchalant elegance. Her features seemed Spanish, but perhaps, if a local, Portuguese was her lineage. The sugar plantations looked for cheap labor and historically experimented with human cargoes from many nations. I am sure she Googled my father's life and recent tragedy of my mother's passing. I fear her plans.

To my father she cooed, her voice dropping an octave.

"The hotel has given you a suite and a separate adjoining room with a full kitchen which you can use for your cuisine preparation." Perfect for his perfection, his own testing, food creation lab. "Also," said all sugar Ms. Cardoza, "I have taken the liberty of having a pūpū luncheon platter served in our private grotto at the beach for you and your lovely daughter. It will be there waiting for you around 1:00 p.m. Just ask any of our staff for directions." I suspected she would be lurking nearby.

Manager Cahill gave a crooked-teeth smile, "Miss Cardoza has had Chef Lorenzo prepare your Lomilomi Salmon Salad from, I believe, your first cook book." He effused self-pride at the personal service of his sharp PR Manager and the hotel's fine dining Head Chef, not realizing this was a dish that Jeffrey and Elizabeth, my mom, had created together on one of their early romantic escapes to the islands. By past examples of his mourning eccentricities, I knew he wouldn't touch any direct memory of her, especially her signature food dishes. I saw Jeffrey's lips purse in a slight wince. Trying to be ever the gentleman, Jeffrey Dayne would have to find a tactful escape from this pupu predicament.

Michael led the bell hop brigade with all luggage to our rooms, situated on the hotel's top floor. Five stories, no high rises around here. And not presidential suites, darn it, but my room alone had twice the floor space of my Santa Monica hovel. Michael told me not to tip anyone, management exception just for us. Out of curiosity, giving him a departing thank you, I did the girlish sort of mumble-stumble and asked if I would see him again. Not a big deal, just chitchat courtesy to the staff.

"Mr. Cahill has made me your father's cultural attaché. If you have any questions, or your dad requires whatever, give the front desk a call, and they will track me down."

He gave the impression, ever so slightly, that the task assigned to him, dignitary babysitting, even for one in the hospitality industry, fell beneath his capabilities. I did not feel offended; in fact, felt better for him, that he sensed loftier goals. And for the moment, thought no more of him.

Recipe: Lomilomi Salmon Wraps

1 pound salt salmon, shredded

4 pounds ripe tomatoes, small dice

3/4 pound Maui onion, finely diced

5 ounces scallions, whites and greens, coarsely chopped

Large lettuce leaves

Mix all ingredients together by hand. Let cool in refrigerator.

To serve place inside lettuce leafs as a wrap.

('Lomi lomi' means "to massage" in Ha-waiian,

so don't be surprised when you hear it used in spa treatments)

Chapter 4
Great Daynes

I have to digress. I am keeping a journal of this trip for future reference, and to organize my rambles. In breaking in my notebook, stream of consciousness worked well, and while back in my California apartment, here is an excerpt of what I scribbled:

My name is Madison Merlot Dayne, Jeffrey's wayward daughter. This will be my first official producer assignment with the Food Television Channel (FTC Network). Jeffrey found himself contractually pressured from the Network big boys to abandon his self-imposed mourning hiatus and finish one more year of food shows. My father requested my presence as one of his conditions of returning. As to the network executives I am on intern probation, shaky at best. They'll have the professionals produce the actual cooking program in the studio with a fake set of the Dayne home kitchen. I have been relegated to shoot the B-roll footage of Jeffrey's travels, tape color background, record Jeffrey's comments for voice-overs. I alone am the walking everywoman of the food show documentary.

Here's the quick history. Their ground-breaking cookbook, *States of Epicurean Delights*, came first. Those in food show television ratings, those advertising revenue number crunchers, took one look at Dad and Mom's photo staged in their suburbanite kitchen and said, "Let's make a show about and around these two upward and mobile traveling bon vivants." The show's substance of recipes hit a chord of public interest, extolling foods from different geographical locales (as in various 'States'). The first season hit high marks, gained top reviews, viewers seeing beyond food prep, enjoying the fun-loving chemistry between the stars. Their Nielsen television ranking and viewer demographics insured a continued run. The television producers rushed out a second cookbook, adding show recipes and higher resolution color photos of food presentation. In negotiations, and under Jeffrey's legal eye, the new book was ordained, *Insatiable: Further States of Epicurean Delights*. Sadly, though the book's first edition press run and literary launch were a success, the only photo on the back inside flap was Jeffrey's somber pose, the book dedication to his departed wife, my mother. I never bought a copy, though he did send me one, and thank God, not autographed. For as much as I saw him during her final year, an inscription to me would make me more the stranger, yet appropriate and well deserved.

The Hawaiian gig will be his return to the culinary world of good eats and fine dining. I assume he bears self-doubt if he can do this traveling without his TV partner, the stalwart, sensible Elizabeth, taken from us by the cruel, goddamn scourge called ovarian cancer. My invitation to join this pilgrimage sparks of Freudian nuances. Several of Mom's features carried into my looks: curly hair and scattered cheek freckles, matching brownish-red hair, posed on facial bone structure, more rectangular than round. My body, proportioned well enough, certainly not a beanpole as I have daily fights against adhering ounces of body fat. Other similarities were in our speech and mannerisms. We flipped our hair alike, using head throws instead of hand flings. We both used the word 'exactly' for agreeing emphasis, and if in dispute, most invariably got in the last word. Whatever. That's his problem. Trying to recapture her memories I would make a bad ghost for him.

I signed on, in retrospect, because I was an unemployed media school graduate with several years of bumming through boring assistant to the assistant director of home-spun corny used auto commercials, and more so, I had one parent left and had not done a very good job in being the loving, caring daughter. Or, maybe it's this internal drive, the female chauvinist out to show up the production side of the entertainment industry. I want to someday be a damn fine producer. Doing a few segments of a nationally televised food show, even if a second unit for the color filler, would still be a highlight in my resume reel. I'll do this trip, maybe another, then shop my talents to Hollywood. Kick open doors. Shove Spielberg and Scorcese aside.

Chapter 5
The Grotto

Within an hour of my arrival, after unpacking, bathing and primping, refreshed, though jet-lagged, I stood naked in front of a full-length closet mirror.

I wondered aloud. "Is this the body that could launch a thousand war canoes?" I gave myself credit for being shaped and toned. Lugging camera equipment and incremental jogging in wet Santa Monica beach sands gave me stamina and a hard-body physique. Okay, I feared the worst. I feared premature butt sag, and lately my food intake had gone more toward fast Mac-attack than gourmet. That was my secret life. I did not yet appreciate my father's food creation as art, or morsel-tasting as sensual emotion.

My outfit for the afternoon had me looking like a jungle explorer. My straw hat went over a head scarf wrap to keep sweat out of my eyes and the camera lenses. My ensemble included tan shorts and well-worn tennis shoes. For beach attire, I would have gone braless and bounced, small bounces but as this luncheon meant work, expected filming, a sports bra served the purpose of not letting the camera straps rub my nipples raw. Three jostling straps to be exact: the video equipment bag, the sound case, and for still shots, my trusty digital Nikon D80. I had brought three still cameras: my Dad's old Pentax with archaic 35 mm film, shooting 100 ASA for bright sun, an heirloom with good memories; the before mentioned Nikon; and a pocket digital, prepped and ready for any fast draw action.

A walking studio, I traipsed down the path toward the grotto for our afternoon luncheon snack. At several points I paused and took quick background shots of the hotel grounds, the marina in the distance, and various jungle exotic flower species. My still camera photos would be available for a future cookbook as well as create the show's story board and document the food journal diary. Prepared, though weighted down, I turned the corner, discovered a screen of pink-white oleanders and walked into the garden grotto. Beautiful. Serene. Like a Garden of Eden hidden within dark lava rock, a view of whitecaps on the ocean, a perfect day for filming. And someone was eating our lunch!!

Not just anyone. A humongous man. Not fat. Not large. Gigantus. What was it, beyond Sumo wrestler size? This guy had to weigh over 300 pounds, maybe closer to 400 pounds. Definitely Hawaiian, not dressed in any costume, just casual in T-shirt and cargo shorts. Still, the fabric stitched to make his clothes alone could have made a circus tent.

And he was stuffing his face!

"Hey, if you don't mind, that's our lunch!"

Most of the food had been devoured, more torn apart. He turned to me, and I took a step back, fearful. Something was off. His eyes were wrong. They seemed glazed, twisting in his sockets. His head lolled back and forth on his shoulders. Whether in contempt or utter rudeness, he picked up a community bowl of a purple paste-like substance, the Hawaiian staple dish called poi. The bowl half-empty, he took his short-stubbed fingers in a big scoop, stuffing the remaining poi into his mouth with a slurping sound, followed by a guttural ugh of primal satisfaction. He faced me without seeing, his eyes rolling back into his head, and like in a horror movie, zombie white egg orbs stared out. He fell forward with a gigantic thud, King Kong high-diving from a skyscraper, bringing himself to the ground along with the entire table of food, all crushed and blended into garbage disposal gook.

I looked to the giant's face, hidden behind a dark violet mask of poi.

Chapter 6
Pūpū Surprise

Struck dumb for the moment at the man's collapse, instant recollection of my college swim team and life-saving classes kicked in. I dropped my equipment, shouted for help and ran to his aid.

Even with what athletic ability I thought I possessed, I couldn't turn over the beached whale-like Hawaiian. He had to get over on his back, he just had to. I had to clear his breathing passage. If he stopped breathing, dare I consider it, would I have to perform mouth-to-mouth resuscitation? Yuck, could I do it? How much worse could that be from French-kissing my last boyfriend, his tongue tasting of cheap liquor and foul cigarettes, just before he puked over my only Donna Karan sheer black party dress? An a-hole, long gone and good riddance.

All these rushed thoughts as I pushed and shoved with no results. I grabbed at my camera tripod and attempted leveraging his body to flip him. Damn, only one large arm flopped and went nowhere. Desperate, racing toward panic when another set of hands pushed alongside me. Michael K. Teamwork.

Oh, Michael, you are so heroic. He shouted into his hotel walkie-talkie calling for paramedics. A final pair of hands supplied the last needed effort and the stricken man rolled onto his back. I looked to the new Samaritan and his strength, my father; two heroes side-by-side. I am privileged.

Thank the saints, I saw poi-colored air bubbles from the man's mouth, and his chest was rising and falling, but perceptively shallow. I sensed, even for the man's physique, he was not breathing to a normal rhythm, more jerky spurting to his normal lung flow. I cleared the man's mouth of slimy obstructions. From deep within there was a hacking gurgle. His whole massive form shook, his body arched in rigidity and then went limp, back to a stomach slightly quivering and a chest whispering air in and out. My fingers stayed in his mouth to keep him from swallowing his tongue.

The inner-hotel communications from Michael initiated a rush to the accident scene. The house doctor responded with hotel employees carrying some sort of portable defibrillator. I guess their first assumption was that some old fogey guest had keeled over. Michael gently eased me away while the professional caregivers took over.

Manager Cahill arrived and soon after the Cardoza woman, who to my surprise, burst into tears, and started mouthing in semi-hysteria, "Oh, my God, no. No. No. Not like this." If it weren't such a sorry situation, I would guess she was worried about the hotel's PR image and potential liability. But that is crass of me. Next on the scene, an odd group of young people, three boys and a girl, very unkempt, a walking gallery of tattoos and body piercing. Trash-fashionable in scraggly black rag attire. And, if everything was not already surreal, two out of the four freaks, who you'd think would be joking cruelly at the big man's illness, were themselves, like Ms. Cardoza, crying. What was going on?

Michael at my side whispered, pointing to the prone man now fitted with an oxygen mask, "You know who this is?" I shook my head, not really in tune with anything, feeling claustrophobic, a descending panic as the grotto we stood in shrunk, filling with strange gawking people.

"That's Oli Palalū."

Now, above what I had been through, a real shock set in place. I whispered back.

"You mean that's Oli?"

"Yes, he was to sing tomorrow night as part of the Lūʻau Challenge Opening Ceremonies. That's his band over there."

I looked to see, devastation in their eyes. I mean, I just had my fingers in the mouth of the most successful torch singer across the entire Pacific Ocean, certainly a megastar in Hawaiʻi, if not to any music lover who appreciates island melodies. His style was similar to that of ballad crooners Don Ho or Israel 'Iz' Kamakawiwoʻole. From what I had read, Oli was destined to be the next Iz, the late, venerated singer who had at one point weighed 750 pounds and died too young at 38. I knew somewhere in my CD pile back at my apartment was an Oli disk of him singing 1940 ballads, doing an over-track duet with Frank Sinatra, and another with sultry-throated Peggy Lee. Romantic melodies. Oli's lyrics from one hit song rose quickly to mind:

Fathomless, deep is my love — To thee, my passion, my mate

Ah, on a future day, to sing that true to someone special. I took note of the onlookers, who I now realized were profusely worried about the singer's condition. My eyes came to rest on something disturbing. My Father had his arm around sniveling Ms. Desi, patting there-there comfort.

The running arrival of the fire department paramedics changed the scene. Security guards, upon Manager Cahill's command, started escorting everyone out of the secret garden enclosure. The paramedics discussed first response action taken by the house doctor. They ran protocol in their steps of stabilization not knowing what true illness had befallen this singing idol.

Milling in the spectator crowd away from the grotto I heard someone say the words, "Heart Attack," and another person murmur agreement. Probably, with someone carrying that much poundage, I am sure his beating heart would strain under a lot of pressure. Most Hawaiian music fans know Iz died of respiratory failure. Having seen Oli's collapse, I can say that it looked like some kind of seizure. Too much engorged food? Could my surprising him have been the long-awaited trigger of the seizure? No, by the time I arrived Oli seemed swaying, freaky in his expression, eating without focus, out of it. His convulsion was already in process.

More distant sirens. An ambulance arrived. Why two medical teams? Then, it dawned on me; I saw their dilemma of getting Oli and his dimensions safely to the hospital. How would they lift him? A regular stretcher gurney would not accommodate.

Could the ambulance even hold him? To that concern of logistics came Michael, and another man, both pushing large flat luggage dollies, but not from the hotel. The man with a scruffy beard looked seafaring, wearing a jumping-and-hooked marlin T-shirt, and the distinctive battered marina hat, white with gold-back braided scroll work. If he got too close I might smell week-old odors of sweat and chopped bait fish. He must have been from the hotel's small harbor marina and I guessed the carts they pushed were for hauling fishing equipment and yacht luggage from shore to ship.

Placed together, side by side, both luggage carts made an adequate carrier of the ill singer. Within a few minutes, the paramedics, the doctor, and a squad of employees assisted the dual cart gurney up the path to an awaiting ambulance. Much of the crowd followed, all now silent, like a cortege in dirge march, a macabre scene in the midst of vacation brightness.

A policeman asked me to stay behind to make a statement. In a few minutes, I was ushered back into the garden hide-away. Deep harrow marks showed where the carts had etched tracks in the grass carrying away their precious human cargo.

Jeffrey stared at the mess strewn on the ground. At least, the perceived confrontation of munching the lomilomi salad had been put to rest. To move the singer the glop went through secondary foot mush blending. The sight brought a queasy feeling to my stomach. Two hotel maintenance personnel stood on the sidelines with shovels and trash containers awaiting orders to restore everything back to the pristine image of resort serenity. My father squatted and with a chopstick poked at the luncheon turned garbage. Pūpū poop.

Michael stood with a policeman and another man, one dressed in an understated off-white short-sleeve shirt and grey slacks. Michael beckoned me over and made the introductions.

"This is Detective David Kee. He's in the Investigations Department. He'll be the police department's community liaison. Needs to make sure this accident doesn't become some sort of tabloid frenzy." The men exchanged sly smiles of unstated secrets and Michael saw I had noticed. "You should know Detective Kee is my cousin, second or third cousin, on my mother's side.

"And this is Officer Kinkaid. He will take your initial statement of what happened. Try to remember everything."

"Yes, I understand." I said demurely, bowing to officialdom. I found it interesting that both men deferred to Michael, and didn't throw around their cop weight. I relayed my story as Officer Kinkaid took notes. Detective Kee scribbled bullet points in his own notebook, making me nervous about what I had said that might stand out as extraordinary beyond a straight story.

I found it odd Detective Kee, being of Chinese ancestry, did not look like a relative of Michael's. Where Michael was all Hawaiian except for his eyes, Detective Kee, a good ten years older than Michael, stood short, his face shaped like a valentine heart, but pushed in and narrowed. If I were doing a studio photo shoot, a period piece, I would dress him in costume as a gaunt nineteenth century opium den smoker. I thought this because his yellow-dark skin had a pasty pallor suggesting a long-time chain smoker. He drummed his pen on his notebook and chewed gum in staccato bites, the signs of nicotine cold turkey. I knew the clues well, my own nasty habit two years behind me, knock on koa wood.

After giving preliminary who I was, why I was on the scene, we arrived at the expected what I had witnessed of this medical accident. "And you feel," asked Officer Kinkaid, "Mr. Palalū had been at this table quite some time before your arrival?

"Yes. I glanced at the table and saw most dishes were half-eaten. Like he tried each dish but only consumed a portion."

"And when you saw him, he became sick?"

How rude. He could have worded the query slightly differently. Sounded like he implied my looks caused the singer's illness. Like really.

"Probably from inhaling the food. Yeah, grazing at that speed I saw anyone, including him, might have consumed too much, too quick."

Michael helped as he could. "I think the officer is trying to ask: was he sick a few moments after you arrived and confronted him, or did he seem sick the minute you saw him?" They were splitting hairs.

"I'm pretty certain he had been getting sick before I arrived. He looked ill, and after eating the poi, he immediately collapsed. If you want a guess, his convulsion started prior to my arrival."

"Miss Dayne," offered Detective Kee. He spoke slowly as if I needed to translate his English, which he spoke perfectly with no dialect. "You see, Oli, Mr. Palalū, had been sick the last several weeks, from what we so far gathered. Perhaps the flu. We feel he could have had a relapse, and the fall started the seizure."

I dug into my memory. "No, it looked like a convulsion just as I arrived, before he fell."

"Thank you, Ms. Dayne, for the clarification."

When I completed a few more background questions, as to estimated time of my arrival, what room I was staying in, things like that, they seemed satisfied and put away their note pads. Only then did Jeffrey ask as he circled the food dump, "Is anyone going to test the food?"

"I don't think that will be necessary," said Detective Kee. "Everyone has the highest respect for Chef Lorenzo's cuisine, including myself. Besides, I think we are reaching the conclusion Mr. Palalū had an episode from his earlier illness."

"You certainly can reach that conclusion, Detective. But see that pile of pink food? That's the Lomilomi Salad presumably made from my recipe, out of my cookbook."

"Presumably?" countered Detective Kee.

"Well, if it was made to my recipe's ingredients, they got it wrong. There are garnishments that I did not use. And did anyone notice the poi?"

We all looked to him. Jeffrey Dayne bristled, disgusted. Not at the mess, not at the crisis of the very sick man who ate his luncheon snack, but that the kitchen might have adulterated his creation, a high crime to any artist. You don't enhance a Mona Lisa with an added mustache. We looked at him, the police officer with irritation.

"About the poi?" queried Detective Kee, accepting he was playing straight man to what Mr. Dayne saw as the obvious.

"Like the Lomilomi, there are green flecks in the poi. One doesn't add green sprinkles to poi."

Officer Kinkaid's side radio crackled. Detective Kee's cell phone buzzed.

"Call for backup," barked the police officer. "Arrest everyone who gets close to the hotel." He looked to our curious faces. "The crowds outside the gate saw the ambulance rush out and heard Oli had been injured. They got it all wrong. Yelling that the hotel is at fault. They've broken into the grounds and are headed this way. I don't know if I have enough personnel to control them."

Detective Kee ended his phone call. "Oli Palalū died on the way to the hospital."

"Madison." In the midst of individual tragedy and civil uproar, my father turned back to his food rummaging and said quite nonchalantly, "Run to the hotel kitchen and find me at least two or three half-pint plastic bowls with tight lids."

Chapter 7
Recipe for Fear

I returned from my so-called life-or-death task carrying a lumpy sack of storage containers. I felt demoted to waitress-in-training. In my walk to the grotto, I passed a lot of tossed and tumbled action. Security guards chased orange and green-shirted trespassers. Some chases were comical with hedge-jumping or tag games, like trying to lasso scattering rabbits. Others suggested frustrated anger as security guards and interlopers, most with orange shirts, exchanged punches and in turn were maced or jabbed with batons and kicked when the subdued cringed on the ground. Any dissenter philosophy of pacifism may have forever vanished. It would be a 'them or us' line drawn in the beach sand. I did not see any white shirted protestors running helter-skelter and guessed civil disobedience was not included in their job description. I clicked off a few digitals with my palm camera.

Not my fracas. To hell with local political squabbling over lost causes. With the short week ahead, my priorities were clear: shooting foodie footage, B-roll pics of Hawaiian touristy sunsets, foamy waves, volcano lava spurting, maybe a jungle waterfall, carve out my own time for scuba dives, searching among the coral reefs for Nemo fish. I'd find a private cove where, topless, I could baste my skin in coconut oil until I was SPF 4 tolerant. To hell with eroding ozone layers and UVB rays; they're for sissies.

I could see with Oli's death the grotto garden had been sanctioned an official 'investigation accident site.' Michael wisely secured rope, looking like white sail rope, probably from his buddy, Barnacle Bill, the sea captain honcho, since both men were stringing the lines from palm tree to tree, roping off the grotto. Hotel employees, beefy and heft, maybe from the marina and valet staff, stood as uneasy guardsmen. Following Michael's direction, the curious hotel guests or sullen orange-green shirters were asked to bear respect for Oli Palalū. Still, the morbid hung back on the fringes exchanging speculative gossip.

I returned to find my father and Detective Kee in a turf battle.

"You are informing me it will take ten days for your Honolulu lab to return an analysis of the food this lūʻau singer ate? That won't do. Won't do at all."

"Maybe in a week since they know who it concerns?" Meaning Oli the singer, not my father's own niche popularity. And Dad, Oli Palalū, known as Oli, is famous worldwide, not some Tiki lounge lizard.

"And the autopsy? Another week?"

"No, that might be as soon as tomorrow. A separate agency, not County Health. Considering the victim's immense girth and how this might be accomplished I don't know if staff here are adequate. We may fly in more qualified people from Oʻahu."

"Immediate lab analysis is essential. I don't want to be the cause of false rumors," stressed my father. "I can express mail out my samples to the Illinois Bureau of Investigation. They can give me telephone results by tomorrow night." He took the plastic containers from me.

Detective Kee felt no civilian should be giving orders, especially a tourist. By right he did have concerns of the public welfare in mind.

"It's better to shut down all food services at the resort than have food poisoning hit elsewhere."

"Food poisoning," was my surprised comment. Like everyone else, the crowd vote was for an accident based on Oli's past medical history; the autopsy diagnosis certain to be heart attack or brain aneurism, something like that, with body weight a contributing factor.

My father warned me to silence with a frown. I had seen that parental look before when my curiosity interfered with his mental gymnastics.

"Your father," said the detective, "believes the food might be tainted. It does happen in warm climate conditions. And this food had been sitting out at least a half an hour before Oli Palalū and you arrived."

"And, if there is tainted food," Jeffrey's tongue rolled off these words with disgust. "All I am asking," he was at his gathering task, "is for less than a teaspoon of several food items. Your forensic people are welcome to the rest. And you get immediate access to my data. Better safe than sorry if I can turn it around sooner than your State Department of Health. And I'll give you this, trace the food prep back to the proper kitchen area and only shut down that one facility until I get my results back. That will be only a day of inconvenience. Shutting down all the resort's restaurants on an unproven assumption would have severe economic repercussions. I feel their problem. If bad food exists, there can be containment, and the culprit ingredients isolated." Like a sleight-of-hand magician, he had the containers with his small samples filled in a flash. Luck assisted when Kee's attention became diverted by several police officers appearing on the scene asking for command instructions.

Detective Kee should have asserted his authority, even acted like an arrogant officer of the law, but he might have known the reputation of Jeffrey Dayne, his specialty and intelligence when it came to food. Perhaps unstated, Detective Kee further knew that Food Meister Dayne lay under the tour protection of his young cousin, Michael K., and family ties could have unstated obligations.

The detective aggravated at his failure to rule the scene of his own inquiry, scanned the horizon with a goal to reassert a Captain Queeg meanness and pointed for the benefit of the two police officers awaiting his leadership commands.

"Go arrest that man for trespassing against a court order." Maybe family blood had little clout in this crisis.

Down from the grotto, standing on a worn sea-pounded rock that jutted out from the foam of the ocean's turbulence was the white-haired Hawaiian I had seen at the front gate. His arms raised above his head, ti leaves in one hand, extolling the blue-sky heavens, obviously chanting, but unheard from where we stood. Michael's uncle, Joe Coffee, seemed to be invoking distant and ancient gods. But to what purpose?

Chapter 8
Foodie Detective

I don't like to be beholden, but we are. Ms. Desi seemed diminished, a world-bearing slump on her shoulders, definitely reeling, I presumed, with the ramification of Oli's death on the hotel's reputation. Still, by her consummate skills from Jeffrey's request, she directed the hotel concierge to use all methods available to help expedite our parcel to Illinois. She immediately exited the scene, flashing at my father a dramatic grief-sob. Her power lingered over all her minions who jumped to her commands and Jeffrey's samples of collected ick were boxed and express-mailed into the aerial ether.

My father told no one outside of Detective Kee what he was shipping back to the mainland (in Hawai'i it is bad form to say, 'back to the States,' since the locals remind you that you are in a State and they are not foreigners!). I think Jeffrey was worried about Hawai'i's Agricultural Department that guards vigilantly the comings and goings of plants, animals, and I assume, messy food, especially when shipped in black plastic garbage bags surrounded by dry ice.

I am always amazed at my Father's networking. He is an artist in cultivating friendships, solidifying connections, reminders to drop lines, email and snail mail stay in touch, be in the loop. He's a mental, walking rolodex.

"How are you going to get the higher ups in the Illinois cop lab to jump to your beck and call? For Pete's sake, you were an anathema to them, a defense attorney, no less."

His genuine smile of all-knowing made me feel good.

"In life, the best relationships are the quid pro quo of helping and being able to call in favors. Ray Platt from the Illinois Police Lab has a son, second offense DUI. I fast tracked him into a detox program. As an appreciative father Ray will get me quick turn-around results. Besides, he's a closet foodie. Sent me a thank you jar of his wife's homemade elderberry jelly."

"So, you think spoiled food got Oli sick? Food poisoning from the lomilomi or the poi?"

"That could be an answer. But the food seemed to be well handled. Perhaps you didn't notice the muslin cloths wadded up on the ground. They were soaked. This Oli probably ripped those off the table. Even with silver chafing dish coverings for the food, ice had been placed around the food on the cloth. The ice now melted. Somehow I couldn't see the fault being from Chef Lorenzo's kitchen. He is Cordon Bleu. Several Michelin awards. With the Ho'oilina Kai just opening, he's goal driven to obtain a Five Star rating, sit at the gourmet pinnacle. I'd expect him to be obsessed with cleanliness. Still, the Lomilomi and the poi were tampered with."

"Tampered? As in 'intentionally'?"

"Maybe. Or maybe some sous chef took it on his own to create a pièce de résistance with flair. To any Head Chef like Jacque Lorenzo, modification without approval would be a firing offense. And to put green plant flecks in the poi when not called for, yes, I would call that tampering."

We were walking through the resort past the main pool. The upper gentry lounged in cabanas sipping mimosas, reading their novels of romance and swashbuckling. I thought I spotted what's-his-name, the actor from last season's TV hospital comedy hit.

When I could break away and lie by this pool I would spy on the who's who from behind my sunglasses.

Graciously, my father carried my equipment load while I retained the small cameras. We had not walked the resort grounds on arrival. The place looked placid with strolling guests as if there had not been an earlier contentious confrontation from the gate crashers. Looking less at the flora and fauna and beach-clad tourists my mind digested, so to speak, what my father now suggested.

"If intentional, and not just fancying up some dish, you're saying someone tried to poison Oli Palalū? What are those green flecks?"

"Definitely plant or vegetable matter. The lab results will tell, and we can't jump to conclusions, but we must be careful."

A bile of hysteria rose in my throat. "Careful? Did Detective Kee come to that conclusion? Is he shutting down the kitchen? Investigating staff? Not food tampering, what you are saying is that this could be a 'poisoning'? Who'd want to kill a beloved Hawaiian singer?"

Jeffrey Dayne stopped in the pathway and turned to me. He had this patrician air about him. I could see him elsewhere, white Panama brimmed hat, a silk ascot wrapped to his neck, standing on the veranda of a Caribbean plantation, a Scotch in his hand, no, a glass of French appellation cabernet, certainly no crushed grape younger than twenty years. More than a father to me, he stood as an ideal, a Grecian god, and I had failed him. His fallen angel.

"Madison." His hands gently on my shoulders. I hoped someone would take a photo of this gesture. I would create a wall hanging of the father-daughter moment. I needed this.

"Madison, you don't see it. This Oli fellow stumbled across our hidden luncheon, and with his appetite, and certainly his star-ego, took advantage of free food. No one knew he would be there. No one knew he would stuff his face. If it is poison, and that is a big 'if,' but if it is poison, it was meant most certainly for me, and by happenstance, you. We were supposed to be poisoned."

'Pop' went the balloon of the tender scene.

"Poisoned? Us? You've got to be kidding? No one tries to murder a foodie star!"

"Ah, dear Madison. I certainly have fans. The New York office sends out form 'thanks-for-your-letter', even secretarial signing them, Insatiably yours, Jeffrey. But central office of the network is reluctant to show me the small stream of hate mail. It does exist for anyone in the public eye, even food show celebrities. It comes with the territory. A soufflé fails to rise for a perfectionist, or a husband rejects his wife's cooking because it is not the normal meatloaf fare, and the wife casts her anger on the gourmet recipe I recommended. An unhappy fan will annunciate nasty comments, and yes, threaten bodily harm. They write, hoping that during the taping of a show I might choke on the bone of my chicken al fresco. Or that it would be a fitting demise if a garbage truck ran over me. I'm new in this business by three years and only starting to have my own watch list of kooks."

"You mean you, us, we're being stalked by a deranged foodie fan?" Fear prickled the hair on the back of my neck. I shivered at a cold draft while breathing tropical heat. My eyes wandered the manicured landscape, searching for what? "What does a poisoner look like?"

"Let's hope the lab tests don't substantiate my concern. That probably will be the case. Let's go to Merriman's tonight and have wonderful organic vegetable soup, and a Parker Ranch steak."

No, I will never eat again until I am locked securely in my Santa Monica apartment with take-out pizza. At least, I'd die from self-inflicted obesity. And, that thought comes full circle to the vision of my trying to save the dying Oli Palalū, perhaps murdered, perhaps murdered by poi.

Recipe: Poi

Poi is made from the popular taro plant: the 14th most cultivated crop on earth,
and although taro is eaten around the world, only Hawaiians make poi.
Traditionally they cook the starchy, potato-like taro root, or corm,
for hours in an underground oven called an imu.
Then, they pound the taro corms on large flat boards called papa ku`i`ai,
using heavy stone poi pound-ers called pōhaku ku`i `ai.
The taro pounds into a smooth, sticky paste called pa`i`ai,
then is stored air tight in ti leaf bundles
and banana sheaths for storage or future trading.
By slowly adding water to the pa`i`ai,
which is then mixed and kneaded, the perfect poi consistency is created.
Many Hawaiians love their poi fermented slightly, giving it a unique,
slightly sour taste. A bowl of poi to many is considered such a sacred part
of daily Hawaiian life, that whenever a bowl of poi is uncovered at
the family dinner table, it is believed that the spirit of Haloa,
the ancestor of the Hawaiian people, is present.
Because of that, all conflict among family members
should come to an immediate halt.

Poi:
Taro root, peeled and steamed
Water
Mash the taro with a stone pestle, or "poi pounder."
Add water until the poi is smooth and sticky.

For those liking their food "Westernized," they can try Poi in the following adjusted dish:

Poi Pudding
1/3 C milk or whipping cream
2 T brown sugar, molasses or honey (to taste)
1/3 C poi add vanilla (to taste)
Softly whip cream and stir in sweetener and then poi. Serve cold.

Chapter 9
Ghost of the Mermaid

What was I to think? My first day on The Big Island and I was waist deep in some major macabre shit. What should I do? Swilling scotch from the mini bar a ready answer. I leaned on the railing of my balcony and absorbed this paradise, now turned weird. I felt the trade winds slam my body like a frizzing hairdryer on max power. On this side of the island, there were few days without the leeward currents, varying in their undulating levels from subtle wisps to pre-typhoon blows. You get used to them.

Not meant to be, but this trip is an anniversary of sorts. This is actually my second island trip, the first a little rushed and not pleasant. Last year this time, in February, up the coast, I stood on the beach at Pololū Valley, with the island of Maui hazed in the distance, and watched my father kayak beyond the surf onto a green-blue mirror of ocean. Amidst a choir of hump-back whales I could see him through binoculars scatter my mother's ashes among the sea-shouldering leviathans. Upon his return he said to me, "She frolics again, a mermaid."

Let me back up a little for the short bio of Mr. Jeffrey Dayne, foodie star. In the beginning, pre-fame, post-college and post-law school, my father struggled in the caverns of the Cook County Court House in Chicago as a neophyte in the Public Defender's Office, a court-appointed defense attorney, protector of the downtrodden and presumed innocent. Most incarcerated, of course, were street scum, definitely guilty, but Jeffrey Dayne (remember, never "Jeff") rode every day on the L, his fierce graffiti stallion, ready to do battle against the Lord High Executioners of the District Attorney's office.

One court docket day twenty-six years back, entrenched now in family folklore, a miscreant purse snatcher appeared for adjudication. Usually, these sort of meddlesome cases were plea-bargained behind the railing before the judge took the bench. In Chicago courts, case paperwork burdened both sides of the justice scales and dispositions of cases were settled by poker face bluffs and horse-trading. In the case of this purse snatching, the victim would have none of this compromise. She demanded her day in court against the protests of the ADA, a lowly assistant district attorney paying thankless, long-hour dues up the career ladder. The purse snatcher's victim had shown up seeking justice, making an enduring trip from the suburbs, believing the wrongdoer would not receive proper punishment without her presence as condemning witness.

"But he stole only $35! And, we recovered the credit cards before they were hit," stressed the worn junior city prosecutor, facing another twenty-five cases to resolve before noon, and this five minutes too long of his time. "Mr. Dayne, the Public Defender, will be asking for a release based on his client's twenty days already spent in lock-up. Time served. His client will still be on a short probation leash."

The victim, in her twenties, for the first time, eyed the young Jeffrey Dayne and likewise he acknowledged her with a nod, surprised, intrigued, deciding she was out of place in this bureaucratic carnival. She seemed an angel among the scallywags.

"It's not the money," she said with firmness of purpose. "It is the violation of personal property, of one's freedom, yet perhaps more important, it was the tube within my purse. Likewise stolen but not recovered."

"Tube?" Both ADA and PD went to their file report of the incident. No tube listed. She saw the male species about to exchange glances with some unsaid sexual inference.

"It is a tube of ume paste. My girlfriend brought it to lunch that day we met at Le Colonial on North Rush. The paste goes with a recipe she brought from her Hawaiian trip. Ume paste is impossible to find in a Chicago store. It is the central ingredient in Li Hing Mui vinaigrette."

Neither attorney had ever heard, let alone tasted, Ling Hing whatever. She noted their barbaric ignorance.

"My girlfriend loved the vinaigrette in a cucumber salad with blanched tomatoes, created by Hawaiian chef and restaurateur, Alan Wong. As I have not been to Hawai'i, she brought the islands to me, only to be hijacked!"

The ADA liked his supposition better, that this paste was a lickable aphrodisiac or heated incense for kinky massage. Vice would know more, and he made a note wondering how to spell "yumi." Vice knew all things kinky. The ADA shrugged, helpless to her anguish. Spokesperson of the people, he could not fathom how to represent women with lost feminine playthings.

Jeffrey Dayne, always with this penchant for quick analysis of awkward situations, jumped to her assistance.

"Miss…"

"Child. Elizabeth Child."

"If my client…" he pointed to a hodge-podge of orange-garbed prisoners sitting behind protective glass in a holding room awaiting their fate. Dayne had no idea which one was his client.

"If my client would promise to do his best to stay out of trouble, not repeat this offense, and if we were to find and replace the contents of your lost tube of 'paste', would you accept that my honorable friend here and I would work out the details of the proper punishment to be meted out to this vile and despicable creature?" He gave her his patented twist of the head, bent, pouting smile, like an endearing puppy, cute yet blinking behind mischievous eyes.

Elizabeth Child considered Jeffrey Dayne and took stock of his character, if not his looks that gave her an inner-feeling, a tingly warmth not before felt among others of the human male species.

"Yes, that would be acceptable. But this paste is rare and hard to find and the tube is labeled in Japanese." She threw her evil eye toward the prisoners, wondering which crook among the pack had defiled such an ingredient, aghast that it might have been spread across a microwavable macaroni and cheese concoction, would one dare say it, like ketchup. The horror pained her expression.

My father, at this point in the storytelling, usually in front of Mom, would say with that twinkle eye stare, no longer the puppy, more the assured golden retriever comfortable by hearth and fire, "and, I said to myself: 'yes, indeed she is a rare spice.' And, I never have gone back on that opinion."

Sheesh. He admitted proudly that his entire afternoon the next day was spent in search of this Rising Sun of a Holy Grail delectable, including an hour drive across the state line to an International Market (and weird animal parts apothecary) in Indiana. On a late Saturday afternoon, he entered the Prince & Davidson Kitchen and Cooking Emporium in Naperville, Illinois, and presented Elizabeth Child with a squeeze bottle of Neriume nectar, holding the prize in his hand, but back from her grasp, his own form of temptation. Jeffrey had discovered this magic edible, light-rust in color, sprang from Japanese apricots.

"Show me how to make your Li Hing Mui vinaigrette. I got around to reading the police report where it noted that you punched and kicked the perpetrator while he dragged you along the sidewalk by your purse strap until it broke, thus making his getaway. What food could be so worth dying for?"

And, together in the store, after hours, side-by-side in the demonstration kitchen, Elizabeth and Jeffrey made glorious food, and later, made glorious love on top of the prep table.

Recipe: Li Hing Mui Vinaigrette

1 whole egg
2 tablespoons Ume paste
2 tablespoons Li Hing Mui Powder
1/4 cup rice vinegar
1 cup salad oil
1 teaspoon fresh lemon juice

Place all the ingredients except the oil and lemon juice in a mixing bowl.
With hand-held immersion blender on medium speed, slowly add the oil in a
steady stream to create an emulsion. Continue until all oil is incorporated.
Finish with lemon juice. Chill until ready to use.
[we are using a recipe different from the book...author]
Place ingredients in blender, combining, adding in salad oil until smooth.

Recipe: Blanched Tomato & Japanese Cucumber Salad
(One Serving)

2.0 ounces Japanese Cucumber 8.5 ounces Red Tomato, skinless
.5 ounces Basil Sprig
.25 ounces Chives
.25 ounces Kaua'i Salt
2.0 ounces Li Hing Mui Ume Vinaigrette

Score the bottom of tomato with an X.
In a saucepan of boiling water, blanch tomato for 10 seconds. Transfer to an ice bath.
When cool, peel to-mato skin, keeping the flesh smooth.
Cut each tomato into 3 horizontal slices.
Keep the slices of each tomato stacked together.
Slice the cucumber into thin slices:
Arrange on salad plate in circular design.
Place the tomato in middle of circle.
Pour the vinaigrette over the arrangement.
Sprinkle salt (or Kosher salt) on top of tomato.
Garnish tomato with basil sprig and chives.

I adjusted my camera waiting for that mysterious green flash
when the sun's final rays edged below the red-lined sea. . . a sailboat passing
by within focus would be a postcard moment. . .

Chapter 10
Captain A'hoii

I decided to shoot the sunset, waiting for my father who was off on a tour of Chef Lorenzo's kitchens. As I passed through the lobby I spied the humid atmosphere of tourists bustling, doing their resort thing of checking in and out, placing names on the activities signup sheets. Whoa. I spotted the Beautiful People from the airport. So, they were staying at this hotel. What were the odds? Of all the places on island, they had to be here to remind me daily of fun I could be having.

They were gathered at a table in the hotel bar, off in a corner. Sipping wine and beer and not boisterous, actually somewhat serious, staring and taking notes off a meeting easel board with various numbers and letters written, set in three columns. I guess they had found a business trip way of deducting their travel costs. Smart Beautiful People. Their smiles were contagious. I smiled at their easy merriment and just then Mr. Rugged Leader himself looked up and caught my brief stare. His countenance widened to a full grin. A question posed drew his attention elsewhere, too fast for me to throw a responsive flirtatious smirk his way. Oh well, his loss. I continued my journey to the beach.

Oceanside, I adjusted my camera waiting for that mysterious green flash when the sun's final rays edged below the redlined sea. This is the phenomenon where the color spectrum is filtered out on the horizon. The red goes first, the atmosphere absorbs the blue, leaving last the prism's green — poof! — visible in a nano-second flash. Some see it, some don't.

This was the second of three handheld cameras I brought, Dad's reliable forty-year old Pentax, fitted with an 80 mm lens and 10% orange filter, using good old fashion negative film versus digital chip. A sailboat passing by within focus would be a postcard moment, but the sea sat still and empty of man. I was sitting at the beach bar with a few other sun setting aficionados. It is an island ritual; have a drink on the beach, and see nature's beauty, perhaps recharge internal batteries or see our lives as insignificant grains of sand on the cosmos shore. If the sun doesn't rise in the morning, I can say, "But I saw it just last night, and it looked fine to me."

I was debating whether to ask the bartender to whirl me up another Lava Flow. It would be my second on an empty stomach, having missed a suspicious lunch.

"Did you photograph Oli's death gurgle?" Not a pleasant voice. "What?"

"How much are the tabloids going to pay you?"

"What?"

"You're a shit if you take blood money."

The angry, slurring voice came from a young tattooed man, one I recognized as a band member in Oli's backup group, Pāhoehoe Sounds. Loosely translated, Smooth Lava. With him the girl band member; I think I heard she played the keyboard and sang backup vocals. The band member staggered toward me. Definitely, he was under the weather. The girl held onto him, more propping him up. A few feet away, swaying, pointing, shaking his hand at me with a fist and extended finger gesture.

"He is" — he choked — "was one of the greatest singers ever. He doesn't deserve to have his name, or his image, dirtied by you pappa— rizz-ee creatures. Give me that film!"

He made an ungainly lunge my way, and I yanked the camera, holding it outstretched over the bar, safe. He tripped and fell to his knees.

"Listen, kid, I took no photos of Oli. I was the one trying to save him. My only photos are of the resort before and after he got sick. And I don't sell my photos to anyone." My response harsh, more pissed at myself, realizing I could have made a bundle selling photos of 'the singer's death scene' to all the less-than-moral media. Too late. Walking down to the beach for the sunset I saw the local press and several stringer freelance photographers snapping away at the grotto for the AP, CNN, and the supermarket checkout stands. Instead of clicking away a roll of film I tried to save a man struggling for breath? And for that a dopey kid yells at me.

Another voice, pleasant and calm.

"Kukui, take Johnny Rocket over to a pool cabana and let him grieve and pass out with some dignity."

The man speaking stood tall, sunned, a few leather-skin wrinkles around the eyes showed character, yet I sensed breeding. Forties somewhere, I guessed, younger than my father, not by much. We watched the Goth girl cart off her stoned companion.

"I'm sorry, but they're all upset. It's an island tragedy, if not for the whole world. Oli will be a great loss to us all. His mythology begins today."

The man dressed in immaculate white, cotton shorts, unbuttoned shirt, a fine nest of tangled chest hairs, like I like. He carried himself well, and looked me in the eyes, clear and sharp, as if he could gain my heady thoughts.

"Oh, let me introduce myself," he said, his smile entrancing, teeth definitely bleached and sculptured. "I'm Jimmie Cooke. Cook with an 'e.' I work and live down at the marina."

Ah, yes. "You're the boat captain I saw earlier at the grotto. With Michael."

"Yes, I saw you there also. What you had to go through, very courageous."

He had cleaned up for the evening. That's why I couldn't place him at first. He had shaved off his beard stubble, and his hair, without his scrambled egg captain's cap, was washed, fluffed, and combed, no longer stringy and perspiration-matted. Looks could be deceiving, since I paid him no attention at the grotto.

"I'm Madison."

"Yes, I know. Madison Dayne, producer of the Jeffery Dayne TV show."

Elevating me to 'producer' flooded my mind, a feel-good feeling.

"A while back, I tried one of your father's New England chowder dishes. Small world, and now I will finally get to meet him. A rare privilege."

I wanted to be the center of attention, not in my father's shadow. I moved the subject matter elsewhere.

"You and Michael certainly were a help today. Everyone seemed in shock."

His eyes took me in. My casual outfit for the night, a light lime-yellow dress with floral print, bought on sale at a Fresh Produce store. No bra, feeling perky, easy comfort. I knew I was no alluring siren for sailors, but confident, if luck arose, I could stray a few ships toward a dangerous shoal.

"And, as Johnny Rocket asked, didn't you get an urge to shoot up a roll of film, all the excitement? It'll be a front page story."

I told him the truth.

"I shot some landscape photos of the hotel, the beach, the marina, just before I reached the grotto. After that, as you said, in the excitement, I forgot all about the camera. Everything was a blurred rush."

He took a bar stool next to me and ordered a Mai Tai. I noticed with band member Johnny Rocket's outburst, I had missed my sunset show. Was there a green flash? I noticed because Captain Jimmie Cooke sat in front of my perspective, the blood-red remnants of a perished sun, streaked behind him in the sky, as if a fiery halo. I longed to shutter that image.

We sipped our drinks, me more slurping the white foamy concoction.

"Johnny Rocket. That's a strange name for someone in a Hawaiian band?"

"I think, if I recall, his first name is Claudio, and Claude doesn't have that musical panache as a Johnny Rocket. I heard he wants to be a hard core rock 'n roller. Playing guitar and singing backup for a super star like Oli Palalū was paying his dues, his first step to his own recording label. I guess, with what happened today, he and Kukui have their careers at risk. I can understand him being zonked out."

"Kukui." I pronounced her name lilting. The Hawaiian language is rich with vowels. "She's an attractive girl. Very Hawaiian…" I paused, wondering how far I could take it with this stranger, "If she could lose the wiccan costume."

He gave me a strong, healthy laugh. It made me comfortable, happy that someone appreciated my wit. But I was right. Tear off Kukui's heavy metal hip couture, dye away the raspberry streaks in her black hair, and tone down the multi-piercing including the nose ring, and you might just find the girl-next-island.

"Kukui is a rarity. Her formal name is Kuikahi. One of the few pure Hawaiians. Her family is from Ni'ihau, the only protected island with pure, original Hawaiian culture. Accents you hear on Ni'ihau have similar word dialects heard in Tahiti. They sent her to get an education on O'ahu, to the Kamehameha Schools. Somewhere along the way she rebelled. She has a good heart, a lost soul trying to find herself."

"Aren't we all?" Said about me, not Kuikahi. For the first time, I noticed behind him on the ground sat a large white-green cooler on wheels, with a pull handle. "What's that? Your beer larder for a sunset sail?" The sky's blues purpled toward evening.

He laughed, lighter, more serious.

"Health Department shut down Chef Lorenzo's kitchen. I had to dress up my act and run down the coast and peddle my fish catch to the other hotels. Today, I was lucky. I had a run of dolphin fish, mahimahi to you food people, and hotels can't get enough. One of my boats is on charter. By unsaid law, and extra money, we keep most of the fish tourists catch. I've been selling direct to Lorenzo's kitchen. You can't get any fresher for the menu."

"You said boats, plural. You have more than one fishing boat?"

"Three ships, one sailboat."

"A fleet. Risky with bad weather? Or, if the fish aren't biting."

"I always work the averages and the angles. Try to make it profitable. It's more a retirement hobby."

"You're too young to be retired." I spoke too quickly, too eager to be charming. Age in an active man adds distinction. Jimmie Cooke, in my book, looked hottie in a beach bum rakish sort of way.

"Thanks for the compliment. For my present condition of self-induced leisure I have to blame a wealthy family, and a father who kicked the bucket for working too hard on Wall Street. He left his only son a fine inheritance. For a short time, I was a stockbroker, trying to follow in Papa's footsteps. Pity. Wanted to show him I could be one of the best, like him. Lose a parent, and we rethink our life goal priorities."

I said nothing, nodded to him, thinking of my own circumstances.

"I still dabble in the market," he continued, "and it's far more fun doing day trading off my Wi-Fi computer while trolling fishing lines behind the stern. You and your father should come out with me tomorrow, since you have time on your hands."

"Time?" I had a plate full of taping tomorrow, thinking ahead on perspectives for the lū'au shots.

"Oh, maybe you hadn't heard. With Oli's death, they've postponed the Lū'au Challenge for two days, out of respect."

"No, I hadn't heard." I had been in my room gussying up for my dinner with Jeffrey. I better track him down. Dad and I needed to discuss the ramifications of rescheduling.

"Yes, maybe we could do that. I'll ask him. Some boating would let me do some photo work from the seaside."

"In Hawaiian, toward the sea is called 'makai,' like Ho'oilina Kai. Toward the hills is 'mauka.' Please, accept my invitation. Tell your father he can teach me his fresh catch dishes. I'll supply the fish. We'll make them onboard. And tease him with the fact I stock some excellent '86 Jordan and an unopened case of '90 Opus One." He laughed. I matched his smile. He seemed to know the right buttons to push to entice a foodie star.

Captain Jimmie Cooke excused himself, graciously picking up my bar tab. We shook hands, slowly, he covering my dainty hand with both of his, encasing, swallowing. Something left unsaid, so I felt.

As he walked the path back to the marina pulling his dolly chest of fish smells, I pulled out my camera and focused on the back of his head. I zoomed in and snapped a quickie series when he made a side glance towards the vacant grotto of today's tragic adventure. With the evening embracing the warm land, the natural light sleeping, and without klieg back lighting, or spotlighted flash, his photographic image would rise from the processing chemicals, vague and shadowed.

Interesting, the oddity. Jimmie Cooke. Owner of charter cruise service. A ship's captain. Captain Cooke. I got it. Like Captain James Cook who discovered Hawai'i. This man, not that old, probably appreciated me more than I realized, since upon introduction, I did not play off on his name and make some smart-ass joke. Captain Jimmie and First Mate Madison. Cute. I toyed at mental possibilities. But, then I remembered what happened to the original Captain James Cook. Made chopped sirloin by the natives.

Recipe: Lava Flow Cocktail

1 1/2oz. Light Rum
2 oz. Pineapple Juice
1 oz. Cream of Coconut
1/4 cup Strawberry Puree
1/2 Banana
1/2 cup crushed Ice

In blender, combine all ingredients with ice. Blend 20 - 30 seconds.
Pour strawberry puree into a hurricane (or wide rim deep) glass
and follow with the blended mixture to create illusion of lava flow.
For the island spirit, add the cute little umbrella and garnish with pineapple slice.

Chapter 11
A Tangled Net Woven

Instead of my Father waiting for me in the lobby, I saw Michael K. Out of curiosity, earlier I had asked around and discovered his last name was Ka'aiea. Michael L. Ka'aiea. Hotel Resort Manager Cahill, I was told, called him Mike Lake, for what reason I don't know. Probably the 'L' was some long Hawaiian name and Cahill anglicized it. After all, the state fish is the: Humuhumunukunukuapua'a. Or easier said, the Trigger fish.

Michael was showing hotel guests a display of war weapons situated on the wall as colorful if not dangerous-looking object d'art. His animated personality held his listeners enthralled, a wide-eyed African-American couple draped in Tommy Bahama outfits. I could see their excitement at history-o-rama images of savages pummeling each other with strange tools of lethality. As he sent them on their way, he noticed my aloof presence.

"And what do those lovely toothpicks do?" Teasing, with a Lava Flow buzz, I pointed to the mounted array of weapons, spears and such, some nearly six feet long. He took a weapon from the wall display, balanced it in his hand and mimicked a throwing action.

"The polol ū, the long spear." He replaced the spear and retrieved an evil-looking club, with white razor points. "The lā'au pā lau. The shark teeth war club. Sometimes called the Lei'O-Manō. And here are the daggers. Bludgeon. Curve-bladed. Take your choice. Most of these had olona fiber string attached, used in close fights. The slashing weapons were designed to gut the opponent." He bantered friendly. "I don't think you want the mauling, bloodletting definition of these war implements."

"What does that one do?" I pointed to a small, honed, gray lava rock, like a small lifting weight, larger on one end.

"That pounds the taro root into poi." We exchanged stares imagining a man dying, his face poi-smeared.

"What goes unsaid," explained Michael, taking my view and mind back to the display, "is that these weapons are pre-Cook discovery. After that came the iron implements, cannons and guns. When King Kamehameha the Great invaded O'ahu in 1795, he used European advisors and cannon in the Battle of Nu'uanu Pali. Technologically improved killing won the field of battle."

"At least, you didn't say the 'white men' brought the killing machines."

"No, against all stories of simple native innocence, Hawaiians were killing each other in battles long lost in history, long before Captain Cook dropped anchor. But Cook and his men brought an unstoppable weapon. Disease. Poxes and venereal disease to a virus free people. By accounts, 400,000 Hawaiians lived on the islands in 1798. 26,000 Hawaiians, core survivors, survived by the 1920s. One might call Hawai'i's discovery by modern civilization an act of biological genocide."

Even in education, his intensity seemed hardened. He had to lighten up. I gave it a try.

"Speaking of Captain Cook, I met the modern Captain Cooke with an 'e'."

"Jimmie. Great guy. He and I go way back. He gave me my first good paying job, working summers on his boat, the year he arrived. He knew nothing of tying a half hitch knot, splicing line, or which side of the boat port was on."

"My father would say, 'Port is a sweet wine, but I prefer Madeira.'"

He smiled. A sweet smile. Like Captain Cooke's.

"As much as you might visualize a Captain Ron, or Gilligan's Skipper, don't let him fool you. He's a sharp man. He's been very helpful to us islanders." I did not see Captain Jimmie as the Skipper. Maybe a swaggering John Wayne in the role of Lord Nelson.

"Not a haole trust fund baby?" I said this in jest. A cloud went across his face, not upset, again this deep-seeded tone, spirituality in fathoms.

"He's been like an older brother to me since my father died."

"I'm sorry." Sincere about the loss of a parent. "You grew up around here?"

"I grew up on Kaua'i. My father worked in the last of the sugar cane mills. He was an important man on the island, because, though pure Hawaiian, he treated everyone alike. Hawai'i these days is an immigrant island, everyone traveling here looking for a better life. My father could have retired and headed up the Kaua'i clan of Hawaiians, those pledged, not to take over power, but to maintain the culture of the old ways, before women danced the hula, before songwriters spoke of little grass shacks in Keala-kekua."

"Sadly, he made one mistake." He went silent and returned the weapons to their quiet repose as art.

For some strange reason, perhaps a silly gesture to offer empathy, I put my hand on his arm. His silence festered. We Daynes are cursed to pry out hard truths. I took a guess.

"You came along," I said. He smiled, and in turn touched my hand. Warmth flowed.

"Something like that. My mom made her grand entrance on Kaua'i."

I could make the time, my father could wait and not to lose the moment, I sat on a lobby couch and patted the seat next to me for him to join, both oblivious of the hustle of tourism around us. My head tilted, inquiring, as the attentive listener. I sensed he required a neutral audience, one without preconceived prejudices, a confessor. He began, his voice easy in a sing-song fashion, a born storyteller, captivating.

"Kaua'i is a spectacular, beautiful island, a Hollywood producer's dream of the real jungle setting." He rattled off several names of well-known movies filmed on Kaua'i, the Garden Island: *Jurassic Park*, *South Pacific*, and *Blue Hawaii*. Even the obscure campy: 1958, *She Gods of Shark Reef*.

"My mother was, is, one of the top Chinese actresses, out of the Singapore movie colony. A classic artiste, personified rare jade. In her early film career, people would go to the cinema to watch any film she starred in. On Kaua'i, she came to make a Chinese film, a jungle war epic of Chinese fighting Japanese, both sides fighting against magical, soldier-devouring dragons, and thrown into the script, one endangered princess. This period was early kung fu days. A hit in Asia, the film never made the video store rentals in the U.S. Somewhere during the steaming days of camera action my father, who was hired as an extra, as a strong muscular guard to the imprisoned princess, found himself trapped in a hut during a tropical typhoon with this gorgeous woman, she in gossamer silks, he in loin cloth."

Michael leaned back on the couch and closed his eyes. My own vision of pounding rain on palm thatch, a man and woman trapped by hormones made me cross my legs and wipe the sweat from my palms.

"I get the picture." Not wanting to dwell on such an image.

"Anyway, filming ended and off she went back to Singapore only to discover to her surprise nature can storm within as without. My mother was, is, a remarkable though calculating woman. She feared a Chinese abortion. Perhaps she had a Taoist philosophy toward life. First, she hid her expanding stomach, then at an appropriate time, created a role for herself as the Christian nun raped by the warlord. Her belly swelled and I became a prop on the world's celluloid stage."

"I'm so sorry."

"Well, don't let me get ahead of myself in the telling."

"You look well-adjusted by the end of the story." I think I saw him put color to his face with a light blush of modesty.

"A month before I arrived, she flew back to Kaua'i, met with my father, told him the news, and demanded he marry her."

"A happy ending?"

"Define 'happy'? I said she was calculating. No, she brought legal papers for a subsequent quickie divorce, saying that after my birth she would relinquish all parental rights, that my father would be my sole caretaker, and she would settle on him an annual amount of dollars that would help support he and I until my 18th birthday."

"The epitome of a woman where career came first." Both our smiles bittersweet. I wondered if someday I would let my fledgling career dominate my heart.

"You have to remember my father was in total shock. The news that he was to be a father never entered his mind. But, he held inner core beliefs. He said he would do her bidding. However, he had his own demand."

"Okay, I'm hooked. She would have to commit hari kari after your birth."

"Madison, that's a Japanese custom. For excruciating pain, Chinese are meant to suffer a thousand paper cuts, not slice open their own stomachs."

"Go on, please." Interesting, he called me by my first name. For sure staff rules violated. I let it ride. I'm not a by the rules sort of person...

"Both of them went over to O'ahu, and when the time came, they drove to Kukaniloko, and she gave birth naturally, a mid-wife present, in a rock-strewn field on a large flat rock hidden by a red soil pineapple field, a night wind howling to hide my first cries."

"Why there?"

Michael, for a moment, sat silent. I understood he held more secrets within, but that was okay, for now.

"Let's just say, my dad had his old Hawaiian traditions. With my lineage Hawaiian-Chinese with American citizenship thrown in, I needed spiritual help more than others. Old people say Kukaniloko is the place 'to anchor the cry from within.' My mother, I think, loved the whole dramatic 'strang und durm' ambiance, the brutality of hard birth, the paganism. From what I heard, she used it in a movie a few years later, but the scene became the outer steppes of Mongolia and she again a deflowered princess.

"So here I am."

"Sad, and, your Mother and Father never saw each other again?"

"Are you kidding, she told my father it was the best raw sex she'd ever experienced. Every few years on her way between the Orient and Hollywood she'd do a layover, spend a weekend at Turtle Bay Beach, getting waxed outside by attendants and inside by my father. He never took me, always considered her visit a personal vacation earned by being a single child-rearing parent. I grew up accepting she'd tolerate cruel, insulting movie critics easier than motherhood. About ten years ago, a week after they announced the shutdown of the sugar mill, my dad dropped dead. Heart attack. A great beast, a good man, he could not live without hard toil on his brow."

"And your mother?"

"She'll never die. Plays the film roles of the prying mother-in-law; the aged dynasty queen. Beyond my 18th birthday, once a year, I receive a small stipend check, no note. More a reminder of my father's memory than any token toward my existence. We've never met. No reason to do so."

"But Detective Kee? He's related?"

"Are you really that interested?"

"Lore of the islands is required research." A vague answer masked my up-close curiosity of one of its inhabitants. Curiosity, the Dayne curse.

"My mother's family came to Hawai'i in the 1860s. Made money in real estate on O'ahu, branched out to the other islands. My Chinese great grandfather and grandmother were trapped when they went back to see their ancestral home in the 1930s. World War II intervened. Post war, and around the time of the Korean War, my mother was born in Singapore."

"Have I heard her name in films?"

"Tsin Kee? I doubt it."

"But, around here they know you as, what, 'Number One Son of Tsin Kee'?"
He laughed, seeing I teased good naturedly.

"Undeserved notoriety. The Kee side of the family tree sees me as a direct link
to her mysterious allure. She represents the memories of their ancestral home land,
their vanished Hakka village. I have Kee relatives everywhere. An extended family
of distant cousins. It's like a support club, whenever required. In Chinese Mandarin,
they say the word as a 'táng'."

I knew I was prying but what fun.

"And, somewhere, Jimmie Cooke entered your life?"

"Right on cue after my father's death. On his first circumference of the islands,
he sailed to Kaua'i and into Hanama'ulu Bay outside of Līhu'e, where John Wayne
filmed Donovan's Reef. His crew got drunk on him, and I was one of several hired
to get him back safe and dry to the Big Island. I stayed, took up hotel odd-jobs,
helped on his fishing charters. His foundation paid for my entire Nevada education
at hotel school."

"Foundation?"

"J. Cooke Foundation. Yeah, he set it up, not his old man. He's been quietly
funding education for those he personally sees as potential good citizens. The whole
litany, regardless of race, creed, color."

"Very noble of him."

"A captain among men. He says I'm his protégée, a Dale Carnegie success
story. Whatever that means, but if it's bragging rights I turned out fine by his expectations, so be it. I think the outcome of his investment still remains to be calculated."

We looked down to find I had my hand resting on his. Politely, he stood up.

"I better get back to my hosting jobs. The hotel hired me as an assistant to an
assistant, but where I want to succeed in management they don't seem to have a
clue on how to run an executive training program. Right now, I am doing a lot of
self-teaching."

"Best of luck. Sounds like you have the drive to get there."

"Thanks. Oh, that reminds me." He seemed hesitant. "Did you hear the Lū'au Challenge was postponed?"

"Yes, in fact, Captain Jimmie told me."

"The real news is that day after tomorrow, the night before the lū'au competition begins, there's going to be a musical memorial to Oli Palalū. The tear-jerker will be the Pāhoehoe Sounds performing at the end of the show."

Seconds of silence, his mind searching, made him awkward, childlike.

"I was wondering if you would like to go with me?" Another pause. "I mean, sort of me escorting you, since you are one of the guests of honor. Your father already said he would be attending."

A let down. He asked me for a date, an almost date, but to be chaperoned.

"My father would be joining us?"

"No, Desi said she would take him."

That woman's grasping plot was afoot, but not if I could help it.

"Michael, I would be honored to accompany you."

It wasn't until I saw my father embracing another man in the parking lot that a thought struck me. Two men in the space of an hour had asked me to join them on outings. If not bona fide dates, the atmosphere would be in place. I only had to add fragrant spice.

Chapter 12
Merry the Man and His Papaya

Concierge Services for Ho'oilina Kai made 8:00 p.m. reservations at Merriman's, a fine dining restaurant up the hill in Waimea. The hotel placed a jeep at our disposal and with the wind whipping my hair we made the climb from coast into the hills. The ride became National Geographic. Island floral changed from salt-sea scrub to rain-kissed lushness. I needed this time out and leaned back as Jeffrey negotiated the winding turns. That's all I wanted to be for the rest of the trip, observing passenger, not active participant.

Merriman's Restaurant, off the main road, looked like a yellow-white plantation house, nothing ostentatious like resort opulent glitter, nor touristy island kitsch of broken surfboards, and hanging fish nets. The interior resembled laid-back French Country. Local artists with their acrylic dabs or water-color swirls were afforded free gallery wall space to accent the décor.

Jeffrey gave me the background as the hostess seated us. "Your mother and I found Merriman's, Peter and Vicki's restaurant, the first year they opened back; when was that, 1988, or '89, I believe. Peter had, as they say, been 'down the hill' working at the Mauna Lani Resort. I think what he strived to do with his own place is what we see as today's standard in upscale restaurant chains, kind of Asian-Hawaiian fusion. Peter made his name by stressing 'regional cuisine' and meaning it."

I was silently swearing off Lava Flows until the next Ice Age, and a little light headed I tried to guess. "Something like: you are what you eat, right?"

My father did not wish to lecture. He knew I might get abrasive, defensive, as if I knew everything. Patience with me made him a saint.

"Merriman's specializes in gaining produce and food products, organic, if they can, from all the local growers. They've developed vendor relationships to envy, like having your own extended greenhouse and pastures. We can create a dish from a recipe and call it excellent. But seeing first-hand the growth and cultivation of the ingredients develops a meal *par excellance.*"

The waiter proffered menus and a wine list. Jeffrey had his mind set.

"Considering how the palate will wander here tonight, we'll taste both white and red. I'd like to start with a…"

He didn't ask me. I'm just the hired grunt, without class or finishing school.

"Madison, is wine okay with you? I noticed, by your speech, that you may have had a few fru-fru soda pop drinks. Where at the pool? The beach bar? I don't know if you should mix alcohol."

I should have ordered a Longboard Lager beer from Kona Brewing and gained his outright displeasure. *Chill, Madison, you're too uptight from these strange first day 'festivities.'* This was a working vacation, under his influence, I could be flexible. Who knows, maybe I'd learn something that would upscale me back in west L.A. nightlife.

"I'm fine. I'll stick with one glass of white, whatever comes out of the spigot."

He eyed me, gauging my sobriety, I'm sure.

"We'll try your '04 Grgich Hills, Fume Blanc."

When alone, after the bread delivery — offered with multi-flavored butters — and after the bottled water was served, I had to ask, "Okay, you were in this clutch with Chef Lorenzo. I saw tears in his eyes. Don't tell me this is a new version of Brokeback Volcano?"

"He's certainly emotional. More temperamental than most other chefs I've met. His father was a line cook at the 3-star Maisons de Bricourt and his mother sang chorus in the Venice Opera Company. The world's been his to prove his talent. He slaved and suffered to become world class, and then, the Health Department shut down his kitchen. To say he's devastated is a mild statement. He and I had walked through his entire operation, from refrigerator to checking all condiment jars. He knew it was I who was having the pūpūs. He personally supervised. No, I can't fault Lorenzo or his staff. Somewhere, from the minute the meal was ready to be served, to wheeling the cart down for grotto delivery, a distraction occurred, and someone acted. A sleight-of-hand to pour in liquid with those green plant flecks and a quick stir."

"So, you don't think Chef Lorenzo has it in for you."

"Of course not. I'm participatory in the culinary arts, not a food critic."

"If the food was tampered with, he could be sacked, as a scapegoat."

"Yes, sadly possible. He swore if he caught the culprit, he would kill him."

Such thoughts of revenge brought momentary silence to the table.

"That's comforting to know," I said, tired of this bad day. "A crazed French-Italian Chef with carving knives ready to exact judgment."

"What's more interesting about his wailing is that he begged me to help him find the guilty party. As a compatriot connoisseur, and a guest at the hotel, I feel an obligation to help where I can."

The wine served, I caught the glances of the wait staff paying close attention to our table. They knew who I was sitting with. Television exposure will do that. No extraneous fawning words would be said, though above any current impeccable table service, I sensed the ultra-treatment would be laid on thick.

Jeffrey and the Cellar Master/sommelier launched into discourse on the new additions to the Merriman bottled inventory. Jeffrey, as they conversed, went through the proper rituals of smelling the cork, swirling wine in the glass, a deep sniff of the bouquet, the mouth swishing taste, and the thoughtful pronouncement. "Excellent with an edge; a light tannic tart, but not bitter." The sommelier agreed, understanding the vino language I could not translate. My glass was filled, and then his again. To get a rise I should have asked for a straw.

"Madison, wine, a gift of the gods, is an individual experience. No taste buds are alike, so the taste has to be for your senses, no one else's. It's totally acceptable to be a snob, for your enjoyment is what they are here to achieve, not vice versa."

I sipped seeking holy enlightenment. It did taste good, a little bite to it, maybe a smidge of tartness.

As we munched bread and waited to order, I asked, "So, how does my father discover the culprit who tampered with our pūpū food? You're no detective. And still keeping active your attorney license does not qualify you for a police badge."

"Alteration of food is a proficiency of mine. How much to add and subtract is deductive logic. And, the word 'detective' suggests 'detect,' and one detects by asking questions." He paused and looked around the room. "As we are about to do."

Manager Cahill of the Ho'oilina Kai Grand Hotel Resort approached our table.

"Mr. Dayne, I should have known you would consider this one of the best eateries on the island. After the bloody fiasco today, heads will roll, I can assure you."

The sacrificial lamb search had begun. I felt sorry for Chef Lorenzo. Maybe my father could indeed help him, point blame in another direction.

"Mr. Cahill, I notice you have a large table gathering over in the corner. Are those guests of the hotel?"

My eyes poked around a grouping of palm fern dividers to see a table of Oriental gentlemen chattering in animated conversation. Japanese, by my guess.

"Those are the big boys who own the Ho'oilina Resort. The Kiyoshi Corporation."

Jeffrey sipped his wine and gave me that eye, implying, "Watch this."

"The death of Oli must be bad karma for them," commented Jeffrey, casual as if disinterested.

Cahill smiled in confidence. "You can say that again. More than you'd know. The Resort is under contract to be sold, some real estate trust in Europe. These guys had to get it open after the years of litigation. The opening established the base purchase price. Now, with this bad news, which the buyer somehow already heard about, there's pressure to reduce the price. They're over there crying in their sake."

"Wasn't the Lū'au Challenge supposed to help smooth over the island trouble? What was it all about again?" Jeffrey, I'm sure had heard the story.

"Oh, I really don't want to talk about it. I wasn't around when it happened. I came on board only to open the resort."

"What's a 'heiau'?" Jeffrey sipped his wine.

Cahill looked uncomfortable and stared at surrounding tables. He looked at a waiter passing by. His voice went to a gruff whisper.

"The Japs blew it by bringing in a west coast construction firm going cheap, hiring a boatload of Mexican illegals. They go about tearing up the land for the golf course, and one of the bulldozer guys sees this pile of rocks and tears it down. Turned out to be one of the largest religious temples of ancient Hawaiians along the Kona coast. The local eco brownies, all of them a bunch of island Talibans, went ape-shit. Pardon my language, Miss Dayne, but it is so infuriating the time and money wasted. Five year shutdown on the project. They sued the Kiyoshi Corporation. Filed injunctions."

"Didn't the issue go up to the Hawaiian Supreme Court before the State Legislature stepped in?" Cahill's expression showed surprise at my father's knowledge about this Hoʻoilina construction fiasco.

"Yes, the politicians created a compromise bill no one's happy about. Kiyoshi paid a hefty cash fine. Public access land has been set aside for the locals, and the hotel has to demonstrate more sensitivity, like the Lūʻau Challenge. We paid a fistful for the rights to host it this year. Still no peace with Old Joe Coffee on the warpath. And now, Fat Oli drops dead. I hope the new owner can grease the right palms."

With such snide cultural arrogance, nothing could stop my frothy response.

"Yeah, I took photos of the crime scene with the hotel in the background. Tomorrow, I'm going to sell the lot of them to all the tattling gossip media." I said this with a face of benign innocence, leaving Cahill shocked.

My father ignored my snide jab.

"Is that why Michael Kaʻaiea works for you and the hotel? Appeasement to the locals?"

Cahill might have felt he was whipsawed by the two of us. He sought to define Jeffrey; like, is this hotel guest a friend or foe? I could sense the hotel manager moving into a political cautious mode.

"Mike Lake has his degree in hotel administration. He's well thought of in the community. And, Mr. Cooke recommended him. I've not been disappointed in my decision."

Jeffrey nodded.

"No, I agree; he seems to be the right person to quiet down his uncle."

A waiter appeared and hovered for our entrée decisions, and Manager Cahill used the moment to retreat, bidding us a lovely evening and to enjoy the meal.

I whispered to my father.

"Was that racism I just heard? Right in the middle of the world's most ethnic melting pot?"

"Madison, what you heard was a man who misses the good old days of Victorian colonialism."

On dinner selection, I bowed to my father's wisdom. He had eaten here religiously in times past, so one could not ask for a better menu guide.

For appetizers, he ordered:

Kālua Pig & Sweet Onion Quesadilla

Big Island Goat Cheese & Mango Tart (served with Arugula and Strawberry Vinaigrette).

Vine Ripened Hamakua Springs Tomatoes.

I felt full at this moment without even opening my mouth.

"We will split the entrées; see which one you like the best for the next visit."

For the fish he selected: *Sautéed Kampachi with Red Pepper Coulis, Chuka Soba & Lop Chong Sausage Stir-fry.* For a red meat, he had changed his mind on steak and decided on *Kahua Ranch Lamb, with a side of Cabernet & Foie Gras Sauce.*

I had glanced briefly at the menu, amazed at all the exotic sauces. That's when I saw one menu fish selection, served with Li Hing Mui, an ingredient to a Tequila Butter sauce. Could a food bring back painful memories to mind and tongue? Yes. Jeffrey most likely intentionally skipped this choice. I hurt with him, helpless to know what button to push or unlocking key to find a happy tomorrow. I knew it wasn't what's her name, and that sparked me.

"I guess ol' Desi of PR is working late trying to crank out the official line for the hotel about Oli's death. A 'freak accident' sort of thing." I sipped my wine, using the glass as a shield.

"I think she's spending the evening with the surviving band members, the Pāhoehoe Sounds. All are devastated and in deep mourning. You know her son's in the band?"

"Her son?"

"Yes, calls himself, 'Johnny Rocket.' Sounds more suitable for a roller-skate hamburger drive-in."

I was in mid-sip. He handed back my sass with a full blast, tactfully, in a careful thrust.

"Did you know she had taken her son's garage band," he said, "toned them down, and negotiated them to be the backup group to this Oli when he was trapped in Hawaiian karaoke, one hundred pounds less, two years ago. According to Michael, Desi became the ad hoc band's manager and promoter. Oli's rising star, his hit songs, had a future to make them a lot of money, and now this. I'm sure she's trying to keep them all on an even keel. Who knows what young people do with grief?"

He wasn't talking about me. Or was he? Was he condemning me? No, I think he was focused on time present, thinking who might have mistakenly caused the death of Oli Palalū.

"Yes, I saw Johnny Rocket down by the beach. A little drugged out."

"Aren't pills and drugs and groupies a requirement with rock bands?"

He was not prudish, a little old-fashioned, but his flat humor returned us to safe ground.

"I don't think Oli's sort of ballad music invokes guitar breaking and hotel wrecking. But Johnny Rocket certainly comes across as a headbanger."

First course arrived and we moved in to important truths: starvation abatement.

During the salads I realized to my surprise my plate was scraped clean.

"What was that dressing? That was fantastic."

The server, on clearing plates, replied, "Banana Papaya Sauce." The salad had consisted of papaya, macadamia nuts, and baby greens. I found myself asking for the recipe, something out of the ordinary for me.

By dessert, which honestly, I can't repeat or I would gain immediate pounds, our host, Peter Merriman, dropped by and accepted accolades for a dinner fit for a star. Jeffrey went through each meal item and gave comment, not rating, more as with a wine, a discussion on the various creative flourishes. Mr. Merriman complimented my Father on his best seller, *Insatiable: Further States of Epicurean Delights*, and Jeffrey responded in kind to our host's compilation cookbook, *The New Cuisine of Hawaii*, produced with eleven top chefs of the islands.

Once outside the restaurant, Jeffrey said,

"Next time we venture forth up here we'll go to Daniel Thiebaut's restaurant, just blocks away. Imagine. Two outstanding gourmands extraordinaire to be found in this small burg, originally founded as a cattle ranch town."

We did not drive back to the hotel resort, more a corpulent rolling down the hill from Waimea. My extreme compliment to Merriman's came from patting my tummy, wondering where all the morsels could fit.

When I returned and opened my hotel room it was in shambles, ransacked.

Recipe: Banana Papaya Sauce

1/2 ripe papaya - peeled and seeded
1 banana
1/3 C. plain yogurt
1/3 C. lime juice
1/3 C. lemon juice
1 Tbsp. honey
Put all ingredients in a food processor and process until smooth.
Yield: 2 Cups. Use with fish and/or salad.
- from Merriman's Restaurant

Chapter 13
The Shag Story

I slept with my father; rather, in the adjoining suite they'd given him, the one with the kitchen. I could not sleep in a room where I felt personally violated. Just because hotel security changed the key code, how could I feel any more secure?

Very strange circumstances. Nothing appeared to be stolen. Loose change and traveler's checks were on the dresser. Losing the camera equipment spiked my immediate panic. All accounted for, though someone tossed the place, apparently looking for something. Film canisters were opened but the unexposed film untouched. The Pentax camera had been opened, exposing and ruining the fresh roll of film I had loaded for my sunset visit to the beach. Clothes had been yanked from drawers, or apparently rifled. I got this feeling that a sicko might have broken in, because all my panties and bras were removed with some gentle order in mind. Other clothes were dumped unceremoniously on the floor, but my personal unmentionables were merely rearranged, like they were fondled and laid reverently down. God, I hope not sniffed. How disgusting. I planned on having the hotel, on their dime, wash, iron, and sanitize all my clothes.

The night manager expressed sympathy but could do little. This was petty crime, breaking and entering, vandalism at the most, and hardly that. I was to file a report with the police in the morning. I could see it going nowhere. The break-in didn't reach the fingerprinting level. The police would hardly roust the entire hotel and start grilling suspects. So strange. Beyond HDTV camera equipment, owned by the Food TV Channel, not mine, what did I have worth the risk and effort?

As I said goodnight, Jeffrey informed me of his, our plans, for the next day.

"I made the calls. We've accepted Cooke's invitation to go fishing, boat touring, and perhaps a *safe* luncheon, in a secluded cove."

"Is there enough room?" My mind conjured up the small charter fishing vessels I'd seen at the marina, little deck room, cramped steerage.

"I heard it was adequate. I've invited Chef Lorenzo along, with Cooke's blessing. We are going to fix one of the Chef's dishes. I'd like you to shoot the food prep. Giving him an international audience, via a camera lens, might return him halfway to sensibility. Goodnight, Madison."

"Good night, Dad."

I felt squeamish, a kid on a camp-over, warm recollections of my childhood, wanting to recapture the snuggle value. I could not sleep right away, all nerves. Working on settling down I took the elevator down to the lobby for a little jaunt around the interior flower gardens of the hotel. A janitor buffing the floor and a night clerk doing paperwork were the only people in view. It seemed the tourist crowd crashed early from their day romping exertions. Even the parrots had covers over their cages. I passed the walled weaponry display, all accounted for, still looking lethal. The main bar was closed. In the corner, leaning against the wall, were the flow chart notations from the Beautiful People. I studied what they had written down. For some strange reason, like being drawn in to an unknown labyrinth, I went back to the lobby, found a sheet of hotel stationary, returned, and copied down the two columns.

N 36° 06. 381'   W 115° 10. 348'

N 36° 07. 573'   W 115° 11. 538'

Don't ask me why. Maybe my hidden urge to be part of their pleasure and mirth or wondering what they were up to intrigued me. Stock quote machinations? Real estate formulas? If I could get one of them alone, I would put on an act of 'silly me for being so nosy,' but....

My walk downstairs dissipated my high-strung energy, the cause still apparent: not knowing who had broken into my room, and for what purpose. I had no answers.

When I returned to my new room I opened the sliding glass door to listen to the ocean's repetitive melodies, wishing I could add to those sounds some strong medicinal relaxant. I saw my father on the next suite balcony leaning over the railing, silent, deep in thought, a brandy snifter in hand. Above us a billion stars danced. I watched as his eyes focused on the dark and restless sea, longing for his lost mermaid.

This was their island.

Here's another of my journal stories, this one from the dusty files of long, long ago.

So, Elizabeth and Jeffrey are hitting it off. Jeffrey believes she is the one, the ever-sought soul-mate, so he constantly reminds all with this oft told reminiscence. To ingratiate himself into her world since he certainly did not want to bring the drudge of rampant crime into their intimate conversations, Jeffrey begins the trek to Naperville, to her kitchen store, Prince & Davidson, where she was manager. Strategically, he began the love conquest, coveting her time and presence, in the subtle pretext of taking cooking classes, which by fate, he is quite good at.

This rutting ritual went on for a one year dating cycle. Commute and cook, and for dessert, if not also as hors d'oeuvres, nibble at appetite engorgements of love and lust. In short time, they joined in those little habits that become endearing in couples. Sunday mornings, after reading the Chicago newspapers in bed, they would go through her accumulated pile of food magazine subscriptions tearing out recipe sheets. As a couple they did all things epicurean; as example, attending wine tastings to learn snobby phraseology like, 'the wine has oak wisps with hints of green apple bouquets.' Jeffrey would surprise his sweetheart with out-of-print 1930s and 40s cookbooks for her extensive foodie library. They discovered common enjoyment in regional cuisines. Sometimes, they'd order their vente seven-pump vanilla lattes at the mega bookstores, browsing and buying, seeking the latest in gastronomical challenges from far distant places. And thereby, most above all, they would cook together, experiment, create, laugh and hug, and sup in each other's ardor.

As fairy tales dictate supposed happy endings, they did everything proper regarding engagement and marriage rituals to please all parental sides. The new Mr. & Mrs. Dayne embarked on their honeymoon to the state of Hawai'i, an inaugural trip for both, to the island chain's largest land mass, also called Hawai'i. They spent ten days languishing, I presume, in rapture at Mauna Kea Resort, off the Queen Ka'ahumanu Highway, just a few miles from where my father and I are presently staying at the newly opened Ho'oilina Kai Grand Hotel Resort.

When not behind a 'Do Not Disturb' sign, the besotted honeymooners toured the island imbibing in cooking classes at one gourmet restaurant after another, offset with menu sampling at local bistros, going native at spam-laden greasy spoons, or savoring odors of Kālua pig smoldering in wood-fired imu pits. Somehow during all such distractions of palate I was conceived.

Mother, once in a fit of giggles, with her attempt at the birds and bees dialogue, which I knew enough of, thank you, let me know that I germinated not from a normal course of human reproduction methodology, but a riotous evening of honeymoon debauchery after consuming one, though I think two bottles more accurate, of an expensive 1984 California merlot, rolling around in the beachside condo like—I don't want to even think of the animal allusion.

Nine months later, in the miracle of pain and joy, both having equal choice of names, I became Madison Merlot Dayne. My father took the high road considering the lawyerly integrity of James Madison, a founding Federalist and U.S. president, explained Jeffrey, the proud new father. And, he had heard, President Madison's wife had something to do with early American colonial food. Like ice cream. Haha.

Mother, on the other hand, remembered that island night of sweat and sweet bliss, alternating passion in crescendos like the rolling, crashing waves heard from inside and outside the bedroom. Feelings, though inebriated, were being expressed in soul-seared whispers, commitments made of volcanic duration. 'Merlot' came added to the Madison name. Mom, in her innuendo humor, of course had to go on and tell me I could have been called 'Claire Murray Dayne,' from that night, same name as the rug designer they shag-burned across from floor to heavens. Sometimes, children need less information rather than more.

Chapter 14
Pursed Clues

A shark bit at my shoulder as I struggled in frothing water, gasping, being dragged down to the murky ocean floor. Not a shark, but a flailing Oli, dropping into darkness as I opened puffy eyes.

My father, already dressed for the day, tugged at my shoulder. No Jaws. No drowning singer.

"What did you have in your purse last night? Where is it?"

Sleep deprived, I pointed to the floor, under some salvaged clothes. My canvas tote, stitched with yarn flowers, he retrieved and brought bedside. The bag, a cheap souvenir from Cabo San Lucas and a forgetful wanderlust Spring Break. Before I could protest he dumped out the contents. Praise be the saints! The condoms, unopened, and my morning-after pills, a full bottle, always were secreted in a camera case pocket, even the thief had not discovered. My makeup lay scattered and revealed me as a minimalist in facial construction. The stars got make-up; behind the camera it mattered little.

Jeffrey picked up a roll of film.

"What's this?"

"From your old Pentax. Keeps me in the dark room practicing. What I shot yesterday on arrival. Using the hand digital I popped the demonstrators at the front gate."

"I didn't see you taking photos."

"A good photo journalist has to catch his quarry unawares. Besides, digital shots are usually silent." Not mentioned was I got off a few surreptitious pics of Michael K. carting our luggage on arrival.

He gave that consideration. "With the Pentax camera what did you photograph?"

"The front of the hotel on arrival; behind the hotel on my way to the grotto, the grounds and the marina. That's about it. I changed film for the beach bar at sunset." He pulled my digital camera from the purse dump.

"This the digital you are referring to?"

I had to think, reconstructing yesterday's timetable.

"Walking back with your plastic evidence containers, I think I snapped a couple of shots of the guards chasing the interlopers, maybe some rough stuff pushing and punching."

"Trying for your Rodney King Pulitzer?"

"Interesting situations intrigue me. Family habit."

Jeffrey balanced the film canister against the digital camera, weighing importance. I showed him how to pull up the photos on the smaller camera and let him scroll back and squint at the postage stamp display screen.

"Maybe your burglar didn't get what he was looking for. He exposed the film in your camera left in the room, correct?"

"That was a clean roll I loaded and yes, ruined. No exposures." Well, except the fuzz composition of the Captain Cooke head shots. Not important.

"But, he didn't get the photos you took, that's important, I think. Maybe you took a photo yesterday that compromised a protestor, or worse, caught someone where he or she wasn't supposed to be, like near the grotto."

I threw back the bed sheet eager for the chase. "We need to get the 35 mm film developed as soon as possible. And print out the digital card."

At the hotel front desk we found the photo development service required courier service to Waikoloa Marketplace, with delivery back by early evening if not next morning. So much for this detecting jazz and a quick solution to the crime, whatever crime it was. Standing around, I spot the Beautiful People beginning their raucous day. Interesting. They were loading into three different Jeep Wranglers.

All wore white ball caps with a red marking. ⊕ Was this a religious-like symbol? Great. Probably a bunch of missionaries out to proselytize for the flock.

Several of them were holding some hand held device, waving them at each other, laughing. As they drove off I realized I could wait no longer with not knowing.

"I have a question," I asked the valet, who had just seen off the Jeep caravan. "I saw these people earlier and note they are off on some sort of… excursion. Do you know what they are doing? Just in case my father and I might want to try it."

The valet, dressed in his hotel uniform of white shorts and short sleeve white shirt, ever helpful, saw no harm in the question.

"I am not sure, ma'am. But, they have GPS units. I think it's one of those geo-cash games." My blank face begged more knowledge. "You know, it's a treasure hunt sort of thing. Like a scavenger hunt, but with technology. They are given some coordinates and the GPS leads them to find a treasure. Like On-Star in cars. Nothing of value, I hear. Sign their names when they find the hidden box, or whatever."

I thanked him, the mystery thus solved. They were playing a game, with three teams. Young affluents at leisure play. Means nothing to me. Did their leader choose the teams? Did he put that athletic top heavy blonde on his team? I could not recall if I saw her in the jeep with him. It's of no consequence.

Chapter 15
Shaken Not Stirred

Back in the room I dressed for a day on the water, a two-piece under shorts. I scarfed down nuts and potato chips from the room mini-bar since eating food from any hotel restaurant left me wary. I went off in search of Jeffrey who told me to track him down at the hotel's fine dining restaurant. Chef Lorenzo had named his gourmet showplace the Uakea La Reve, loosely translated, 'white mist dream.' The front desk called the place Lorenzo's, while I heard valet gossip about the shutdown over at Larry's Pub. So much for high-faluting name branding.

As I walked through the resort's floral pathways toward the restaurant I saw Michael and waved. He threw back a friendly grin. Heads turned. He had been in a meeting held in the beauty of the warming morning, the humidity yet to appear. Excusing himself, he bound with athletic leaps to the top of the grass-stone amphitheater to join me where I stood on the over-looking path. It was an open air amphitheater, comfortable for 200 people, with grass seating, designed for convention seminars, wedding ceremonies, and, as I saw, a concave of secretive Hawaiians.

"Conducting a class for senior citizens?" My playful question meant to match his buoyant mood.

"Diplomatic peace talks."

"Manager Cahill said you were community liaison for the hotel."

"More like his 'token' ambassador; but hey, I'm making progress."

"No more protests, goodwill among men?"

"Far short of peace in our time; let's say a shaky truce is at hand."

"Your Uncle going along, willingly?" I glanced down at the old men, among them Michael's uncle, Joe Coffee. He glared back. Though my father might have to, I didn't have to make friends with all of the unruly natives. I winked at Michael's uncle, throwing at him an exaggerated grin of gritted teeth, lopsided and dipsy.

"These men are the elders representing all the islands. They're the kahuna, the senior priests to the old religion. Keepers of the Kapu. In ancient times, their will was ultimate law. Back when the gods gave favor to the islands. Except for my uncle, they have no political agenda. The death of Oli Palalū is a bad omen. It does no one any good. I've convinced them to let tomorrow night's memorial concert for Oli and the day-long Lū'au Challenge be used to reestablish harmony between the land and its people."

I liked listening to him, a man of purpose. My problem was in gobbling up all the rigmarole of ancient deities. Being from L.A., all our gods are tarnished and self-serving.

"Your uncle was on that surf rock yesterday, I assume invoking the spirits. Was he bringing down a curse upon the Ho'oilina Kai Resort?"

"Joe Coffee believes that someday a new heiau will be built somewhere on this property to replace the one destroyed by the hotel's construction crews. He must keep the gods appeased that the sacrilege soon will be atoned and made right. In other faiths one might compare his quest to bringing the Israelites back to Jerusalem and rebuilding the destroyed temple."

"Aren't the Israelites back in the promised land? With daily violence? Will it be the same for the Hawaiian people? Restoring the old ways, that is? At a bloody cost?"

"My uncle's beliefs lack practicality. Merely invoking Kāne, Kū, and Lono won't gain dominance over his promised land nor see his monarchy restored."

"You live and work here. Do you see a new heaiu being built?"

"Not with the current owners. If the Europeans buy the place, who knows? They might want to make a peace offering, continue this truce. All the heiau rocks remain stored on the other side of the maintenance sheds. Looks like rubble. I find no fault in hoping some day we will rebuild a sacred place of worship. Our history is the central thread holding together this society's fabric; it's not the whole cloth to wear. Uncle Joe has yet to realize these islands have evolved into a multi-culture. I can help calm these present troubled waters, miracles take a little longer."

I laughed. Perhaps this shaky peace would ease my mind as to the more sinister events.

"I'm sure if anyone can conjure up a miracle, you probably could." Now, why did I say that? It almost gushed out.

His smile turned mildly serious, less harsh. A feeling emoted of being unsatisfied.

"These old men are true to their beliefs. But, I don't see any miracles on the horizon that will answer their prayerful incantations. These days, to create workable solutions it takes cold hard cash and the juggling of political enemies to forge alliances. Today, miracles must be preceded by a business plan. That's what Captain Jimmie says, 'the business plan comes first'."

I touched his arm and looked into his eyes, seeking that depth he spoke from.

"Michael, what do you want?"

"Why can I talk to you so easily, Miss Dayne?

He tried tactfully to avoid my question.

"Michael, remember my name's Madison, and you were about to make a profound statement." My sincerity infectious, he laughed, accepting my intent to pry.

"Okay. Madison. I need a direction, my own soul-seared cause. I feel I'm drifting miles from shore." He made light of his personal burdens. "Where's divine guidance when you most need it?"

Old Joe Coffee stared up at us with an evil eye. His lips moved slightly in unheard chants. A cloud moved across the sun, a gust of wind swirled my hair. I wondered if I was recipient of some mumbo jumbo spell, amounting to no good.

When I arrived at the restaurant I found my father. As usual, he had placed himself in the midst of turmoil. Two police officers, Detective Kee, and Chef Lorenzo followed Jeffery as he exited the back of the restaurant.

"As Chef Lorenzo showed you the procedure of food prep, and with his oversight, the pūpū platters left without those green flecks mixed in."

Detective Kee's inscrutable face and his look to the restaurateur bore the silent accusation, 'if one accepts Chef Lorenzo was not the culprit in the first place.'

Jeffrey, ignoring the chef's rising anger percolation, continued his analysis of the crime as he saw it. His eyes studied the loading dock area where we stood, all of us inhaling the smell of rotten lettuce mixed with spoiled and trashed leftovers in the dumpster, the antithesis to my perfume walk along the floral pathway.

"So, any adulteration of food took place from this point down to the grotto. And you questioned the porter who made the delivery?"

"What can I say," acceded Detective Kee. "Nothing about him suggests a desire to taint the pūpūs, if that's what happened?" The detective came across as a stickler for police procedural.

"I did not do it and my staff is trés loyale." Chef Lorenzo issued his umpteenth cry of innocence, hoping that my father was wrong about the food being the root cause, and a simple explanation would make his nightmare disappear. My father is seldom wrong when it comes to food.

Jeffrey inspected the smears of garbage along the backdoor to the ramp. "Here," pointing at a microscopic dark green gob.

Detective Kee, exaggerating a suffering act of being imposed upon, put on white rubber gloves and pulled evidence tubes from his pocket. He scraped up dried particles, pasty green flakes.

"And in the bush, there." I looked, as the rest of the inquisitive, and sure enough, a fork lay on the ground, a greenish tint on the utensil's prongs.

Chef Lorenzo protested.

"Mon Dieu! My man could not have done this, and no one else was here all the time. The food was placed on the cart and he pushed it. No one else."

Detective Kee dropped the fork into a plastic bag.

Jeffrey pondered. "Let me reconstruct. You and your people brought the food out and placed it on the delivery cart? Serving dish covers placed over the food? The muslin cloth over all. And everyone went back to their kitchen duties? The porter assigned delivered the food to the grotto, set out the food, covered it with the cloth and departed?"

Lorenzo recalled and nodded to the sequence.

"But, the porter did not leave here immediately because of the ice."

"The ice?" Detective Kee asked, noticing Chef Lorenzo's Gallic expression change to surprise.

"As I said, to keep the food cooled," explained Jeffrey, "I assume the porter went back in to get a bucket of ice, which was placed on the trays surrounding the covered food, and then sprinkled over the cloth, melting, keeping the cloth cool and damp. The porter stepped back inside long enough to leave a window of opportunity opened one or two minutes. Enough time for the fork to stir in the mysterious ingredient."

Keeping up with Jeffrey's mind clicking, I saw some issues, and never born to stay silent, I interjected.

"But the opportunity could not be coincidence, a chance occasion? Someone had to know what was happening with the pūpū luncheon, even how the food would be delivered." The word, *premeditated*, seemed too evil to utter.

Detective Kee gave my father the benefit of his suppositions.

"Are you suggesting an inside job, a hotel employee?"

"Perhaps a devious tourist signed up to watch the Lū'au Challenge? What I'm suggesting is that here lay opportunity, and someone took it. And Chef Lorenzo and his restaurant are blameless."

"If indeed these green flecks are chemically sinister." Detective Kee could not let it go, that my father's expertise could trump an investigation.

"We shall see. Tonight, I should have a call on the results."

I needed no convincing. A poisoner lurked at Ho'oilina Kai Resort. And my father and I were still targeted to become victims like Oli Palalū. To hell with cheeseburgers in paradise, we were talking poison poi in paradise.

We were all walking through the resort to the lobby when I noticed the palm trees swaying but no wind. My legs were shivering, no, the ground was moving, slightly. I stumbled…into the arms of Detective Kee. *Wong man*, I thought, as he put definition to my clumsiness.

"Earthquake."

The earth went silent. We stopped and waited for an encore from beneath.

"You can't feel most of them," explained the detective lecturing with his geology lesson. "On this island, there are at least two hundred micro tremors per day. After all, you're vacationing on a living, breathing volcano."

The way things were going, I considered, this was no vacation. We resumed our stroll, my legs shaking without the help of Mother Nature or the Goddess Pele.

Chapter 16
Sea worthy

Later that morning, the seafaring conga-line wound its way down toward the marina dock. The porter pushed the cart with my camera equipment and our beach bag. Jeffrey, Chef Lorenzo, and I brought up the tail end of today's new adventure.

Jeffrey pointed to the two orange life vests on top of the luggage pile.

"What's that for? If we hit an iceberg?"

"Michael said Captain Cooke's boat had sprung some leaks recently. I borrowed these from the Sports Activities Desk."

My father regarded me with amusement and shook his head. Chef Lorenzo gave me an odd look. But, I believed, better safe than sorry, all things considered.

We passed a beach volleyball game in progress. The semi-naked, sweating male form in all shapes and sizes should have attracted my rapt attention. Tattoos on three of the players did draw my Dayne curiosity. They seemed skin-etched identical to what band member Johnny Rocket wore on his upper arm. A flower with thorns, petals of yellow and green. If I could recall faces from the grotto craziness, perhaps these were the other members of Oli's band. For people in mourning, they were euphoric at the game, wild and shouting, perhaps their method of grief release. Shouldn't they be practicing for the memorial to Oli? And, what were Kukui and Johnny Rocket up to? Probably somewhere, wasted.

The Ho'oilina Marina, situated in a large man-made lagoon, held a variety of boats, sail craft to cabin cruisers. Three docks went out in the sideways letter 'LLl' allowing for maximum dockage. We entered a gated area requiring a pass code and walked to the end of the dock to a sign reading "A Kupu'eu Point Tours." Found here were two empty berths, their signs advertising the boat name and availability as fishing charters, with one sign reading "Tahitoa's Rehab Grins," the other, "Raw Tolo Oceans." Hawaiian names were beginning to bug me.

At the end of the dock a large sign read "Pirates of the Caribbean," and a smaller notification of home port, "Antigua." A world traveler this Captain Cooke. Below such an announcement bobbing low in the water was a small speed boat.

How were we going to all fit? And why should I risk my expensive HDTV equipment in a rolling ocean in this Sunray teacup? On closer inspection, the boat builder was Craftsman, and the side panels had to be expensive polished mahogany or teak. Still…

A young Hawaiian man, long black hair pulled back in a pony tail, hefted coolers into the boat, further crowding and over-loading. I felt uncomfortable, more so, when I saw on his arm the same tattoos as the band members. He looked familiar, but I couldn't place where I had seen him.

"My name's Larry. Let me load your stuff and we'll be on our way."

I had to state my displeasure.

"We can't be going out on the ocean in this?" He gave me his silent quirky appraisal and dismissed me as haole tourist, but being the hired help Larry had to politely deal with me and my whining.

"No, ma'am. This just gets us out to the mother ship." And, with that, he pointed out past the lagoon, beyond the breakwater jetty. Behind the masts of sail boats I saw a sleek white yacht in the deeper water, gigantic in length, graceful in styling, a couple of inches short of being called an ocean liner.

Jeffrey's laugh was to remind me that I had been duped by two men, each who thought it would be fun to make me look like a doofus. My father, and Michael. I'd good naturedly take their in-joke, but I'd get even.

I pulled out my camera with its telephoto lens, using it as a telescope, and focused. Above the bridge I could see a miniaturized helicopter strapped down on a pad. I scanned to the stern and viewed an oversized outdoor living room. There stood Captain Jimmie Cooke, beaming, drink in hand, awaiting our arrival. Next to him, likewise holding liquid refreshment was Desi Cardoza.

I smelled something and it wasn't the odorous stale harbor water where fuel and floating garbage mixed with fishy oils. Did my father know the P.R. lady would be onboard? It could not be chance. Within her temptress clutches lay conspiracy. How was I going to keep them apart? What subterfuge to keep cabin doors left open? I slunk down on a boat seat in a foul mood. My vacation getaway was now a day cruise on the S.S. Poseidon. Topsy-turvy.

Our launch eased through the nautical city motoring toward the "Pirates of the Caribbean." Seagulls squawked overhead to the bustle of deck cleaning chores on the sailboats and water taxis making deliveries. Seals basked on a bell buoy. Daybreak charter boats returned to berths, hoisting flags to announce their successful catches: marlin, dorado, tuna.

"Not a bad water home for a capitalist robber baron," said Larry, standing behind the wheel, catching the mist spray as the boat accelerated, hitting wave bounces and skipping like a slow stone across the water. "Captain Cooke will give you both the full onboard tour. You guys must be special. He seldom has guests. But then all the rest of us are the minority oppressed."

"Ah, I recall," said Jeffrey. "You are Larry Tutapu. You're the leader of the People's Party of Free Hawai'i. I see you have found a pretty good job while awaiting the coming revolution." Larry took the recognition as his due.

"Hey, don't get me wrong about Captain Cooke. He's one of the few who helps our people and doesn't seem to want anything in return. Probably white man guilt; who am I to complain?"

His comment triggered a thought.

"Is he financing your education?" I had to shout above the boat's roar. "Like he did for Michael?"

"You mean Laka Ka'aiea? Yeah, Captain Cooke's foundation has paid for a hundred scholarships around the islands. I'm honored to be following in Laka Ka'aiea's footsteps."

"Why 'honored?'" asked Jeffrey, pulling my digital camera out of my beach bag and casually taking my photo, and then one of Larry Tutapu. He seldom did camera work. He had no sense in depth of field or aperture settings. Lucky for the novice the digital self-focused.

"Anyone who works for Captain Cooke gains his personal support to make it in the haole world. He takes an interest in them. I took over the position of the ship's First Mate that was once held by ali'i Ka'aiea. People treat me with respect."

I said, "Because of Michael Ka'aiea? Or because of Jimmie Cooke?"

"Didn't Lord of the Manor Cahill tell you?" His pigtail slapped in the rushing wind and he shouted his story, relishing his role as teacher to the uninformed. "No, of course not. He'd rather see the plantation workers in servitude. Mike Lake, as Cahill calls him, is Hawaiian royalty. In his island clan, he can count back over 35 generations on his father's mother's side to Pili, one of the great chiefs who came to the islands in 1100 A.D., a part of the great second migration. Ka'aiea is short for Pilika'aiea. As the legend goes, once when the Hawaiian kings were all corrupt, a priest brought Pili from the home lands of Samoa, fresh royal blood, to restore island justice. Laka Ka'aiea's line goes back that far, and is recorded in chant."

Wow. I swallowed the shock.

Who would have thought an Assistant to an Assistant Hotel Manager had lineage, royal blood in his veins? To me, crowned royalty meant England or European castle settings. The visage of Michael carried new inferences. I tried to recall our past conversations, the subtext. I guess I bore fault at first impressions, as Larry Tatapu could justly condemn, my seeing only a sub-servant, and not individuality based on the inner character. And there's this blood line breeding, if that had importance. I had this sudden female cat-like nose-twitching to study and define the real Michael Laka Pilika'aiea. But, then look what happened to the curious cat?

"So, why," inquired attorney-gourmet Dayne, probing, "isn't Laka Ka'aiea active in the Kingdom Restoration movement?"

"The question is: why isn't he with our group, the total overthrow of all systems and the rightful return of the land to the people. We owned the island before King K carved the land into his personal ahupua'a."

We were nearing the yacht, its length eating up the horizon. It was beautiful, fast lines, a great work of marine art upon liquid glass.

Larry Tutapu was not through with us.

"Joe Coffee, his uncle, or as we know him, Priest Pa'ao, was upset at Michael's father for marrying outside his people, tainting the bloodline. As long as Joe Coffee controls the monarchy movement there's no role for Laka Ka'aiea. He must wander around the hospitality industry hoping the haoles appreciate his talents."

"What does 'Laka' mean?" I asked. I grasped Michael's frustration at perhaps his true calling: a spokesperson for his people. I knew it would have caused him silent offense if I called him Mike Lake, and certainly, I had no intention to do so. I said 'Laka' several times to myself, and then 'Ka'aiea,' and then dumbly tried variations with Madison attached.

The boat's speed decreased towards idle as we paralleled against a boarding ladder platform. Larry tossed a line to a crew member, Filipino by looks, not Hawaiian.

As Larry offered me his hand to steady my ascent to the gangway ladder, in my leap suddenly I was close to his face. He gave me a cold, cruel look. "'Laka' means 'a man out for revenge.' That is the type of man we want on our side. Laka Ka'aiea shall one day become one of us."

Jeffrey and I exchanged glances. When the revolution arrived for angry Larry Tutapu it meant bloody battles. By his standards, my dad and I were not expected to be on the winning side.

Chapter 17

The Shipping News

"Welcome aboard." Captain Jimmie looked less the sea bum and more the successful millionaire, a sea-gentrified gentleman. His whole sailor chic wardrobe spoke of Ralph Lauren Polo, his sun glasses Armani.

"I hope you don't mind; I invited along Desi. Ms. Cardoza. Yesterday was an ordeal for her as well."

Of course, I minded. Desi, lounging on the back promenade, or was it the poop deck, waved her drink at us.

We made no attempt to hide our awe at being aboard this floating city. Without fanfare, a tour was to be expected, so we followed.

"Built by the best German engineers, Abeking & Rasmussen. 188 feet in length, 35 ft. beam. Draft of 11 ½ feet. At top cruising speed we can maintain 14 knots, comfortably."

This man-toy looked comfortable for sheiks, sultans, and princes.

"What's your crew size?" asked Jeffrey, interested, but not as overwhelmed as I was. He was polite. Ostentatious wealth never impressed him.

"Depends on guests. Six cabins. I picked this up in the Caribbean about two years ago, and never really made it a party animal boat. It's more like my floating office. For crew, I'm down to five people. The usual complement with 12 guests would be 13 in the crew, a very one-on-one ratio."

"Are we taking this out for a spin today?" My excitement hardly subtle, it came out sounding 'pretty please, rev the engines, let's cruise the coastline,' but wisely, I said,

"Leaving the harbor must be a major logistical undertaking."

"Yes, sadly, Miss Dayne, I would like to put out to sea with her, but not today. Perhaps when the lūʻau festivities are ended, we could do so. Don't fret, the amenities aboard are endless. Let me show you." My imagination as to what amenities meant started to wander, a fantasy worthy of Danielle Steele.

We were led down a stairway to the stern of the boat. Dare I say, the 'basement.' The below-deck stern with a garage exit door close to the water line, they called it the 'tender dock' looked like a sporting goods store. A Hobie sailboat, two wind surfers, two kayaks, two Yamaha wave runners, water skis, snorkeling, and scuba gear, all fit snug below deck. And to top it off, I was told the wood-paneled boat we had come out on, and another small craft for water skiing and cove fishing would be crane hoisted on deck to be lashed down for travel. Amazing.

Ah, the lives of the rich and famous. It would not be a bad life if someone else paid the bills.

The rest of the tour further substantiated what having *kala nui* would get you. Lots of money, as the locals would say. This Tiffany aircraft carrier boasted a gymnasium, 12 seat dining room, and an interior living room that served as the entertainment center. The Captain's cabin, rather office, boasted oil paintings I thought I recognized from my college art appreciation classes. Since his desk top held few papers, I assumed the office, which was a good 12x24, had push-touch hidden cabinets. A part of his credenza held three computers, several phones, one saying Nera Wavecall and a satellite tele/fax. A flat screen TV in the opposite wall held thin bookcases of DVD and CD cases. I started browsing the titles, noting and selecting my ballad choices, the original French movie version of *A Man and A Woman* (*L'Homme & La Femme*), and *Best of Norah Jones*. If a candlelight moment might ever arise aboard this big tub, those would be my choices for ambiance.

"Are you a day trader?" Jeffrey noticed posted graphs and bar charts that seemed to be tracking trends.

"A little bit. More a currency trader in futures. Tests your heart."

"The stock market can be a form of gambling."

Captain Jimmie studied my father, but saw his statement as neutral, nothing political or opinionated implied.

"Yes, but less risk with the more information one can ferret out."

"Ah, information gathering. Yes, that requires one to be all knowing and very international."

"True enough."

I got this odd vibe they were sizing each other up. Jeffrey inspected the massive desk, an ability to eye detail from a great distance, including a skill to read materials upside down.

"Are you dieting, Captain?"

"What?"

"I see one of your file folders marked *Caloric Rapist*. That's an amusing title."

"Oh, indeed," the Captain went around to his desk and picked up a hefty file, feeling the weight in his hands.

"I have a trainer, and yes, a severe regimen against food intake. One might say the man's 'a caloric rapist.' Nevertheless, I promise, I will consume whatever delectable fare you and Chef Lorenzo create today." He thrust the file into a side drawer.

I had made my way over to a wall of leather-bound books and nonchalantly pulled out a heavy volume and read the title.

"Good Lord. Is this the first narrative of James Cook's discovery of Hawai'i?"

"Yes, I am quite proud of that. On the inside front page you will see it was once owned by William Bligh."

"Like *Mutiny on the Bounty* Bligh?"

"The same. He was Sailing Master on Cook's third and final voyage. I like how history is not one story but interrelated episodes."

"Your Hawaiian-related books take up most of the shelf space."

"Everything Hawaiian is of interest to me. After all, this is my home."

Like a random lottery, I pulled out another leather volume, and read aloud, "A *Dictionary of the Hawaiian Islands* by Lorrin Andrews. 1865."

"Madison," my father gently admonished, "I think you will find the books you are holding so cavalier are worth thousands of dollars."

What was I thinking? Reverently, for all to see, I replaced the book.

"Yes, I pride myself on first editions," added Captain Jimmie, "and they are expensive." He walked over to me, his eyes digging deep into mine, pleasant, drawing me in. He tapped at the book I had just eased back into place on the shelf.

"Jeffrey, a side note you might find interesting: Lorrin Andrews spent thirty years writing his dictionary, meaning he started his work in the 1830s. What most people don't know is that as he toured the islands looking for obscure words and their meanings, he also took prodigious notes of Hawaiian customs, including their eating habits. That separate manuscript, which contains recipes of Hawaiian dishes, pure of Western influence, was never published by Andrews. Food was not his forte. Several years ago, the manuscript journal showed up at auction in England, selling for over $40,000. South American ex-politician by the name of Lorca bought it, and the manuscript disappeared from public view."

"A must for your collection, n'est-ce pas?" The accent French. I had forgotten Chef Lorenzo, loitering, seemed to have found bookshelves with Continental works; he, too, in awe as his fingers traced various French titles, in gilded leather, several I could see written by a Dumas. First editions, as informed. Probably stuffy reading.

"Indeed, I would like to see such a manuscript," said Jeffrey. "See how past tastes contrast to the current 'Asian fusion'."

"Yes, of course. Some day that might be possible. In fact, when he is not in Colombia, Mr. Lorca, I hear a man of dubious credentials, some say wealth by drug money, owns a vacation estate in one of the gated resorts near Black Sand Beach. Quite protected and guarded. He's spurned all my inquiries. Someday I will have the Andrews' receipts, that's what they called recipes back then—'receipts'. I will have that manuscript. And I can be quite persistent."

Though his tone light, one felt his seriousness of purpose, a challenge to the successful businessman. It struck me I had heard, or was it read, the name of 'Lorca' and 'Black Sand Beach'. Where?

Jeffrey stared at a grouping of modern books on a shelf closer to the floor.

"This section seems to be themed with controversial topics?"

I glanced. Many titles and subject matter came off as political and argumentative. 'Take back the land — it is ours' sort of hyperbole. Agrarian reform. Hawaiian Homeland. The future beyond pineapples and sugar cane plantations.

"Though a tourist Mecca, Hawai'i is in political flux. I like to be informed."

"They look well read. Dog-eared chapters." Jeffrey missed nothing.

"To some of my young friends, for their education, I have become a lending library." Captain Jimmie beckoned to the door. "For your pleasure, let me show you all my kitchen facilities. I can't wait to see what you and Chef Lorenzo have in mind for our palates."

Later, on the back deck, called the fantail I believe, I inspect Desi Cardoza reclined, oiled, and absorbing the cosmic rays. Somehow, I felt inadequate, body-wise, in viewing her poured flawlessly inside a bikini, the bottom part, that is. She sunbathed topless. Very European. It amazed me to see a woman, who had borne children, show no tummy skin sagging; her bronze belly pilates-taut and accented with pointed grapefruit-sized breasts.

"How are you doing, Miss Dayne?" She inquired from behind sunglasses. She felt my cultural awkwardness, and draped a towel loosely across her chest.

"Fine, all things considering."

A Filipino waiter handed me some fruity slush mimosa drink stick skewered with a pineapple chunk. Perfect. A minute later it was so good I had brain-freeze.

"Yes, yesterday should have never happened. Such a tragedy." Her tears for the singer had lapsed, but her vocal chords emitted thick, raspy emotion.

I sat across the deck from her. Removing my T-shirt to reveal my demure suit top, apparent who was the white lily in the crowd. I was not going to take off more, do a nipple show. My father would have a double cow. I made small talk.

"You're the manager of the band, I heard. How sad for all of them."

From under her sunglasses. "Yes, they're lost for the moment. But as they say…"

"The famous, 'show must go on.'"

"I'm afraid so. They're practicing for the memorial to Oli."

"That's tomorrow night?"

"Yes, the hotel is going to use the 11th hole of the golf course, a par three. It slopes down towards the water. Put the crowds on the hillside, and put the musical groups on platform risers over the green. Like the Hollywood Bowl. It will be fitting for Oli's memory. A couple of TV shows are going to cover the event live. And, I hired a videographer for the band. Maybe we can market a video, give the proceeds to charity."

Since I was going with Michael, I should likewise take some stock footage. I put on my best manners and asked delicately if there was a problem if I shot some HDTV for background for our TV show, the Network national audience, if I gave full accreditation to the band. I stressed 'national audience.'

Her enthusiasm bubbled. She was not as devastated as one might believe. I could see marketing juices eek from her slimy pores.

"No, that would be fine. Exposure is important now. The band has to decide its future."

The band members did not impress me, character wise, her son specifically. But I did have the Dayne curiosity. I made my voice sound concerned.

"The band won't breakup?"

"No, not a chance." Desi spoke sharp and immediate. No question there. "They have to go forward with their own brand of music while honoring Oli's hit songs."

It was she, no doubt, formulating these young kids' future. One false step and they'd be one-hit wonders. She wasn't only the band's PR Manager, she was a stage mom. Something struck me.

"Wasn't 'Oli sick before he died? Flu or something? He missed a couple of dates I heard, and the band went on without him. How'd they do?"

She dabbed her face with a wet hand towel from an ice bowl.

"Actually, quite well. Without Oli, Johnny Rocket has a tendency to go more rock 'n roll. At first people missed Oli, but you get caught up in beat dance music and a party atmosphere."

The proud mother.

For the next half hour, trifle talk was exchanged, my asking touristy questions, she with the answers. I closed my eyes and leaned back to feel the sun's power at charbroiling flesh.

A shadow gave me a start. Jimmie Cooke, owner and Captain of the Pirates of the Caribbean, leaned over me, the Prince hovering above Sleeping Beauty, unfortunately, bearing no kiss.

"Madison, your father wants you." It figured. Didn't anyone else want me?

One of Captain Jimmie's early morning charters had brought back to the dock swordfish, hours fresh, and the meal to be prepared by two chefs on the pinnacle of the culinary mountain must appease all taste buds. And, it became so. Likewise, the footage I shot was short of its own masterpiece.

The marinade prepared by Chef Lorenzo gave the flavor over any fishy smells. Since the Chef created his work impromptu from ingredients within the yacht's well-stocked kitchen, I jotted down the results in my journal. I thought I could do this at the apartment if a special occasion ever arose.

We ate outside under the veranda awning, imbibing a Ferrari-Carano Chardonnay from Sonoma County. I had mike'd up Jeffrey and Chef Lorenzo for the prep, shooting HDTV footage, but for the luncheon, I used the Nikon capturing the table setting, the casual bonhomie of host and guests. These color stills might be photos for the next cookbook: *Insatiable Island?* Who knows, but if so, my photos would be predominant in the book, perhaps a source of side income.

Table conversation was light with nothing dramatic forthcoming. Desi sat next to Jeffrey. I found myself seated next to Captain Jimmie, which I did not mind one bit. He was articulate, witty, paid me and the other guests equal and proper attention, no fawning my direction to make me uncomfortable with my father present. Captain Jimmie was the personification of the perfect gentleman, the suave admiral. I admit my frame of mind floated to the ambiance of the Rich and Famous setting, so when the Captain asked me if I wanted to go for a ride, a nod of acceptance was like, sure, why not. I looked off the yacht's side for the motor launch. I should have looked up to what was lashed on the landing pad.

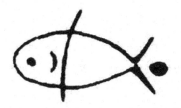

Recipe: Pirate Zest Marinade

1/3 cup lemon juice
¼ cup dry white wine (Captain Jimmie supplied a 2002 Sauvignon Blanc
from his shipboard 1,000 bottle wine 'cooler')
1 tablespoon grated lemon peel
¼ cup minced green onions
¼ teaspoon black pepper
3 tablespoons safflower oil
1 tablespoon finely minced fresh ginger
2 cloves garlic, finely minced.

The sword fish steaks went into the combined marinade ingredients for at least an hour.
The swordfish was then grilled, brushing on the marinade.
Jeffrey added the final flourishes by wrapping the swordfish in something called
a Peking pancake (he prepared this from scratch in the galley though a Chinese market
can provide the pancakes premade. Tortillas or won ton wraps might work).
Finely chopped avocado combined with diced papaya as a garnish and the remaining
marinade was sprinkled liberally around the wrap.
The swordfish, on my own reflection, would have looked good by it-self on a bed of pasta.
This was Iron Chef creativity at its best with Chef Lorenzo and Jeffrey Dayne spontaneous.
I would write the recipe into my diary journal, 'feasted on Swordfish à la Lorenzo-Dayne.'

Chapter 18
Rotor Rooted Ride

Exhilarated and at the same time terrified here I was in the two-passenger helicopter buzzing yards above the ocean. Well, maybe a hundred feet or so, but with my view unobstructed behind a bubble of plexiglass, I trembled as one with the wind, man's technology barely holding me from free-falling. The rotor and engine noise required us to talk through headsets, and Jimmie's voice crackled loud in my ear.

"See the spouts up ahead?"

Against the reflective glare on the ocean, I saw spigots spraying mist upward, two or three humpback whales at the surface.

"This time of season the females are here to calve. The males are seeking to make a family. There's a lot of activity. They've come down from Alaska where they're engorged on krill, their basic food staple."

He seemed a competent pilot though I got nervous when he turned in his seat and pulled out from beneath a cover, a telescopic camera, more accurately a Nikon with an 82 mm Fieldscope sport optic attachment. With this camera elephant gun, he could pick up the wart hair on a whale's back. Hovering in the helicopter, we waited for the world's largest mammal to seek a breath of surface air. A whale tail slapped the water, the form of mating communication. Jimmie took a couple of shots and then we resumed our journey to the Mauna Loa volcano and its National Park.

"Each tail is distinctive to a whale. Like fingerprints. The Whale Society uses them as identification to plot whale migration, study how many have survived each year. I'll send my photos on to them for record keeping."

"With a lens like that, you could find a cavity on a whale tooth."

He laughed, knowing my ignorance, treating me gently.

"As you probably know humpbacks don't have teeth. They have fibrous baleen for sifting out their food." He paused. "Killer whales have teeth."

He studied my nervous features. If I ever had a fear of flying, it was then and there. I had not wanted to go, but everyone urged me, pointing out that it would be a once-in-a-life chance to shoot aerial views. Once in a life sounded portentous. The locals, Desi and Chef Lorenzo, all said Captain Jimmie could fly helicopters and was proficient in fixed wing aircraft. I acceded reluctantly. My father never had a son who would do dauntless deeds. I had to provide that lost bravery.

Before I strapped myself in for my rotor-rooter ride, I had some shenanigans to initiate for protective measures. First, I tracked down the revolutionary Larry Tatapu and found him below deck working on scuba gear.

"Is Desi Cardoza part of your New Order?"

A dead look of questioning to my statement.

"My father is making the moves on her. He usually gets what he goes after. So, what I'm wondering, will he steal her away to Chicago, or do we both move here to the Big Island and make life miserable for you and the Pāhoehoe Sounds? I'll be honest; I don't want her to become Mrs. Dayne Number Two. Maybe we have a common cause."

I could see him swallow the bitter pill of an outsider snaking a local off island. That was anathema to Hawaiians, their people leaving for greener pastures, or to a better prepared table, as Mr. Dayne might provide. And I figured Larry held blind fan loyalty to the Pāhoehoe Sounds, that they were going to write his movement's anthem. I continued to set my hook.

"I'd keep an eye on them both. Make sure you're in the middle of their conversation before it gets heavy, keep them an embrace apart." I left him hoping he would run scam interference, but if not, Plan Two was my last desperation idea.

The Filipino head steward was polishing the luncheon silver in the paneled dining room.

"Are you missing this?" I handed a silver knife used at our luncheon over to the steward, which I had palmed in my napkin. The knife bore a crest of a two-sail schooner stamped into the soft metal, real stuff, not plated.

"I must tell you this in the strictest confidence. Can you keep a secret?"

The butler-styled man, dignified, in his impeccable white blazer, expressed confusion.

"I'm sorry, I don't understand." His English accented, but secondary school educated.

"My father has this sickness. I do not wish Captain Jimmie to know; it would so embarrass my Father, and hurt me terribly if the secret's found out." I actually fluttered my eyelids. "My father has this bad habit of collecting things not his. He doesn't mean to; it's this sickness. I usually go around after we visit some place and return all those things he has picked up. Like this knife."

The steward's eyes bore the startling news I had brought to his calm chores. Indeed, a serious confession, and I hoped a secret requiring the tact of a gentleman's gentleman.

"I think I understand."

"Thank you. Thank you so much. You do not have to do anything. Just keep an eye on him, and let me know later if he picks up anything else. I will certainly return any item before we depart the ship. Here's a small gratuity for such watchfulness." He did not protest the money.

I left the head steward, dropping his polishing task, to take on his new job in surveillance. I returned from my excuse of a long run to the ladies room to find the luncheon party breaking up and the Captain poised to invite me to venture skyward.

Zipping along in his private VW sized helicopter, too close to the wave caps, too close to the clouds, he overpowered me with his devilish grin.

"Would you like to fly?"

"You've got to be kidding?"

"Here, hold on to the throttle; I'll keep my feet on the pedals."

I wanted no part of an act of immediate destruction. Lightly, I put my hand on top of the throttle and found myself thrilled, not so much with the vibrating power within my hands, but that Captain Jimmie had placed his hand over mine for guidance. The helicopter immediately dipped to the right. I panicked, but left my hand where it was.

"A helicopter will yaw right when there is a new feel to the controls. Flying a helicopter is more difficult than a regular single engine. The collective control stick to my side will cause the craft to climb or descend. Controlling the throttle is harder; as it changes the pitch, one has to keep the engines at the same power level as the rotor speed. The pedals are the rudder to control the pitch of the tail-rotor."

With that ounce of instruction, he brought my lunch to my throat as we dipped sharply and swung left toward the coastline. Only his hand on mine kept me from losing my cool and the digested swordfish luncheon. When my eyes adjusted to the horizon, I saw smoke on the ocean. Steam, rather.

He banked the helicopter inland and up.

"Mauna Loa, 13,700 ft., is obscured up there behind the vog."

"Vog?"

"Twenty-five hundred tons of sulphur dioxide daily spews out of the Kilauea Caldera. Mixed with water and carbon dioxide, it gravitates up the mountain, volcanic mixed smog. Vog."

I had seen what I thought was fog above Kailua-Kona town. I accepted being the tenderfoot educated by the big white hunter guide. I gripped the side of my seat as he swung the helicopter and raced across Hawai'i Volcanoes National Park towards the Kīlauea Caldera.

"Better get your camera ready," he said and reduced air speed to allow me to capture a documentary sweep. Steam from vents, lava fireworks exploding skyward, made the landscape eerie and hellish. Tourists hiked designated trails to find the best perspective as my HDTV shot them tight from panorama to closeup. As the camerawoman, I felt exhilarating pleasure capturing these flaming arterial veins, torturous and destructive. From deep earth the magma fire boiled to the surface as lava causing the creation of new earth spreading across a black-landscaped panorama down to the blue white-tipped sea.

Captain Jimmie, I could call him that, pointed down toward an approaching ridge. I could smell the sulfuric rotten eggs in the air.

"The lava flow at the Chain of Craters. Present flow is from 2003. Sometimes called the Mother's Day flow. Down the coastline we've had more recent eruptions and flows. Houses burned and buried."

Drips of fiery red melted stone driveled from underneath a black blanket of rock, a crust likened to burned sugar, and dripped in small streams into the Pacific, generating steam. Did I say I was amazed and terrified?

He hovered the helicopter at a sideways angle, the air currents bouncing us up and down. I grabbed the shoulder HDTV camera and began recording the birthing of new land. Through my lens I watched in awe. Magnificent and glorious to behold: Nature's omnipotence. Or to be politically correct, we were watching mood changes from the goddess Pele.

"Tourists try to stand on the outer edge, the overhang, and lean out to capture the moment the molten rock hits the water. There have been times when the crust breaks off with someone aboard. You don't swim away. You're scalded to death; tourist soup."

He shot the helicopter down the coast where, like army ants, trails of visitors walked the lava for better views, returning to tell tales of buried Kalapana Village they had seen. Moving down the coastline, away from the crowds, Jimmie located a landing site near the ocean. When I put my camera in the back seat I noticed for the first time a leather satchel with a bottle head sticking out. Champagne. My heart raced. Romance may have at last found Madison Merlot Dayne.

"Help me land." He went through the explanation of aerodynamics, telling me to watch the indicator speed, showed me how to hover, and I felt the landing skids touch warm terra firma. Captain Jimmie was not finished with my lessons nor as ready as I was to move on to personal objectives. He made me change places with him. With his direction I felt a surge of courage, self confidence in my capabilities. I did a check off list with him: establish the right RPM with an open throttle; pull in the pitch and depress the pedal. The aircraft moved slightly to the left and right. I was off the ground, hovering, if mere feet. He talked me back down, idling the engine. Taking off the earphones, listening to a ringing in my ears, I could only absorb my inner feelings.

Over the rotor noise, I shouted, "What a rush."

"That's why I'm here," he responded, into my ear. I could not wait and gave him a quick hug.

There's a lava river underneath me!

Chapter 19
Lava Flow — and not the drink

"Let's get your photo shoot out of the way… first." Enough said.

I pulled my Nikon out and went rummaging for my pocket digital. It wasn't there. I was certain I had packed it that morning. Yes, I had. Dad used it when we were in the motorcraft. Perhaps it fell out on the yacht or I left it in the runabout boat. Misplaced for the time being and with other things on my mind, I gave it little thought as I scurried with my more powerful camera, less professional, more the zany tourist. I froze.

Beneath my feet in the cracks of carbon hardened lava I saw and felt a moving stream of liquid fire.

"There's lava under us!" I yelled as the wind gusted off the churning ocean. More smells of rotten eggs invaded my nostrils. Sulfur from the earth's core.

"The lava will break to the surface and crawl until it cools. Beneath there's a faster flow that moves toward the water. The rough rock on the surface is called 'a'a lava, the smooth, ropy lava is known as pahoehoe." I remember: the name of the late Oli Palalū's band.

"And, we are not going anywhere near the edge?" My caution returned.

"Not a chance." He moved off, exploring, and I snapped several exposures as he walked, jaunty, a man in control. So be it. Men came before boys.

I found a slow flow and saw and heard the molten rock cooling, crackling the rock, stretching, popping, and being overwhelmed by the next layer pushing against the new rock, overlapping, like pancake batter on a skillet. Pāhoehoe. The fresh rock was both fire and skillet.

"I think I'll use the HDTV." That was back at the helicopter.

"I'll hold your camera," he offered. "Take a few memories. After this there's a secret beach I found, no one else around."

Our eyes judged the invitation together and both accepted. I smiled, stood back, and he caught a candid that would show, I'm sure, heat rising from the soles of my shoes, and other less frequented places. I trotted off to the helicopter. Digital video on the lava field I knew would be used in the Jeffrey Dayne food show, and with it, my byline assured in the show credits.

In a violent shake, I weaved and fought to maintain my balance. Another tremor, this one long, reverberating; I actually thought I saw the land buckle in a wave-like motion. This was no tremor but a Richter jumping earthquake. Thrown to the ground, my shoulder hit first with a sharp pain. I hugged the ground and rode out the gyrations. Less than a minute, feeling like eternity, before the quake subsided to sputters; but then, I heard this terrible noise like an avalanche, distant, growing closer. Cra — aa — ck! A crunch breaking-type noise. All at once, around us, like a football field of plate window glass with fast-travelling spider vein cracks seen everywhere, the sound building into rumbling breaking.

I saw Captain Jimmie trying to stand a hundred yards away, his eyes bugged in disbelief. The earthquake had spawned fissures and separated the rock, and lava flowed up to separate us. I rose to my feet and saw worse. The black rock had broken into a diamond shape around him, an inverted triangle, clear to the ocean, the lava oozing up. I ran to him, but a good eight feet of molten rock kept him from running to me and both of us to the helicopter, and escape.

Mega-phoning my voice over the fiery rock canal I asked, "Can you jump?"

"Too far apart. I'll see if there's another route." He went running off to the far side where I could see a yellow-red stream bubbling and making popping noises like small firecrackers. The lava was eating into the sides of his horror predicament. He returned negative, not fearful, but obviously concerned on how he would ex-tract himself. Or, if he could.

Another noise, a ripping sound, and he fell. Back on his feet our eyes met, his eyes darting. The whole slab of lava rock under him was moving, toward the ocean!

"There's a lava river underneath me!" The steam at water's edge increased in its ferocity defining a faster flow. Captain Jimmie was heading slowly yet steady on a black-crusted plate towards the burning sea.

"Do something!" I yelled, fast walking parallel to his movement, my voice anguished. He couldn't perish, he just couldn't. I saw him then unique, above the doom of a fearful trip, weighing his options. *O Captain, My Captain!*

"Go get the helicopter." A steady voice.

"What?" My scream barely above the din of grating, tumbling rocks.

"You'll have to fly over the lava to reach me. It's my only chance."

"I can't fly."

"Like an angel. I'll teach you. Just listen to me carefully."

Did I have a choice? Did I stop to think of my inadequacies, my frailties? I found myself in a strange twilight zone, numbing, watching each step, my tennis Sketchers scorching, following his own unsteady trip as the rocks under him moved like a slow motion roller coaster, undulating, up and down, toward a one-way plunge. I could hear the hissing ocean ahead. He shouted out the basics. Told me to repeat them and when satisfied, said only 'Good luck.'

What could I do? I ran to the helicopter. Flipped the switches he told me, listened to the blades increase their whirring speed. Revved up the RPMs, put on the collective lever next to me. The helicopter vibrated, the noise deafening since I chose not to put on the earphones. Use the radio, my mind screamed. Talk to whom? To shout a 'May Day?' A frantic call that would bring rescue too late. I advanced the throttle, depressed the pedal — racked my brain — what else?

What else?! The helicopter moved, light on its skids. Lighter. I was hovering a helicopter, hot damn, then a hard lurch as the helicopter hit the ground. Again, try again. I had forgotten to adjust for collective pitch, so when I rose again the aircraft actually moved forward in the air but skidded to the ground with a noise of scraping that left me scared shitless. I had just crash-landed a helicopter! Again, for God's sake, try again! If the previous steps gave me forward momentum I would repeat the basics, go no further. The Wright Brothers made practice perfect, after twenty years! I would have only one chance to hopscotch the lava flow, and reality reared its ugly head; I envisioned the aircraft becoming a sea craft, exploding, and me melting.

Again and again, I bounced imperfectly toward Captain Jimmie. I did not even glance his way, knowing the instructor in him was cursing his worthless student. Here I was and I knew I had to hover, move upwards, pitch forward and reach the required 15 knots to get what Jimmie called Effective Transitional Lift.

I caught my breath and held it, and prayed to deities yet to be born. Hovering, higher, forward motion, pitch — the helicopter wove from side to side. That's expected, he told me. Beneath me and out the window I could see fire between black rock fissures. In a second I was over the lava stream, barely. I reversed procedures, and felt the skids skidding, rocks hitting. I powered down the engine whine as soon as I felt I was upright. I looked up and saw I was only a hundred yards from the ocean, the rock in front shearing off into the steam.

Jimmie's hands grabbed and tugged me from the pilot's seat. Of all things, I had forgotten to put on the restraining belt. I was embraced rough, lips found mine, powerful, sweaty, thankful.

"Let's blow this party!"

Heady and floating more from his kiss than my solo flight, I ran to the other side. As I did I saw where Jimmie had put down my camera on the rocks. I raced over. I could see him yell at me, mouthing the words: 'Leave it!' Perhaps I should have thought safety first instead of material possessions. As I heard the rotors again build decibel to increased speed, I grabbed and retrieved the camera an instant before a lava glob would have devoured it. No time left. The steam column almost upon us, I flung myself into the passenger seat, and not a second too soon. As we lifted and dove forward toward safety, the floating fragment that moments earlier held Jimmie captive moved to its final outcome, shattering and tumbling into the obscuring and heated swirl. Ever while the ultimate producer, I turned back, leaned out the door, my belt now on, and with no fear, ran video at the small lake of moving lava left behind.

Moments later I placed the camera on my lap and cried a typhoon.

We agreed to immediately return to the yacht; me with my shoulder bruised, my legs like campfire marshmallows, and Captain Jimmie worried that the helicopter might have been damaged and we might be at further operational risk.

My father greeted our return.

"How was the volcano outing?"

Captain Jimmie had asked me to say nothing of our incident. I wondered about that, at first thinking he didn't want my father's wrath at putting his only child at peril. Nagging at me another interpretation surfaced. Perhaps he did not want me to babble out our harrowing story, his persona emasculated, an inability to be the hero who saves the day. I agreed to the gag order. I could care less. I wanted to see him again… on that secluded beach.

"Outside of being assaulted by an earthquake, bruising my body, burning my lower legs, sure, I took a couple of instamatics for your damn cooking show." He said no more to avoid confronting my grumps. By the time I made it back to the hotel I felt my temperament boiling, and there he stood, smiling Mike Lake.

"You don't look so good." He, at least noticed.

"Did you have an earthquake here today?"

"A few hairline cracks in the plaster, no serious damage."

"Well, I was at the National Park, probably at the epicenter, and my body took a hit or two."

"Yeah, you got some scrapes on your legs. Are those burns?"

"And my shoulder is an ugly shade of purple."

I hated it. His concern so sincere.

"Why don't you go up to your room. I know some special herbal remedies, medicinal roots, taboo in pharmacies, but the local kahunas swear they're miracle cures. Get ready for an all-body massage."

I perked up and hurried to the elevator, limping but eager. A day of passion might not yet be lost. On my bed lay a hotel envelope from the concierge with the processed film from yesterday's candids. I didn't have time to study them. A quick glance and when I saw no masked person with a forkful of green poison, I dropped the photos on my nightstand.

I showered, hot water melting me to a sensual readiness. Not too overt, but past shyness, I lay naked under the bed sheet. A pleasant knock came to the door.

"Come in, Michael."

"He said not do deep tissue, lighter Swedish." The Asian Mamasan in her mu'umu'u held several jars without markings.

"Where's…?"

"Michael Pilika'aiea sent me. You're very special to him. He no do this for anyone, ever."

She threw back the sheet and slathered me with goo that smelled like a stopped-up Venice Beach bathroom. I opened my mouth to protest, but under her heavenly fingers exploring, evaporating knotted muscles, no words to halt were spoken. My mind sought to focus on the day's events and rationalize on my failure at seduction, twice over. No use. I lost my train of thought, and in fact, lost consciousness.

Chapter 20
Trumpets of Sick Angels

Lightning cracked the night apart. Rain whipped sideways. The thatch roof dripped and the fronds heaved and flapped to the storm's cries, but the tiny hut held. I feel my clothes, gossamer silk, clinging to all the nuances of my naked body. Downpour soaked, I have fled from the Beast in the jungle whose blood-stained teeth demand further sustenance. The soldiers who have survived the Beast's attacks were out there, searching for me, the princess, ordered to kill me on sight, and if caught I know they planned a fate worse than death. My sole protector, my last valiant warrior, entered from the storm. Water ran from his rippling muscles, a flap of leather barely covered his engorged manliness. I see his face in the fire light, Captain Jimmie, matted grey-brown hair, eyes eager.

"Wake up."

Why did he say that? *I turned to hide my desire, passion pumping my breasts. When I turned back, the warrior's body had changed. It was Michael, blood stains on his spear; I saw his shoulder, wounded. I would heal him with my secret power. He whispered.*

"Madison, wake up. You're on TV."

There is no TV in the jungle, not even cable. I heard a commercial. I blinked my eyes open

The warrior face was my father, and he was dressed, the spear in his hand a channel remote.

The news lady reported the 5.5 earthquake and the rockslide damage to area roads, cracked masonry, no deaths, few injuries, and the daring helicopter rescue of a tourist from the lava fields by our own, James Cooke.

"What?!" I sat up. Somewhere in the pillow world of massages, panties and a night shirt had slipped on. Under the sheet, drowsy, I watched the tube.

The television image showed footage from a great height of a small landed helicopter and a young woman could be seen running from the lava field [getting my camera!] and climbing into the passenger side. The helicopter dashed up and off just as the rock bench facing borne by the lava flood smashed into the tempest boiled sea. The news commentator narrated to the end sound bite.

"Mr. Cooke was unavailable for comment, but local emergency officials are calling it a miracle rescue." Jeffrey muted the news as images of earthquake damage updates continued.

My father filled me in on the hot-breaking news.

"A sightseeing helicopter tour filmed the life-saving. Probably will be sold to the national networks and we'll see it forever on the reality 'harrowing escape' channels. Why didn't you tell me?"

I bit my tongue to the truth.

"I thought you'd worry. And it's no big deal."

"I hope you thanked Captain Jimmie."

"Yes, of course." And more so later, I did not say.

"But it's odd, the rescue that is. The press is assuming you were stranded. But Captain Jimmie wouldn't put you in harm's way? Would he?" My father arched his eyes awaiting my answer.

"No, he did not."

He saw my Dayne backbone end the conversation.

"Well, thank God, you're okay. My only excitement after our luncheon was talking food with Chef Lorenzo and Desi telling me how she cultivates her own organic garden. The ship's crew I can tell you are slightly deranged. They hovered near us all day, less service, almost like spying, though our conversation was quite boring and benign. Strange behavior. Not as stimulating as your day among Pele's brimstone."

I touched my body, surprised. I was indeed beyond just okay. No pain from my bruising, my leg burns and blistering barely visible, less ugly. What happened? Michael's gift of healing; a witch woman with magic glump, who had said I was special to him.

I caught myself. Two men, different in character and stature, had burrowed in my mind within my last sleeping minute. My feminine wiles sensed trouble brewing. My father confirmed my trepidation.

"Nanahonua."

"What?"

"Datura candida."

"Are you mumbling?"

"Kurt of the Illinois Lab came through. He mashed out the chemical compounds but had to put in a call to the Bishop Museum Botany Department on O'ahu." He pulled his note-taking from his pocket.

"Angel's Trumpet is the plant. Tree-like, flowers are dramatic colors and trumpet-shape, hence the name. And guess what?"

"It's a poison?" I was fully awake, remembering I almost died two days running.

"Lethal in large quantities and quite available along the Kona coast. From your room you can see two clumps used in the grounds landscaping."

A let-down of sorts: a poison available to locals and tourists.

"Let me read off the symptoms: 'blurred vision, restlessness, disorientation and hallucinations. Severe exposure may result in seizures, paralysis, coma,'" and, he paused for effect, "'Death.'"

"Symptoms I saw in Oli Palalū."

"True, but the mystery remains."

"Oli was poisoned by this Angel's Trumpet." The 'how and what' to murder solved, or so I thought.

"No, from what I saw and gathered in the grotto, there was not enough quantity of the ground-up leaves to be a lethal dosage."

"What killed Oli?"

"We have to wait for the autopsy."

"Great." Crime-solving moved too slow, just like…. The word 'lava' came to mind and my stomach tensed.

While he talked, Jeffrey picked up the photos beside my bed, browsed them, held several up for better lighting. He shrugged. Though still sleepy, on my turn a similar shrug of dismissal. Nothing suspicious stood out. I replaced the photo packet on the night stand.

"Madison, you're not taking into account the planned victims."

"You and me." I had not forgotten.

"That quantity of minced leaves alone would not kill, but it would sicken. We should be asking: who would want us merely sick, and if only sick, what result or who is benefited?"

My thinking cap went on as I went to a drawer for a night gown. It was late evening. My nap without effort could stretch to morning. In the darkness below our window, like crying cats, I could hear small tree frogs croaking. Coqui. Coqui. I offered my perspective.

"Not me as the targeted poisionee, they wanted to stop you, remove you from the scene, but not kill."

"At that point, until Mr. Palalū ate the poi and collapsed, we were dealing with the crime of malicious assault, and even with the singer's death a defense attorney could argue accidental circumstances leading to manslaughter, not homicide. Judgment is less harsh for premeditated hallucinations."

My light bulb brain cells brightened.

"The Lūʻau Challenge." He accepted the premise.

"But would a lūʻau participant go to this length to force a judge to retire?"

"Another foodie star, jealous of the attention this event would garner?"

"Most of my fellow foodie TV celebrities are making more money than I and have published more cookbooks." He laughed. "However, for ratings, they might kill."

My light bulbs became stadium halogen.

"The Hoʻoilina Kai Grand Hotel and Resort."

"For want of a nail, the kingdom was lost," he said, quoting an obscure poem, perhaps Shakespeare. He explained the analogy.

"I like this direction better, but for what plan I don't yet see. I get ill, the publicity hurts the hotel's reputation."

"Only Oli's death by accident does it one better. The food service is shut down. Hotel reservations will take a hit, revenues tank."

"But the hotel is being sold? The end result of damage is only temporary."

"Disgruntled monarchists? Joe Coffee and his royalists punishing the hotel for the heiau destruction?"

"But they wouldn't want to damage the Lūʻau; that hurts the economy of fellow Hawaiians."

"Then how about Larry Tutapu?"

"Possible. Revolutions are launched in chaos and anarchy. But poisoning a foodie star doesn't achieve the level of headlines that would fit his ego. No, we're missing something. The autopsy results might help as well as our bus trip tomorrow."

"Bus trip?" The Oli Memorial Concert was the next night. I wanted a few hours on the beach to give my skin a base reddish hue. I didn't need to be a sightseeing roadie.

"The Pāhoehoe Sounds are going over to Hilo to give an interview at the radio station. Desi invited me, and I invited you along to take some photos. They have some beautiful water falls off Highway 19. Besides, finding out more about Oli Palalū from those who knew him best might give us insight."

Was my father that naïve? He had a chance to be alone with her. I couldn't let the black widow spin her web. I did not want to go. If he was surrounded by the band deviants, maybe they would be distraction enough.

"Michael is going to be driving the hotel van."

"Yes, I'll go." I rolled over in bed, and Jeffrey turned out the lights. My thoughts sought cohesion, trying to put all these puzzle pieces together, but my mind soon drifted off…visualizing… *a thatched hut in the jungle, the storm's ferocity, my heart echoing the rain like savage tom-toms pounding on the roof…He enters with a wildness never tamed, my warrior. I feel my own wetness…* Even in this wonderful, needful dream, reality tethered my imagination. I tossed and turned into another thought: how did I lose my digital camera? Where was it?

I was falling . . . nothing below except the stream flowing through large jagged, broken rocks. . .

Chapter 21
Akaka Falling

Next morning, I asked Michael why he was strapping a ladder to the top of our tour vehicle. "If you're shooting film during the day, some of the shots might require some higher angles."

That was very thoughtful of him, thinking about my needs. I knew it was not just hotel service he was demonstrating. His second act of camaraderie remained unspoken. He said nothing about my highly publicized "rescue," front page in the morning papers, with Captain James Cooke, apparent island hero.

We motored up Highway 19, the day crisp, a night rain shower providing dew soak. With upper winds blowing, you could see the snow cover on the extinct Mauna Kea volcano and spot white domes containing an array of astronomical telescopes, each spying on the mysteries of the universe. By their claims there are no empty spots in the heavens. I heard the view at night toward the stars was the closest feeling to what an astronaut would see in deep space.

All in all a perfect day, but I have said that before about other days where circumstances changed unexpectedly.

The Hoʻoilina Kai Resort van could crowd in ten like sardines and our entourage of nine fit snug. I was the most comfortable in the passenger seat up front with Michael. Dad and Ms. Desi together in the next seats back, her smiling low octave chatter designed to draw him closer. The female singer of Pāhoehoe Sounds, Kukui, next to singer slash guitarist, Johnny Rocket, and in the way back, the musicians whom I met with quick greetings: Paka on lead guitar; Digger the drummer and his ever-tapping drumsticks; and Lolo, the bass guitarist, bald with henna-colored neck tattoos. They were the clowns. Joking, jabbing each other's shoulders, giggling at their silent farts that caused side windows to open. A lot of their chatter in an island pidgin: Howzit, brah surf-headbanger lingo that slipped past me. Under their breaths I came up in the dialect as being 'broke da mouf ' and my yesterday escapade on the lava being an 'okole squeezer.' They seemed young and harmless. Johnny Rocket was not.

"Hey, Miss Dayne, what's this about you being an almost French fry at the volcano? And Captain Cooke swooped in and rescued you?"

My ordeal on the lava had morphed into a glamorized public version. I started to protest but knew I couldn't without damaging Captain Jimmie's reputation as the local hero. My Father would think less of me if I demeaned someone, regardless if true circumstances reversed hero to heroine. I held my tongue as the three-man chorus in the back seat kicked in with their scatological put-downs of the hapless girl.

Michael intoned a severe, "That's enough." The malicious ribbing fell silent, and I was grateful.

Desi chose this silence to give the band their public relations direction on how to act while giving their radio interview. She made the point to downplay any frivolity in the tone of the concert. After all, this was a memorial to a well-beloved native Hawaiian singer. My glance caught Johnny Rocket's slight sneer to his lips and guessed he held another opinion, at least about who was now the group's anointed lead singer. I turned in the front passenger seat and found myself looking at Kukui, who returned my look, giving me a hard stare, uncomfortable, as if prying into my thoughts.

Our first stop did not add to the festivities, at least for my father and me. We said nothing. The van stopped at the overlook at Waipi'o Valley, a grey-black sand beach with lush cliffs in the background. Seven valleys to the west along this coast was Pololū Valley and the beach where my mom's ashes were scattered. Both views seemed identical. Dad stayed in the van.

Michael off-loaded the ladder and held it while I snapped away. The ladder helped because it put me above the fence line that protected showoff tourists from sliding down in hundreds of pieces to arrive at the valley floor the hard way.

Akaka Falls, our next stop, plunges 420 feet from top to the bottom. The walk is a botanical garden trek and our party crossed several streams. I was surprised the band members were tagging along, actually curious. Desi informed Jeffrey, and thus me, that the band members seldom took in the sights that the tourists have on their brief stop itineraries. The youthful noise makers were intrigued. My father lugged my HDTV equipment. Michael carried the ladder. The walk back up the steps was going to require strength and sweat, an event I was silently eager to witness. With Michael Ka'aiea, that is.

I could see why the ladder was necessary. The falls were gorgeous, but tourists must stand back behind a chain link fence. With the ladder, I had an unobstructed view of the falls from top to the rocks below. The ladder was sturdy and I didn't go all the way to the top. I couldn't see over the drop-off below me.

The others, after admiring the plunging falls and mist sprays, began to wander down the steps to smaller waterfalls. I was left alone.

Changing lenses on the Nikon camera I went for wide angle. I took another step up the ladder. After a minute I switched to a fish-eye lens to capture artsy dimensionals.

Back in my bathroom darkroom in Santa Monica I might experiment with some high contrast chemical impressionistic styling, suitable for framing.

I was falling.

A wobbling slow motion tumble and I grabbed at the ladder as it teetered and then slid over the fence. A sharp yank to my shoulder, the ladder nearly pried from my grasp. The bottom rung of the ladder, upside down, now the top rung caught on the fence post. I regripped and looked down. Nothing below except the stream flowing through large jagged, broken rocks, a couple of hundred feet below. My camera dangled from my neck, choking me, the least of my worries.

The ladder rattled but held as I shifted my weight. The ladder step was not hooked, it was lodged, and a shift of the whole ladder might break it free. Think fast. I didn't have a lot of time to wait for a rescue party. If I tried to pull myself, crawling the ladder to the top, my weight, changing the fulcrum's balance, probably would be the cause of the ladder's break-away.

The fence, from the ground toward the falls was not entirely a cliff. It sloped slightly with mossy vegetation from the waterfall's constant misting. Vine root appendages stuck out of the dirt and rock like...like stringy thick hair, like rope.

I did a flip to the inside of the ladder against the cliff. I held my breath to see if the shift sent me plunging. My hands were sweaty, slippery. I am not good at gymnastics, but past history of the swim team, gave me upper body strength. I grabbed at the rung above and did a chin-up a few feet. Catching my breath, I grabbed at another rung. Turning, I reached out, grabbed, and gave a tug at a root vine. It came away in my hand.

A new thought to my dilemma: a rope is made of many twines twisted. One-handed and swinging to the cliff, I gathered a fistful of slimy roots, twisting them together as best I could. The tug grip to them felt strong, and I put my faith in the floral braid. I let go and slammed against the cliff, my lifeline slipped a few feet to my weight but held. I could not return to the ladder.

Hand-over-hand I inched upward. Unused muscles strained my arm sockets. In high school gym rope climbing, I never made the required top for a high grade mark. Struggling with dirt flying into my face, I was close to the metal strand fence when a hand poked under the fence between grass and dirt. I reached with one hand and the hand pulled me up farther until I grasped the links of the fence and leveraged myself up, hauling my body over to collapse on the ground, exhausted, scratched, safe and thankful.

Kukui stood looking down at me. My rescuer. Not Michael. Not my father.

"My gods sent me."

"Thank your gods for me." Relieved, I leaned back against the fence and the ladder chose that moment to fall to a clanging, destructive crash into the gorge bottom of Akaka Falls.

I heard tourists walking our way, high-spirited cackling, off-loaded from a sight-seeing bus.

Kukui helped me to my feet and put the HDTV equipment over her shoulder and walked slowly up the trail. I carried the 35 mm camera, rescued like myself, its lightness added weight of my ordeal. In front of a botanical marker that read, "Koali Vines," my terrestrial saviors, she turned and surveyed my damage, finding me filthy, breathing heavy, and worse for wear, somehow buoyant at avoiding my close call. She got in my face, inches away.

"You could not die this day. You're here to serve a purpose." A flat statement spoken with no emotion and with that she turned and took the lead back up the path to the parked hotel van and the waiting voyagers. I shuddered. Women who see the future usually are witches. Was I saved to perish another day? The word 'heebejeebies' came to mind and a shiver coursed through my beaten body.

We met Michael walking to find us.

"Where's the ladder?" Michael asked, a reasonable question, the answer iffier.

"It broke. Wasn't worth salvaging." Quizzical, he looked at me and then to Kukui who said nothing as she trudged ahead and reboarded the bus. As we settled in, and I adjusted bruises, and took handi-wipes to my mud soiled legs, the derision again dripped forth.

"Looks like you were on the ladder when it broke," grinned Digger, the drummer.

"At least, no lava flowing nearby for her to trip into," laughed Johnny Rocket.

In Hilo, at the first moment alone with Jeffrey, I whispered, pissed off,

"Somebody pushed me at Akaka Falls."

Chapter 22
Hilo Highlights

The day in Hilo town brought additional surprises, all perplexing. At the radio station we ran into Chef Lorenzo with Hotel Manager Cahill.

"The Health Inspector has re-opened food service at the hotel," said Cahill, looking directly at Jeffrey, ignoring Michael and me. Desi, protective as a mother beast, had moved her brood inside to tape their interview with the radio host, a famous local named after a bird. Was it Mynah or Cocka-too?

"That's good news," Jeffrey offered sincere congratulations, but he was looking more to the restaurant owner with whom he had culinary empathy.

"I gave my interview, telling them all the new specials I was creating. Monsieur Cahill pitched the Lūʻau Challenge.

"With the Pāhoehoe Sounds giving their interview," I chimed in, "the concert tomorrow night should bring more people who might attend your lūaʻu festivities."

"Probably the wrong crowd," sniffed the hotel manager. "I have asked the police to provide more crowd control.

Michael's cold-stone feature, I could see, barely masked his anger. He chewed on his lower lip as the manager and chef bid their farewells and wished us a pleasant day of touring.

"It takes a mature man," offered Jeffrey to Michael, "to pick carefully his battles and only commit when superior elements are brought to bear."

"The disgruntled of this island are someday going to punch Mr. Cahill's lights out, and no one will have seen a thing."

So much for the tact of the assistant to the assistant, and I hoped it would not be Michael who lost his cool.

While waiting for the band to finish their station interview, we took a run by the Pacific Tsunami Museum. The history of the 1946 and 1960 tsunamis hitting old downtown Hilo added to my misery, wondering if nature disturbed was conspiring along with human evil.

"They didn't report any tsunami activity after that last quake, did they?"

Michael assured me the oceanographic buoys reported no discernible swells.

"The islanders know the signs better than the scientists. When the tide goes out unannounced, and fish are stranded, run to high ground." There went my comfort level as I looked across the street and eyed Hilo Bay, tranquil and serene.

A light rain started to fall, the sun still shining. Scattered fluffy clouds with grey edges hung over Mauna Kea and rain sheets drifted our way from the ocean side.

"The tourists like Kona because they come for the sun. Hilo gets about 70 inches of rain a year, makes the place a tropical paradise, but you have to enjoy the wetness." I liked hearing Michael give the statistical insight, sounded less preachy, more casual as a friend might relay important tidbits.

Michael had to drop off some ad copy for the Lūʻau Challenge to the Hilo newspaper and that's where we ran into the captain of The Pirates of the Caribbean. I thought Jimmie looked a little sheepish and Michael wheedled it out of him; he was there because they wanted his interview of the lava rescue.

"I assume you told them the truth," my voice came out a little cool which I guessed Jeffrey would pick up on. "The island grapevine seems to be spinning this into a James Bond adventure, save the helpless damsel."

Captain Jimmie eyed me with his smile in place, but he could give back as good as I gave.

"And, I'm sure you kept to our bargain of no embellishment of my efforts. In the wrong hands, my story could backfire and be bad for my charter business and all the Hawaiians I employ."

Touché. He got me. I had no desire to impact anyone's livelihood. "You are the hero, you can be the spokesperson."

He kissed my forehead. Michael and my father said nothing to our rapier repartee.

"You were my heroine all the way."

Okay, he was back in my good graces. I could forgive if it led to that secret beach, even if I didn't like being manipulated. I assume he could curry favor with his local protégés to enhance his holier-than-thou reputation. I would be off-island in less than a week, forgotten. Captain Jimmie went his way. Michael gave Jimmie a friendly handshake, and a few good words, both of them buddies. It must be admitted from one of them I longed for a climax, so to speak, during my island sojourn.

As we waited for Michael's return from the newspaper office, my father unlimbered his mind's gyrations.

"If someone pushed you at Akaka Falls, why and who?"

I was at a loss.

"Nothing I've done would seem threatening."

"But if you're mangled or dead, the grieving father can't go forward with the lū'au competition."

"So, we're back to that, but I don't like getting to that conclusion through my disfigurement or freefall finality."

"As to suspects we have to add a few more to the list of those in the van."

"What do you mean?"

"Manager Cahill, Chef Lorenzo, and Captain Jimmie."

"You're kidding?" He wasn't.

"If you note, all three came in separate vehicles. They could have followed the van, followed us down the trail, and chosen a moment when you were unprotected. No witnesses."

I wanted to protect Captain Jimmie but felt little for the innocence of the cook and the motel manager, both who I felt were egocentric male chauvinists. I lumped them together to hide my captain.

"The van occupants are more likely suspects."

He gave me an apprising glance, putting me to his standard of testing.

Let me at them.

"First, Desi Cardoza. Something happens to me, she'd expect you to turn to her for grief counseling."

"Madison." He knew his vulnerabilities in being the Boy Scout. I continued.

"Johnny Rocket. Maybe he or one of his band members feel you are responsible for Oli Palalū eating bad food."

"Johnny does have a lousy attitude. I deduce a chemical imbalance. I saw that strung-out vacant look among the accused in my previous career at the Cook County Court House."

"Any one of them could have separated themselves in the rain forest and made their way back to the outlook and ladder pushing." "You forgot Michael Ka'aiea."

"You can't be serious."

"No one in a good mystery is above suspicion."

"Does that include you? Trying to bump off your only child?" I was being smart-alecky. So could he.

"Madison," he said, offering that tender smile and warm eyes that said he loved me very much. "Whatever you are doing to yourself, it is my goal to keep you alive, so in the not too distant future you can spoon feed me soft nourishment when I'm toothless and senile, living with you."

"Of course, the purée recipe will be mine."

Michael returned. Jeffrey had not completed his observations. "Madison tells me your mother's side of your family tree is Chinese. Called 'Kee.'"

Michael looked to me and I shrugged my shoulders.

"Yes, Kee is my mother's family name."

"Interesting, that when we were at the radio station and now here at the Hilo newspaper, I noted both media outlets have wall plaques stating they are owned by Kee Enterprises. Any relationship to you?"

Michael laughed sweetly.

"My grandfather's brother's son, T'Shai-Shen Kee. His family calls him 'TS2.' His loyal employees in the past Americanized his name to Quillan Kee, nicknamed Quill. I guess because the electronic pen is mightier than the sword, and he wields it wisely."

"Such power of the press does give one power. Does he help his family, even the estranged ones?" Jeffrey aimed to the point and Michael sensed a trap of semantics.

"What I gain from such bloodlines is priority placement of Ho'oilina

Kai Resort ads in print or first mention over the airwaves. That's one of my productive functions that Manager Cahill uses to his advantage." His humor replaced this deep-seated loathing of circumstances beyond his control, of genes and heredity, and not self-accomplishment. I felt for him. He sensed the awkwardness of the moment.

"When we gather up our newly-minted musical celebrities, I have a couple of treats for you all, before we head back."

Recipe: Seared big-eye Ahi with Artichoke-Caper Polenta
(from Chef Joshua Ket-ner - Hilo Bay Café)

Ingredients:

For the polenta:
10 artichoke hearts, cooked and diced
2 tablespoons canola oil
1 ounce capers (drained) ½ Maui onion, fine diced
3 gloves garlic, minced
2 cups chicken stock
½ heavy cream
¼ c. parmesan
2 tablespoons fresh parsley chopped
½ cup polenta grain
Salt and pepper

For shiitake beurre blanc:
1 cup white wine
½ cup heavy cream
½ lbs. unsalted butter
2 tablespoons olive oil
12 fresh shiitake mushrooms Salt and pepper

For the Ahi:
1 ½ lbs sashimi grade big-eye Ahi
Salt and pepper

For the truf fled heirloom tomatoes:
1 heirloom tomato
2 tablespoons white truffle oil
Salt and pepper

For wilted spinach:
2 cups fresh spinach, picked and cleaned
1 tablespoons olive oil
Salt and pepper

Directions:

For the polenta:

In a heavy bottom pot heat oil and sweat onions and garlic until transparent.

Add chicken stock and cream, bring to simmer.

Add polenta grain; continuously stir with wood spoon until thick.

Stir in artichoke hearts, parmesan, capers and parsley.

Taste and adjust seasoning if necessary.

Form polenta in round silicone molds set aside to cool.

When cool, turn out of mold, heat oil in sauté pan and brown cakes on both sides.

For shiitake beurre blanc:

Stem shiitake mushrooms, toss caps with olive oil,

season with salt and pepper, and roast in 400 degree oven

for seven minutes; cool, cut in quarters set aside.

In heavy bottom pot combine white wine and onion and reduce by half

on low heat. Add cream and again reduce by half.

Add the butter one tablespoon at a time, stirring constantly,

until it has melted into the sauce. Add salt and pepper to taste.

Strain mixture through a fine sieve mesh, or chinois,

and keep in warm spot until platting.

For the truffled heirloom tomatoes:

Cut tomato into a medium dice, add truffle oil and season with salt and pepper.

Taste and adjust seasoning if necessary.

For wilted spinach:

Heat sauté pan to medium-high heat, add olive oil and spinach;

cook quickly and then take off heat.

Season with salt and pepper, drain on paper towel.

For the Ahi:

Portion fish into four filets, season both sides of filet with salt and pepper.

Heat oil in sauté pan to medium-high heat,

add Ahi to pan and cook on one side for two minutes, flip and cook one minute.

Remove from heat being careful not to over cook.

Assembly:

Place one polenta cake in center of each plate,

top with wilted spinach, then seared Ahi,

pour shiitake beurre blanc around plate and top Ahi

with spoonful of truffled tomatoes. (serves 4)

Chapter 23
Treat the Suspects

Lunchtime, we dropped the band members off at a locals place, *Café 100*, where they were going to munch big time on a Loco Moco, an island equivalent of a Dagwood sandwich, usually available all the time, and consisting of two scoops of rice, fried egg, hamburger patty, and brown gravy. Extras are usually potato and macaroni salad, spam, and Portuguese sausages.

Michael's choice of luncheon definitely upscale for a young hotelier, but not too country club. *Hilo Bay Café* is well hidden in a shopping center surrounded by Office Max and Wal-Mart, and not until I get inside did I realize the interior décor could work in any major urban setting: chic bistro. I was impressed with the menu and hence impressed Michael held an enlightened range of tastes. Without doing a spouting of menu items (I have now started keeping menus from every restaurant visited), we did a food tasting off each other's plates: beet salad, heirloom tomato salad, French onion soup, cheese fondue, and these were the aperitifs! Jeffrey pointed out this restaurant seemed to get only positive kudos by all the various travel food reviewers.

During the meal, I watched Desi and Michael inter act, and surprisingly, was well entertained by both. Like we were all old friends out to do lunch.

Why this bothered me, I can't put a finger to it.

And Michael's surprise for dessert: two stops! Ye gads!

Dessert: *Big Island Candies*. There went any thought of waist trimming on this trip. Michael pointed out the company was founded in 1977 to specialize in macadamia nut and Kona coffee ingredients, high-grade chocolate and, of course, lots of creamy butter. We tasted sugared samples they were handing out at the door and watched candy being made in their glass-viewing factory. The band clowns wolfed down the free samples, and Jeffrey, being the gourmet, selected hand-dipped chocolate shortbread cookies. Desi said she liked 'da-kine,' meaning a bit of everything, and made selections from chocolate-covered puffed rice, mochi balls, and iso peanuts. I followed suit and had a similar grab bag, and when Jeffrey was not looking, dropped Li Hing Mui cookies into my bag, the ingredient as I relayed earlier, the fountainhead of all Dayne family stories. Michael, on the resort nickel, treated us all to green tea ice cream cones and bags of macadamia nut crunch.

Our second foray off the main road was called *Tex Drive In*, located on Paka-lana Street in Honoka'a. I didn't realize we were stopping to pick up donuts for the next day breakfast. Not donuts per se but malasada, a puffy Portuguese donut without hole, rolled in sugar. We tried one plain, another with raspberry filing. Michael said, "Place the order you think you want, then double it because that's what is going into the tummy."

The trip back took on a jovial air, good spirits abounded. The boys in the back of the van, stuffed from lunch and multi dessert munchies, switched from farts to burps, a compliment in many cultures. But in their sugar-stocked silliness, I observed culture and etiquette were foreign to their repertoire.

Jeffrey took the relaxed atmosphere to wheedle out of the group questions concerning Oli's health, his recent bouts of flu, the concert dates missed. Everyone gave sober responses, everyone except Johnny Rocket who dozed, his mouth dry, his nose runny.

The taped radio station interview came on. I listened, impressed by what I heard. They talked music, intelligently, and made clean fun bringing guffaws from the interviewer. I saw Desi behind their public image, crafting an innocent Beatle period of good nature, boys will be boys. The van went silent when at interview end, the reason for their visit to promote the Oli Memorial Show, the radio played two Oli songs in a row, both plaintive solo ballads. On the last song, Kukui, in the back seat, sang a duet with the ghost of the dead singer. Michael translated. My heart beat heavy; this witchy woman singing with a dead man, and beside me, the man I was growing fond of, speaking the lyrics I wish he'd say to me alone.

He anu e ka ua
How bitter cold the rainfall. He anu e ka wai.
Bitter cold the stream.
Li a kuu ili
Body all a-shiver.
I ke anu, e.
From the pinching cold Ina paha
Pray, what think you? Ooe a owau
What if you and I

Ka i pu-kuku, i
Should our arms enfold I ke anu, e
Just to keep off the cold?

As we approached the Ho'oilina Kai, an emotion surged through my body and it was not passion. Jeffrey's concerned glance in my direction signaled a reality check. I tensed to the significance: someone, presumably in the van, tried to kill me.

Recipe: Crystallized Ginger Chicken

2 tablespoons corn starch
1/2 teaspoon sea salt
1/4 teaspoon freshly ground black pepper
12 ounces boneless, skinless chicken breast, cut into 1-inch chunks
2 tablespoons sliced garlic
1 tablespoon canola oil
1 cup reduced-sodium chicken broth
1/4 cup slivered crystallized ginger
2 teaspoons reduced-sodium soy sauce
1 large sweet potato, peeled and cut into 3/4 -inch cubes
1 red bell pepper, sliced into 1/8 -inch wedges
1 tablespoon chopped fresh cilantro

In a shallow dish, combine corn starch, salt and black pepper.
Dredge chicken in the seasoned flour; shake off excess.
In a large wok or skillet over medium-high heat, cook garlic in hot oil about 10 seconds.
Add chicken and stir-fry 2 to 3 minutes, or until light golden. Remove chicken to a plate.
Add broth, ginger, soy sauce and sweet potato to the wok and bring to a boil.
Cover, reduce heat to low, and simmer 10 minutes, or until potato is just tender.
Return broth to a boil.
Add red pepper and chicken and cook, stirring, 2 minutes,
or until chicken is just cooked through
and sauce has thickened slightly. Sprinkle with cilantro.
Makes 4 servings. Recipe from Devany Vickery-Davidson

Chapter 24
Belly of the Francophile Feast

We Daynes gave support to the reopening of Chef Lorenzo's upscale establishment, *Uakea La Reve*. The food surpassed all my expectations. The event, 7 p.m. to 9 p.m. open ended cocktail party offered tasting tapas on server plates from waiters passing among us. After the day trip to Hilo, I went for light grazing. Tonight, with each bite, I really did try to dwell on the nuances of taste that Jeffrey sought to instill in my education. I opted for snatched pizza bits as the best selection, even if described— 'Duck and Mushroom Pizza with Honey-Hoisin-Cilantro Sauce.' Give Chef Lorenzo his due, he did have the culinary touch.

I let Jeffrey's list of suspects mull in my frazzled brain. Chef Lorenzo could have followed us to the Akaka Falls, unseen, given me the push, and rushed to the radio station to make his alibi solid. Going extreme, regardless of Jeffrey's loyalty to fellow foodies, Chef Lorenzo could have provided the Angel's Trumpet to the poi. Motive? Jealousy. Envy. He would have stepped in and saved the Lū'au Challenge, become a hero, and with Jeffrey incapacitated (with his daughter), he'd hire an agent, seeking to replace the Dayne show on the Food Channel Network. I could see it, but I could not see it. Chef Lorenzo seemed too erudite to be a poisoner, but didn't the Borgias dispatch their victims with poisoned lasagna?

The evening gathering, by invitation, seemed to be the A-list of the Island. I can't remember everyone in quick introductions. Peter Merriman introduced himself to me again. I recognized famous chef Sam Choy (of restaurants and cookbooks). Another chef, Rick Moonen who specialized in sustainable seafood, had flown in specific for the event from Las Vegas. After hearing his spiel on the marvelous taste of fresh Hawaiian fish, I almost believed that he was going to smuggle back fish right off the charter boats into his suitcase. I hovered on the fringe of an animated discussion from Chef Amy Ferguson of Hawai'i Caterers on the benefits of organic foods in recipes.

The fame side of who's who wore on me after a while, after all I was a nobody, or worse a lesser appendage hooked to Jeffrey's star. So, to give my father's TV show a party-type atmosphere for a future montage, I played the part of a public relations photographer, milled around and shot closeups of society in cocktail congress, sought to create tray food as artsy-fartsy, and clicked away at the behind-the-scene kitchen action. Chef Lorenzo went from the dining room accepting accolades for his revived menu to a shouting dictator in his own version of Hell's Kitchen. I am sure all ingredients had been checked and double-checked for their exact moment to be added and stirred. No food tampering tonight.

In the social crowd mix, of interest, was who was not there; Michael, for one. I overheard Manager Cahill glowing on how efficient he had organized the Lū'au Challenge and the Oli Memorial, throwing a backhanded comment that he impressed upon 'Mike Lake' there would be no disruption to tomorrow night's concert memorial. The way Cahill spoke, his tone condescending, sounded like he was going to hold his underling responsible for his uncle's conduct. Was Michael's job at risk? I worried for him.

My father stood surrounded by several women gushing in adoration but here I had indirect support from that Cardoza harpy, hovering near his side, marking her territory, if no one could see the obvious. The Pāhohoe Sounds were absent as they should be. This was not their crowd. A string trio provided what I took to be French elevator music. Off in the corner, into themselves, were the Beautiful People. Beyond the freebie food produced for all guests it seemed they had specifically ordered red wines of what I would guess would be from the St. Emilion and Paullic wine-producing regions, a couple hundred dollars per bottle. My own vintner education, under my dad's tutelage, gave me confidence that my taste bud judgment could match theirs any day.

It was then I noticed the Leader, who at that moment turned from his friends and looked across the room. My eyes followed his. A table of boisterous men and women, definitely moneyed, like used car dealers on holiday. Gold-chain necklaces for the men and large-stoned baubles dangling off the women's décolletage, the ladies looking more hussy cheap than fashion mag stylish. Of that party sitting at their table, most of the talk and attention, centered on one man, dark skin features, like Desi Cardoza in ethnicity. The man seemed to be holding court, his group concentrating to laugh at his jokes.

Suddenly, the Leader of the Beautiful People rose and made a quick advance through the crowd. Intense in his strides, I sensed an altercation in the making. Instead, very strange, the Leader went to one of the dinner servers, a woman in white uniform who had begun serving a plate of stuffed pastry delicacies. He grasped her arm and whispered in her ear. They exchanged stares. She dropped a serving napkin as the Leader escorted the woman out into the kitchen. I saw that she walked with a decided limp. I did not see either again during the event. Did the woman do something offensive like spill wine on the Beautiful People?

I continued my mock photo journalism, walking the room, hiding behind my camera, the detached observer. I snapped photo portraits of each table, acting like a Vegas showroom camera girl. Closer together, please. Smile, please. The table, when I arrived, where the Leader had approached earlier, waved me away, no photo, one of them even giving me the evil eye. Moments later, they hustled out, as if I had caused their hasty departure. Certainly, I did not intrude like a news rag paparazzi. Strange. It was then I noticed the napkin on the floor by their table, dropped by the wait staff server, the woman with the limp. Curious, as usual, I bent down and picked it up. A steak knife fell out among its cloth folds. Strange. What had I really seen this evening? A foodie detective should have a theory on the night's activities. I only knew Chef Lorenzo's food regained customer loyalty from all who attended, but to everything else I had witnessed, heard and seen, and photographed, left me unsettled, pissed off at myself, realizing my limits of conjecture.

Recipes.

(The following two recipes were sent to Jeffery from Chef Amy Ferguson of Cater Hawaii.)

Poisson Cru served with Patacones
Lime Coconut marinated Opakapaka (Pink Snapper) served with Plantain Chips
Serves 6

Ingredients:

1-1/2 lbs. Any Snapper, white fish (skinless & boneless) or
Sea or Bay Scallops, thinly sliced
Lime juice to cover
½ small Red Onion, cut in quarters and finely julienne 1 lg. clove of gar-lic, minced
¼ cup Culantro (cilantro may be substituted), chopped *¼ habanero (aji chombo)
***2 cups Coconut Cream (to make your own Fresh see notes below)
Salt or fish sauce to taste (I prefer a mix of Tiparos and a small amount of salt)

Procedure:

1. Mix the sliced seafood with onion and garlic.
Then cover with fresh squeezed lime juice. Stir and set aside to "cook/pickle".
2. Once the fish is cooked approx 2-4 hrs later,
drain the lime juice and season with the remaining ingredients

Notes:

*Habaneros are not for the faint of heart!
If you have not had this par-ticular pepper
before I suggest you use a smaller amount or change peppers
(Jalapeno, Serrano, even Hawaiian Chili pepper would not burn you like a Habanero)
So, why do I suggest using it? Because of the flavor...
the first time I tasted it...it made my lips swell,
burnt the inside of my mouth so badly that the skin peeled...
I couldn't drink water for 3 days and my lips
looked as if they belonged to a monkey... haha!
Every time I go to a new region something
like this happens... Like here in Hawai'i...I ate raw taro leaf!
That took 3 days for the itching in my mouth and stomach to go away!
Think before tasting should be my motto...
**Fresh Coconut milk: Crack a dry coconut (brown on the outside)
shake to see if there is water inside, save the water... take the split halves
and toast on a burner...this helps to release
the flesh from the shell... then take the water,
flesh and a bit of water and process in a VitaMix blender un-til it is liquid...
strain the milk through a fine sieve...OR buy Medonca's frozen or a good quality
Thai Coconut milk in the can...if you do...
open the can and spoon the cream off the top of 2 cans,
using the cream only and throwing out the water or add to a Thai Soup, cook rice with it etc...

Patacones Plantain Chips

1. Peel Plantain, and cut it width wise into 3 or 4 pieces.
2. I have found that the easiest way to peel the plantain
is to cut rough-ly 1/4" off of each end of the plantain (the very tips),
and then carefully, without cutting into the plantain itself,
slicing the skin down one side.
3. Once you have slit the skin on one side,
you can gently pry the peel off with your fingers.
4. Heat 1" of vegetable oil on medium heat until hot.
5. Fry plantain pieces on both sides for about 3 minutes,
or until the pieces are golden.
6. When they are golden, remove from pan and place
onto a plate covered with a paper towel.

Chapter 25
Garden of Fiasco

Party over, by 9 p.m. I was back in my room, organizing equipment for the Memorial the next evening. Before the earlier restaurant opening and menu tasting I had, by myself, walked the staging area on the golf course and seen the workers installing a trussed stage, covered with bunting, large speaker stands at either side. Lighting towers were placed down each side of the fairway's approach to the green where the stage was being erected. The basin would seat comfortably about 2,000 people in a grass lawn picnic setting, and the audience would enjoy the musical acts with the ocean as the backdrop. During my walk, thinking like a producer, I realized I was inadequate. I could take B-roll of the event but to capture the musicians from all the angles one would expect in a television show would be near impossible. I would have to go supplicant, knees-to-ground, and ask Public Relations Director Cardoza to let me use some stock film from her camera people who were there in force setting up for stationary and shoulder-held camera stage shots. What she would give me, I expected, would be the highlights of the Pāhoehoe Sounds concert. Instead of running crazy with my HDTV apparatus, I should enjoy the night, relaxing with Michael.

My limitations so apparent. I was an intern shutterbug and my presence on island my father's doing, not because a major cable channel thought I was going places. The room phone rang. The front desk.

"Is Mr. Dayne there?"

"No." I forgot the room I had moved over to after the break-in was under his name, not mine.

"He had ordered a hotel car from concierge. Do you know if he's going to use it?"

Jeffrey going out, and late at night? Not a good sign.

"Hold it, someone will be down shortly."

What's going on? Why didn't he tell me? Only one scenario permeated my suspicious mind: a rendezvous. For some reason of stealth, I threw on the only dark clothes I had brought with me: black shorts, dark grey Hang Loose XL T-shirt from Crazy Shirts, Tribal He'e, (a gift for my father) and a Ho'oilina Kai Resort baseball cap. I rushed to the lobby to see Jeffrey's back enter a car at valet, Desi Cardoza driving. How could he? A panic attack hit me. A quick stop at concierge and I had the car keys for our hotel loaner: an open Jeep, white, the hotel's logo emblazoned on the sides. Where were they going? What they — she — was planning I could almost write the script. As I accelerated, catching up to the car's red taillights, my memory did an unpleasant flashback.

Mom had taken ill after taping the next to last episode of their cooking television program during the second season. The heartbreak diagnosis was ovarian cancer. It took eight months of chemotherapy before the words "irreversible" and "inoperable" made their way into the doctor's comments. Ebbing like a summer sun on the horizon, her body wasted away, and she, more courageous than anyone else, decided to end her own life before she lost all motor and mind control.

As the story was relayed to me, she awoke in her hospital room from induced sleep of dripped pain-killers that had worn off far earlier than the nurse in charge had expected of those life-numbing cocktails. Elizabeth had a hit of reality, epiphany of time and place. She kissed her husband goodbye for the last time, he looking drained and haggard from those months during the hopeful surgical procedures, now the uncertain vigil. When he left, she opened a false panel on the inside book board of their first cookbook. At her bedside for the last six months, Jeffrey had read the recipes from this book several times over, reliving the highlights of a meal's creation, never discovering the more sinister potions hidden at his fingertips. She pulled out the secreted letter written months earlier when her hand could write strong before ravished by the chemo, needle poking and tube insertion. She did not leave a maudlin goodbye. She wrote, as was her personality, her own upbeat recipe of continuing life, a fulfilling guide, food for thought, for her husband and daughter. With the letter came the plastic pouch of hoarded pills. Right or wrong, she retained control of her destiny. I admired her for that, though I miss her horribly, and feel cheated by her absence.

At the early stage of the masticating disease, during my last year of graduate film school in California, I visited her as scheduling would allow in the Chicago hospital. During the subsequent months of gyrating job scheduling, I appeared less often when she went into the hospice, my own life too filled with youth and immortality, self-absorbed, immersed in bright horizons without dwelling on someone's debilitation. Perhaps I saw too much of me in her and could not bear to see the talent of her creativity disappear unfulfilled. I think she understood my absence. I hoped she did. But in her legacy recipe for the survivors, she did chastise me, not condemning, but the same nevertheless, for abandoning the living in time of need, my father. From that guilt, well deserved, I swore I would never abandon him again in times of trouble, protect him as I could. This was such a time. My mother's memory would not be besmirched by a hussy's seduction.

At a distance I could hide in the tourist traffic on Highway 11 until they reached the housing developments of Kalaoa and we headed mauka, land side I smartly recalled, up the road where signs pointed to the dormant volcano mountain, Hualalai, 8271 feet in elevation. God, I hoped she did not live on top of the mountain. The road went from cracked asphalt to dirt and the Jeep began bouncing over washboard ruts. The area looked like small farm plots with housing, economically below the middle-class median, a few mini-mansions popping up in the middle of Kona coffee groves. I dimmed my headlights as the road wound higher with sharp switch backs. A road to a wild life sanctuary went off to the left. I barely missed a turn that would have sent me off-road and plunging down into someone's orchard. I thought the moon might throw off some ambient lighting so I could trail their tail-lights from a safe distance.

Fog not vog found me instead. A fine mantle of ghostly mist obscured the road. I could barely see two feet ahead. Headlights back on did little good. The Jeep crept. I strained looking for their car, her house. Ten minutes later there it was: the Cardoza name on a flowery cutesy mailbox, and a road leading up into veiled darkness as the clouds hugged the ground. I found a turn-around and aimed the Jeep downhill, for a quick getaway, if that was my plan, if I had a plan.

I walked up the drive, catching my breath every hundred feet. Through the fog yellow glows set out the hazed windows of the house. I could not be as asinine as pounding on the front door. Was I protective or curious? Both. This woman was not worthy enough for my father; he deserved better. A person like my mother.

Before I reached the house, I skirted off to the side into what I thought was a grove of Kona coffee trees. I used this cover as I circled towards the back of the house where I could see better, gain a view into the living room and kitchen, both brightly lit. I saw two forms in the window. Not sharp enough. I had to gain a better observation point, but I had run into a fence blocking my access. The wired obstacle seemed to run from the house down the hill into the deeper jungle vegetation. A gate provided the solution and I opened it, my feet treading carefully between rows of what I guessed were vegetables. My eyes focused on the movement within a room.

Jeffrey seemed to be admiring her floor-to-wall bookcase, tugging at various volumes, flipping through pages. At a sideboard she mixed yellow alcoholic potions in cocktail glasses. They stood close together, sipped their drinks, and looked happy. What was I doing here? What right did I have to interfere in Jeffrey's basic male hormones for a momentary fling to have his horns rubbed down to the nubs? They were walking to the back deck. I ducked under some giant-size tomato vines and kept skirting sideways through the garden. She had brought pūpūs from the kitchen. She was seducing with his greatest weakness: food. My, God, were there poi fritters on that plate? Taro tacos with salsa poi? Poison poi in the batter?

I needed to shout, throw a rock, distract them, destroy the ambiance of their first hot, steamy touch.

I heard a noise. I ducked down. Another noise, plants being crunched underfoot. Someone was in the garden with me. I could not be discovered; the mortification would be too great. I crab-walked in a crouch, trying to move down the hill, away from the approaching steps getting closer. I stopped, held my breath and started crawling through a patch of onions, Maui onions, no doubt. At a trellis of colored peppers I defined a new noise.

A snort?

I pulled back some leaves and carefully put my face forward, my ears listening for the next...snort.

A giant snout poked me in my face and snorted snot on me. My shouted 'Yipe!' coincided at the moment the pig made a hairy night piercing squeal. Pigs were on the left of me, pigs on the right of me. With pigs scattering around my feet, I stumbled up and downhill through the rows of the garden. From behind me, I heard a shout, a woman's angry voice. Suddenly, large floodlights lit the backyard. If I kept in a running crouch I would not be seen, I could make my escape, easily; yeah, right. Hardly.

Another noise added to the pigs squealing and trampling through the garden, a dog's bark, two dogs, vicious barking, coming closer. Desi had loosed a wolf pack on me; she would have her revenge, she would have Jeffrey to herself!

I hit the garden fence at the back of the lot and bounced to the ground. The hill sloped enough so that I could not see the back deck of the house, but I could hear the voices of two people, Desi shouting. I found a guava tree, climbed a few feet and jumped the fence. My landing was off in the darkness and I started rolling through the jungle vegetation, coming to rest in leafy weeds. Thank God, no thorns, but I was scraped and muddy. Which way was the roadway? My mind took moments to sense my bearings, up was up, the road down, somewhere. Without warning, the mountain side reverberated with a gunshot echo, not a crack of a rifle, a *whoomp* blast. Shotgun! I prayed it was for wild pig scaring, and nothing more sinister. Where a second gunshot might land pushed me away from the threat; paying little attention, I bounced against trees, tore through bushes, tripped over roots.

I sat in the Jeep, drained of feelings, a mess. I released the brake, put the Jeep in neutral, and in the soupy fog coasted down the road with a troubled soul, worried beyond worry about my father's safety. Two Blue Hawai'i drinks later, slurped at the beach bar, I slumped over in such a battered condition that glib male strangers steered clear. My growing numbness was replaced with deep-sighed relief as I saw my father walking through the torch-lit hotel grounds. I called to him and he joined me.

"Pineapple Bomber," he ordered, and to me said, "My second of the night." He gave me the once over, my features lit by orange blazed tiki torches, accented by purple bar neon with assorted flying bugs. In that décor ambiance, without makeup, my resemblance would suggest Goddesses Pele and Medusa, co-joined, an opinion to which Jeffrey concurred.

"You look like hell. What happened?"

What could I say?

"Went walking on the golf course and tripped into the rough." He picked a leaf out of my hair, looked at it with the curiosity of a tenured botanist, and sipped his drink. He leaned over and picked greenish snags out of my white socks. My socks, shorts, hair, my whole body, looked like I rolled in green mulch, as I had.

When you lie, it is best to change the subject to the offense.

"And what did you do this evening?"

"Desi Cardoza wanted to show me her cookbook collection of Hawaiian recipes."

Boy, that really frosted me; he told the truth. "Is that sort of like, 'Want to come up to my apartment and see my etchings'?"

"A very innocent evening until feral pigs broke into her garden." I said nothing when I should have asked to hear the whole story. "But even if it wasn't innocent, do you have a problem with what goes on in my private life?"

There, it was out on the table for discussion. I could ignore, I could yell at him. Instead, he eased me through my tribulations.

"You know, Madison, your mom was that special person in my life, and now it is you. She has been gone for two years. I mourn her daily, but I realize my life goes on. This trip was the symbolic purging. It's not working. Too soon. In a not too distant future, there may or may not be someone out there who shows me life still holds exuberance. But, Madison, when the time comes, the choice, the person, will be mine. Without interference, understand? Until then, your role is to be supportive to a father and a foodie entertainment personality, in that order."

I nodded with alcoholic haziness, the hurts of the day and evening surfacing into my joints. A lone tear fell onto the bar.

He rubbed my shoulder, gently, sensing my bruises, my internal aches.

"In turn, I will try to help your career and protect you from bad influences. Neither of these tasks do I seem to be doing well. In the future, I will be more diligent. You accept?"

I capitulated to his parental wisdom.

"Yes, Father." Not 'Jeffrey' I had answered.

"Good. First things first, when you go up to your room. I want all your clothes into one pile. Do not touch them. I will take care of them myself."

A strange request.

"I can clean myself, take care of my own dirty clothes."

"See this leaf, Madison?" I nodded tired, ready for bed.

"A plant of the cannabis variety. Marijuana. The golf course has some mighty potent roughs. Definitely out of bounds."

He led me back into the hotel, and to the elevator. "I'll be along shortly."

My worry about a late night liaison with you-know-who showed on my face.

"Madison, I have to go and make amends about your Jeep out front. You parked in a flowerbed of azaleas."

Recipe: Blue Hawai'i Cocktail

3/4 oz Light Rum
3/4 oz Vodka
1/2 oz Blue Curacao
3 oz Pineapple Juice
1 oz Sweet & Sour Mix

Mix all ingredients in blender with ice.
Pour into tall glasses and finesse with pineapple slice and cherry,
sugarcane stick, or an edible flower.

I laughed at how hopeless I seemed,
looking for love on all the wrong beaches.

Chapter 26
Plot Stewing

I slept the sleep of the dead. Wrong metaphor. Late morning I woke to angry voices in my head. Not in my head, but outside my window, and we were five stories up. I threw on my robe. My trashed clothes from last night's jungle foray nowhere to be seen.

Below, in a grassy courtyard, ironically near a bush of Angel's Trumpet, I could see Uncle Joe Coffee yelling at Michael Ka'aiea, and doing so in Hawaiian. What surprised me was Michael's response, snapped back, not at the same level of anger, but likewise spoken in Hawaiian. All the more interesting were small clusters of people surrounding the two of them; as my Father would have noted, three groups, each in the colors seen several days earlier at the front gate. I even saw Larry Tutapu in his green-yellow T-shirt with his followers. Every once in a while the revolutionary First Mate threw out his contribution in a cursed epitaph, frustration at not being part of the dialogue.

I felt like I was watching street gangs in strutting positioning, Sharks versus Jets. No one could prevent the old man from waving his arms to enunciate his shouting. Everyone stood poised, on brawl alert. The Monarchy fogies against Green Shirt rappers.

Only the White Shirts stood aloof. From that group, I had yet to pick out anyone of leadership authority. They seemed a protest movement run by committee.

Michael, I could see, paced uneasy, glancing around, cognizant the one-sided shouting match from Old Joe Coffee could be overheard by the hotel guests, staring down, as I was, from their balconies. In his ranting, Uncle Joe saw me and his arm pointed my way, shaking his hand viciously. Noticing me in attendance from on high, Michael let his voice rise to overwhelm the old man's vitriolic spew. His Hawaiian spit out rapidly, showing him to be a fluent native language speaker. No casual pidgin expressions.

Old Joe fell silent. In moments, they all stalked off, three separate pathways, in various degrees of agitation; the only thing in common, each group threw backward stares, looking my way. Michael looked at me and walked off. No smile, more a grimace of pain.

Maybe *my body could cause the launch of a thousand war canoes.*

Ah, from towel to ocean, the sand burned underfoot, the water a tolerable coolness, I stood neck high and let my pains soothe. I would have tipped heavy for the return of the old medicine woman with her magic massage potions? Here I am in paradise and I have only two hours of beach time before Michael is to escort me to the Memorial concert.

Back on my towel the sun rays purged my mini-hangover. I took stock of what happened last night, and what I had rolled in. Marijuana leaves stuck to my clothing. Maybe I did not know all the history of my father that he could recognize the leaf so quickly; then again, he was a former defense attorney and used to looking through evidence exhibits. I accepted that answer.

As much as I could see honorable citizens growing a few plants for personal use, I considered Desi Cardoza more a fashion hound than a pot freak. However, another suspect, rose to mind: Johnny Rocket. He definitely had druggie habits. Desi, in fact, had said casually that Johnny and his fellow merry prankster band members, except for Kukui, all shared the same apartment, for creative purposes. Without going back to the scene of my crime, which I would not, what with wild pigs and guard dogs and scatter shotguns with shells filled with rock salt (as Jeffrey told me the story this morning), I could envision that below his Mother's garden, in the dense undergrowth, Johnny Rocket had his own hidden farm plot of a cash crop.

On this part of the beach, I found myself alone except for a bearded grandpa heading my way, wearing headphones and swinging a type of metal sweeper broom. No, not right, they're called *metal detectors*. Every once in a while, he would stop, drop to his knees, dig with a small childlike shovel scoop with a screen, shake away the wet sand and inspect his find. Focused, he was nearly stepping on my beach towel when he looked up, embarrassed, at the same time his headphones beeped, and addicted to his hobby, made him immediately dig, almost at my feet. A rusty beer can. He threw it into a sack he carried at his side, that looked half full of trash. That was big of him, an environmental beachcomber. I noted his name etched on the handle of his magic searching wand, he was that close to me. I guess for Mr. C.

Cussler, there is still excitement for the retirees around here, even if it holds rejection more than success.

"Good try," I said about his 'discovery,' but with his headphones he did not hear. In turn, when he looked up, he gave me a silent expressive shrug of 'oh, well, next time.' Just then, his headphones gave him another noisy indication, and digging in the same hole, except deeper, he screened out shells and sand, and held up a Rolex watch, and for his sake, I hoped it was not a knock-off. This time, I mouthed slowly, "Congratulations."

He walked on swinging his metal detector, side to side, a very happy man, but determined, not stopping with just one prize. I watched him diminish with distance. What should I think? Is there a philosophical lesson here? — One man's trash is another's treasure. — Don't look beyond your grasp; the answer may be within reach. — Never just scratch the surface. Dig deeper. — Never give up. Or, a worse conclusion by my jaded Californication life style, unfair to him but a truism: always have a good excuse to be around half-naked women. Finding jewelry at my feet was the best come-on I've ever witnessed. An Oscar-winning performance even I would applaud. Did he really find a watch, or was it his? I am getting too cynical. Give him the benefit of doubt. Just harmless, but there was that twinkle in his eye, and I caught myself wondering what he might have looked like thirty years younger. I laughed at how hopeless I seemed, looking for love on all the wrong beaches.

In truth, the curmudgeon beachcomber did track my thoughts back to other treasure hunters. I reflected to my morning online computer search in the hotel's business center.

Posing a general question I was proved correct. The word 'cache,' pronounced 'cash' is part of *geo-caching*, a travelling hunt game using GPS technology. The odd-looking walkie-talkie devices I saw among the Beautiful People being waved around at the airport were in fact GPS handheld tracking monitors. So, this morning, on the way to the beach, and a little more brash, I went to the bar and copied the new set of GPS coordinates left by the Beautiful People. From my beach bag, I pulled out my scribbles and now knew what I was seeing: locations, or they call them, 'waypoints'. Now I recalled, the tee shirt I had seen at the airport and later in the hotel, in casual passing. In full I had read the t-shirt: N 36° 04. 922' W 115° 10. 367'.

Latitude/longitude, with distance geo calculated into degrees (°), minutes (.) and seconds (')

N 36° 07. 573'   W 115° 11. 892'   SG 20-9-16   15-6

N 36° 06. 828'   W 115° 08. 095'   CC1-08

Three sets of clues this time, perhaps the search would take more time, travelling to the other side of the island. They had departed after breakfast on their quest mystery. A basic guess that they might have combined some scavenger hunt elements to energize another Great Race competition. Wonder what was the ultimate prize of victory? My imagination wandered too far afield to prizes of date swapping, harem creation, or erotic bondage. No, I sensed class in their bearing, intelligence in their game creation. Rather, a geo-caching prize so unique I had to believe that it made travelling halfway across the world for a treasure for the winning team worth serious intrinsic value. No travelling trophy with brass plate of achievement for the Beautiful People. My continued envy led to plotting.

I dove through the waves, and swam laps in front of the reef, with each stroke starting to fuse together 'a plan'. If you can't join them, what better thrill but to outwit the Beautiful People or better said, play a practical joke. It would be my in-joke, a surprise without being malicious, especially without them discovering the identity of the interloper. *Think.* Like leave some sort of message, make them wonder: who did this? Hint but not reveal. *How?* I shifted over to backstroke, somewhat comfortable to believe sharks did not feed mid-afternoon, and they cruised further out beyond the breaker reef. So, I hoped. No more adventures, please.

Swimming on my back, viewing only pure blue heaven, again my thinking cap went on. Yes, that's it. I had to find one of their caches before they did and place something in the box, or whatever container it might be. Let them wallow in curiosity. Something we Daynes knew well enough.

When I reached my towel, saw no one near, even the old beachcomber, I slipped off my entire bikini. No tan lines.

Now comes the Heaven-born: The whole land doth shake   (art by Kathy Long)

Chapter 27
Under the Stars, Under the Music, Under Him

Ouch.

Back at the hotel, by the time I turned on the shower to get ready, the shower stream revealed hurting burn splotches missed by sun screen. Body cream greased on helped a little. I eased into a sun dress, tied up my hair, finger-tapped on dollops of enticing eye of newt perfume. I would only take my Nikon, be the tourist. Enjoy myself.

In the lobby, Michael Ka'aiea cut a sharp figure, washed and fluffed hair, Hawaiian shirt and white slacks, sandals. He did not wear his hotel badge of identification. He carried a picnic canvas bag. My thoughts went back to helicopters and champagne and beaches missed. Well, if you can't be with the one — anyway — Michael and I exchanged gossipy pleasures all the way to the hillside concert grounds. Somewhere in our short hike, I came to realize we were holding hands.

What a treat. First, we were not sitting with Jeffrey and Desi, who sat in the V.I.P. section of the who's who on the Big Island. Michael pointed out the Island Mayor, and both exchanged distant respectful nods of greetings. So, the assistant hotel manager knows the mayor. There's more to this man next to me.

I recognized Manager Cahill holding court. Those missing sparked my interest. The Japanese owners of Ho'oilina Kai should have basked in the positive publicity of doing a good deed, making amends. I saw no one like them in the growing crowd. Michael told me Captain Jimmie's absence came from volunteering his ships' crews to oversee crowd control at the front gate. I asked Michael if he considered this night work or play.

"I have my people well organized. Please note my cell phone has not rung once. I told them only if they see a tsunami." He gave me a big smile, knowing how easily my nerves could fray. I looked to the ocean, saw only a solitary whale spout and a tail slap as the sun edged to kiss the horizon. If the whales weren't worried...

The Memorial boasted musical diversity, consisting, according to the program I read, ten local groups, various types of island music from ukulele expertise to slack key guitar bands, two hula dance troupes, and two poetry readings. Each of the performers would do three songs, one of which would be an Oli Palalū signature song. The poets would recite various lyrics he had composed. A kumu hula, a hula teacher, blew the conch horn to begin the Memorial and recited an ancient chant. The last performance, the Pāhoehoe Sounds, would mean tearjerker time. The final song of their set would be a version of Aloha 'Oe. I had stuffed extra tissue in my camera case.

We sat on a blanket and sipped a sweet yet potent drink. "What is this?"

"'Okolehao. A special rum liquor blended with tropical flavors, and extract from the ti root plant. The power of the ti wards off evil spirits and brings goodness and strength."

"Let me chug the bottle." I read the label. "It says the ti plant was the emblem of high rank and divine power."

"Whatever." Michael shrugged off the implications. "The distillers of this particular brand stopped making this elixir of the gods. I could have the last case left."

"The gods seem to favor you a lot." The music began. Several numbers later, Oli Palalū came back on a giant projection screen, eerie and dreamy, from a past music video he had performed as a solo:

Nauweuwe ka honua Ka hana a ke ola nui: Moe pono ole ko'u po — Na niho ai kalakala, Ka hana a ka Niuhi

Now comes the Heaven-born; The whole land doth shake, As with an earthquake; Sleep quits then my bed: How shall this maw be fed!

Michael translated as hula dancers performed, a sense of romantic sensuality building with the lyrics. In between the third and fourth musical group, when the drink and the soothing melodies mellowed us, and on the blanket edging closer together, each leaning against the other, I had to ask.

"What was that row with your uncle this morning? He was dishing it out and you were standing there throwing it back at him. And why, all the other factions in attendance?" I think Michael had come to understand no one escaped the Dayne inquisitive nature.

"All three factions wanted to use the Memorial as a forum for their causes, pass out literature, make impassioned speeches. Uncle Joe wanted ten minutes on stage to demand the hotel rebuild the heiau. If he had the microphone, I sensed he might call a boycott on the hotel, shut us down for good. My response was that it was the time to recall Oli Palalū's soul on earth and the goodness he brought by his music, not create more divisiveness."

"As it should be." I put my head on his shoulder, his arm went around me. "What about when Uncle Joe cast his evil eye my direction? That conversation had nothing to do with protest."

I felt Michael stiffen and silence followed while Oli sang.

A mau i ke kai loa He loa o ka hiki na, A ua noa, a ua noa.

Great maw of the shark— Eyes that gleam in the ark Of the boundless sea!

Rare the king's visits to me. All is free, all is free!

"Michael, it's okay, I'm a big girl." Whatever, I asked for it, knowing I wasn't that big of a tough-skin girl.

"Uncle Joe said if I continued to see that haole girl from Hollywood, he would disown me entirely, curse me among my people, and I would be 'kipaku.'"

"Kipaku?" I pronounced the word slowly, not knowing if I wanted the definition.

"Banished. I would no longer be Hawaiian. In the olden days, it meant I had to go and kill myself."

"He can't be serious. I'm no harm to the Hawaiian people."

"He's worried that our children's Hawaiian blood would be too diluted to be worthy of the Ka`aiea name."

That shut me up. Another act followed. We were silent until Michael spoke, that smile of his disarming innocence.

"Listen to these lyrics, close your eyes, and hear Oli's voice." On the large screen, the visage of Oli Palalū appeared again and as he sang, one plaintive guitar strummed, a backup group on stage hummed and chanted the refrains. "Believe it or not, Johnny Rocket said he wrote this, but I hear in it a lot of influence of Captain Jimmie's free library."

I closed my eyes. With Oli's dove-like serenade, Michael spoke into my ear, his soft voice almost a duet with Oli's singing, putting the Hawaiian lyrics into English. The whispered effect: outright erotic.

Hiiaka, peerless maiden, tell me!

Why fear such tenderness as mine?

Play the game of kilu, hear my kāna mele

O that I, Lohiau were Kanaloa rippling round your dainty fairness Circling about your waist to entice you to a dive!

Then steal between luscious lips and eyelids thin

O that your shining hair was in the sun

Beams distilled in passion thence to run

In loving watery rivulets down a mortal form

To linger on this morning glory shoulder, warm

Between kissing breasts and every charm.

Desire tingled within. The words of that song did not come from Johnny Rocket. Captain Jimmie's fingerprints at artistic romance were apparent, again the behind-the-scene benefactor and mentor to troubled island youth. No. I didn't want to think about the sea captain. Michael's bombshell of Old Joe Coffee's displeasure offered implications, of what? A serious commitment to this one special man? Me, the causal rift of a family destroyed? How did I really feel? Music drifted among the crowd and I felt the warmth of another's arms around me; in such comfort, my mind free floated, drifting among the night's stars. Both of us must have felt this bliss for Michael rose, gently took my hand, and led me to a secret place under the stage.

The backstage security guard, a Maori dance warrior with his tattoos, smiled and turned away as we ducked under stage skirt curtains and Michael gingerly escorted me carefully around metal cross beams to another blanket repose. He turned on a flashlight, and as I sat offered me a glass of champagne. Ah, the man had his own agenda. Talk about sensual highs; what a trip, our own secret grotto. What Uncle Joe couldn't see couldn't damage his cause. I was not going to tell.

The music above reverberated a rumble on the stage, the sounds somewhat muted with the slow songs, and the pure darkness lit by flashlight glow, the adventure I had been longing for had begun.

"The Pāhoehoe Sounds are next. I thought this might be more…"

"Romantic." I said and gave him a kiss, slowly, letting it linger, tasting his mouth, tenderness he returned.

We lay down next to each other. I could hear the stage crew above move the band equipment around for the next set.

He laid his body without weight part way on top of me. The kissing ardor intensified and my arm took hold of his neck and brought him closer, both of us rubbing through clothes, momentarily restraining flesh on flesh touching. The band did some warm up tuning. We rolled on the blanket, side by side in a clutch of exploring. A fire inside raked my body with wanting. His hand moved inside my blouse, grazing my taut nipples. I could feel his excitement harden; I moved to grab hold and let him know this night meant all or nothing, and nothing not an option. We were committed to a wild night under a musical stage showered with love songs to match our animalistic heat.

The crash of the drum cymbals, the high decibel stroke of guitar chords broke our mood, if not eardrums. The Pāhoehoe Sounds jumped around in heavy thuds as the music, if you could call it that, pounded out hard chords of Nirvana rock and roll, the band that is, noise deafening where any songbird's voice would be buried under chalkboard clawing modulation. Johnny Rocket screamed unintelligibly and jumped right above my head. To the pounding, the rude interruption of sexual anticipation, I sat up too quickly, hit my head, and brought down cobwebs into my hair. Michael's hand dropped out of my blouse into the darkness.

"Ouch! That smarts." Unladylike swear words grumbled under my tongue.

"Are you okay?"

"I got a spider web in my hair." I felt quickly to pull it out. Not cobwebs. "Wiring." In my hair, I yanked at it. "Maybe this will short circuit the speakers."

"I oversaw the setup of the stage. We didn't wire under here, against county code."

I took the flashlight from him, the light catching him readjusting his bulging crotch. The light beam streamed to the lower ceiling of pole girders and cross beams. The wires were wrapped to hold a small bundle in place. Battery like. For a closer look, on my knees, I squinted in the murkiness. The band's grinding thuds and jumps had dislodged the wiring, and the package with a small clock attached swung in the shadows.

Holy Shit.

Chapter 28
My Love Life Bombs

"Michael." I said as calmly as I could. "You might want to look at this; please, be a dear." He likewise crawled to where the flashlight's beam shone. He took the light from me, and studied the device. He turned the clock around, studied it more. The timing mechanism, if I saw it correctly, said ten minutes until the alarm sounded, and then...?

"I'm no expert, but..." and without warning, he pulled two wires. I flinched. No explosion. He held the clock in one hand, and the tube-like device in the other. I took the flashlight from him and shone it down the length of the stage. Barely visible, I spied another wiring pack further along, too dark, and I was sure as hell not going to crawl down that way to discover what I presumed was a second battery-size package with timing device.

"Madison, these are a couple of taped blasting caps, enough to be a half-stick of dynamite. If this had gone off with us underneath, we would be mashed and dead."

"In flagrante delicto." said I.

"And that, too. Not good in anybody's obituary."

"I think there may be another...bomb...down that way."

"Let's get out of here, quickly." We scurried and left the champagne and passion behind.

Outside, the leadership qualities of Michael became apparent. From the stocky security guard, over a concert walkie-talkie, in less than thirty seconds, he was being surrounded by a cadre of hard tough men, all who seemed to defer to him alone as being in charge. He barked orders as he took me by the arm and moved me off to the side, next to, and behind a palm tree.

The security people worked quickly, moving to those closest to the stage, and started the unenviable job of telling audience members upfront to abandon their favored spots, shouting above the jet engine decibel music. The crowd grew unruly. Meanwhile, the Pāhoehoe Sounds rocked on, ignoring a few catcalls to play Oli music. A younger group of fans stood off to the fringes bouncing, jiving, body slams into each other. The 'new' Pāhoehoe Sounds led by Johnny Rocket were on the verge of losing one fan base. Perhaps a new strategy debuted tonight, the band so quickly willing to sacrifice the old fogies and romantics for a youth market into punk sound.

Michael walked onto the stage. I yelled at him, but he could not hear. He was walking to center stage with an explosive device beneath his feet. Who challenged the fates like this? Get away! Pull the plug on the sound system, I yelled.

The song fell apart. Digger, the drummer, the first to see Michael's presence, took his sticks off his tom toms, stopped his vibrating cymbals. Johnny Rocket's expression, from my vantage point, drooled seething hate. I could see how a person like this might kill if you got in the way of him or his career. He was high as a kite, the blaring music hiding his stage dance moves, an uncontrollable, diabolical St. Vitus dance from abused chemical substances.

Michael pushed him away from the microphone, which did not help the crowd's shocked opinion at this rude action.

"I apologize for the interruption." A smattering of boos picked up resonance, mainly from the fringe fans. Michael went on. "Our engineers just discovered some issues with the platform stage that requires a temporary fix. For safety reasons, we are asking the people in front to move back. There will be about a thirty minute intermission. We would appreciate your cooperation. Again, the show will resume shortly." The lights on the golf course flared on, destroying the mood of the evening, as I could well understand.

With the strong arm firmness of the security guards, the front edge crowd grumbled complaints, gathered up blankets and coolers and slowly moved back, off to the upper aisles, where they stood, mouthing anger. Had it not been a free concert, the line for refunds would go from here to the highway.

Michael faced a mini crisis of who held the power. The Pāhoehoe Sounds refused to leave the stage. He couldn't just tell the band members a bomb might be under them; no, the word would travel too fast, crowd panic would set in, and in the rush people hurt. Someone stood next to me, my father.

"What have you done now?"

"What?"

"Well, it's a mess, and you're nearby." I began to fume at his accusation, as true as it was. "And, while we are at it, button up your blouse."

I did so. Ah, farewell romance, now so distant. My turn.

"We found a bomb under the stage."

"What?"

"Michael says they're blasting caps taped together. He brought out the one I found, but I think there's a similar one, at the far end of the stage. Larger." I could hear a police siren coming closer, winding through the golf course roadway. That arrival would not set well with the crowd. I saw other people at the back of the concert bowl starting to stand, puzzled.

"Blasting caps would not blow up the stage," Jeffrey's analysis succinct. "But it could collapse it."

"There was a timer attached. Ten minutes, about two minutes ago. Would you think the next one would be set for a few minutes later, not simultaneous, or would there be inner-connected wiring?" It finally hit Jeffrey, the slow-witted parent he was.

"What were you two doing under the stage?" He paused. "Never mind."

He started walking toward the stage.

"Where are you going?!" I yelled.

"Stay here. Michael is getting nowhere with the Marquis de Sade and the Inquisition Band."

"Eight minutes left, if that much." If that was true or not.

"I'll be back."

"Dad!"

I stood frozen, my two men in peril.

Michael stood onstage surrounded by the incensed members of the Pāhoehoe Sounds, all screaming at him, Johnny Rocket slathering and foaming at the mouth, literally. My father crossed the stage to the band members, and when Johnny Rocket turned to face him, Jeffrey Dayne slugged him, hard, and as Johnny fell, Jeffrey went down and hefted the unconscious singer over his shoulder and carted him off. The entire crowd went silent. The band members dazed, followed, except Kukui. She was not a follower, more like me, the smart-ass, independent woman. Perhaps this was her destiny, to be blown up for all to see, to be a martyr and join Oli Palalū in music immortality. Did she see the future? Was she the one who hid the blasting caps?

Maybe less than two minutes on the dial of the alarm clock I held, and Kukui wouldn't budge. By now concert security cleared the crowd back. Local police arrived, doing little except to flash badges, milling about seeking higher authority, not yet privy to the commotion's cause. Muttering stage crews cursed at the delay. Everyone watched the female singer strut her lovely body and Michael trying to be convincing. Finally, as his desperation grew, he grabbed her hand and raised his other, in a fist, as if to strike, implying he could emulate my father's daring tour de force, but I saw their eyes lock in a fierceness of wills. His fist opened to a palm and he broke their stand-off with a slap to her face. The audience gasped. The look on her face was not anger, nor spite, a raw edge to the girl, eyes wild, and before she could respond, he swept her up in his arms and she wrapped her arms around his neck, buried her head into his shoulder, and he carried her to safety.

Chapter 29
Fall-out

That night, I lost any chance of making Michael Ka'aiea mine, if that was my intention.

A minute later, a muffled boom sounded, and the stage in the center rose, the far end of the stage following, and the platform riser collapsed to the ground, bringing all band equipment into a jumbled heap. The bombing was not complete as another explosion was heard, quite clear, a snapping sound as one of the supporting sound towers broke apart at the top, and fell to the stage at the exact spot where the Pāhoehoe Sounds had been performing, where Kukui moments earlier had lost (too easy?) her defiance to a man's domination of spirit.

The crowd, some screaming, stepped back, but did not trample each other to flee. Most stayed with morbid interest as the police descended, ambulances arrived, sirens blaring, the only injuries scratches and a few fainters. Phone cameras brought this breaking news to the world: explosions at a concert on the 11th Green at Ho'oilina Kai Resort. Not the type of publicity Manager Cahill and the Kiyoshi Corporation desired. The word "terrorists" bandied about like a beach ball bouncing a concert crowd.

As I knew I had lost Michael, Jeffrey, if he cared, had lost Desi Cardoza. No one hit her precious son, even if it saved the rocker's life. That rationale did not play well with a distraught woman who pampered her son as he lay on the ground, retching. Kukui was nowhere to be found. I ambled over to the small crowd of investigators, Investigator Kee among them. Two men in white hazmat suits, whom I took to be with the bomb squad, walked carefully among the destruction. Michael, Jeffrey, and I stood as part of the information gatherers. I guess we had either Detective Kee's permission or the blessing of the Ho'oilina management with Michael in charge. Why we were there it suddenly came to me. Jeffrey had shared his Illinois crime lab results with the Big Island police.

Michael gave his statement to Detective Kee and another detective, explaining that he was doing a back stage tour during the concerts. I took this as my cue, and to protect Michael's nobility, said as immature valley girlishly as I could manage that I thought it would be a lark to see what the music sounded like under the stage. I hit my head, found this wiring in my hair, and we both found the blasting caps. If they ever would find the blanket and broken champagne bottle, they could theorize all they wished. That was my story, and I was sticking to it.

Jeffrey restated to the authorities, if they had already not speculated, the blasting caps were not enough to maim, but enough to structurally collapse the stage, as the explosion had. I saw similarities in this accident and the poisoned poi, enough but not too much. Kee was willing to share his local knowledge.

"These sort of blasting caps and dynamite sticks are used by some local fisherman to illegally catch fish by stunning them with concussion."

"I know lazy fisherman who fish in that manner," said Michael. "I'll kill them if I find it's one of them." You don't threaten in front of police officers. I redirected the authorities back to the subject at hand.

"The falling tower would have killed anyone on stage."

Jeffrey, I could see had reconstructed the crime.

"But notice the sequence." He pointed to the clock in the plastic evidence bag. "The first explosion, the bomb you both discovered, if you notice the alarm timing, would have gone off two minutes earlier than the others, at a part of the stage with speakers and not people standing around. That side of the stage collapsing would have forced the stage to be evacuated. The police would not have arrived for half an hour to look for a cause, so someone had to presume the hotel security would keep people away, and the next explosions would destroy, but not inflict injuries."

Yes, but I quietly differed, no injuries in the plan if the bomber presumed people acted rationally under panic. This bomber had an agenda and stage performers and crew at risk would be acceptable collateral damage.

Detective Kee took notes. Gone were his blustery challenges at Jeffrey's reasoning. We walked around to the front of the stage to survey the damage now roped off with police tape awaiting crime scene technicians to do formal evidence gathering. The evening had been ruined in more ways than one. I took in the devastation. It was minor, all things considered, the psychological effect had made its mark. I saw Captain Jimmie coming from the far side walking immediately in front of the destroyed stage. Then I saw it.

I yelped, "Jimmie, stop!" and broke from our group and ran toward him. Everyone assumed I would throw myself into his arms; after all, he was my lava rock-hard savior. Instead, I hit him at an angle, knocking him back and to the ground. The others started toward us, but I shouted back, "Watch it, live wire!"

A dark rubber snake, coiled, slithered from under the stage into a puddle of melted cooler ice. My eye had perceptively caught a spark up the cable at a broken spot, the smashed stage lighting. No one else had seen it. My tackling implemented faster than I could have formed the sentence of warning. On top of Captain Jimmie, he whispered in my ear, "That makes twice you've saved me from getting cooked. This is getting old."

Jeffrey pulled me up. Michael reached us and helped up his friend, the captain.

"I guess this makes you both even in the life-saving contest."

Captain Jimmie and I exchanged shy smiles to the joke, but I saw Jeffrey putting on his thinking cap.

For the next hour, we stood as part of the investigative event, and I enjoyed the hubbub. In observing the departing crowd, I caught sight of the Beautiful People. Even with their concert entertainment cancelled their playful fervor remained intact. In the science of the single world, I observed the group in the process of quietly pairing up. A new girl, a pick-up presumably, added to the mix. If I were in L.A., I would say she was Hispanic by her looks. Odd, she limped.

I sought out their leader and for whatever weird satisfaction saw him with a buddy, cavorting with inside jokes. No woman with him. Was he gay? Why the fates chose that moment to have him turn toward me, our eyes met, or maybe he just saw the bigger picture, a not too-bad looking woman surrounded by police officers.

Like the dying sun's green flash, gone, or never was, into the throng the Beautiful People disappeared, off to play their jet-setter games of longitude and latitude.

That knowing drug of upsmanship coursed through my veins. It was at that moment my plotting coalesced and I decided to find the time to go geo-caching at their expense. First, I had to secure a GPS device, learn how to work it. Next, what would my gotcha gift be for them? It had to be a doozy.

As the police ran their crime scene I chose not to be intrusive or warned off, so I snapped only a few photos. The bomb squad found nothing else. Night guards secured the area and would remain on station until morning. Captain Jimmie and Michael went off chummy. Jeffrey and Detective Kee were back at it, in disagreement. Jeffrey upset that he had been forthcoming on the Angel's Trumpet, why then could not the police give him the scoop on Oli Palaū's autopsy? I left them to their bickering and headed back to the hotel, soon getting lost in the darkness on the wrong trail. Alone and tired, emotionally drained in body, and more in spirit; and to top this off, I counted up the near misses as I sought the right path. Three attempts to date: the poi, the falls, and tonight's staging. Not comfortable thoughts to mix in my fragile psyche, undone when I heard a woman's scream, very close.

Hidden walkways, the one I was lost on, were where the maids and porters traipsed with luggage and cleaning carts hidden from the regular tourist paths. The screams continued coming from a path around two corners. First on the scene, I found a night staff cleaning lady in hysteria moaning, collapsing to the ground when I reached her side. She could only point into the darkness of the foliage. At first I saw trees and bushes and a large stick, perpendicular to the path. I walked closely. I heard feet running my direction, strangers calling out, offering assistance. I pushed back palm fronds and saw the stick was not what it seemed to be. It was ornately carved, a large native spear stuck in a palm tree, and affixed to the tree, speared and dead was old Joe Coffee.

Chapter 30
Say, It Ain't So

Without a doubt a murderer roamed, no longer a person expert in planned accidents. With the police conveniently still in the vicinity, a golf course away, the forensic experts arrived and work moved quickly, the body removed. Nearly commonplace, I had to make another statement, this time glad to be an innocent bystander passing by. I asked Detective Kee if Michael had been notified. I wanted to comfort him, but no one had seen him.

Later, very late, my father found me at the inside hotel bar listening, with assorted bar flies, to the piano player plink out Big Band tunes. I slurped Lemon Drop martinis like soda pop, and in to my third, feeling no pain; heartbreak, yes, but no pain. Where's a shot of 'Okolehao when you need it?

"Rough day for you."

"Michael's uncle being skewered was the clincher to my forthcoming nervous breakdown."

"No one's death is fortuitous; still, there are positive developments."

"As in what?"

"Tragic as this murder was, it wasn't you or me. The stage demolition was not aimed at you or me. A pattern was broken."

"I find that no gratifying consolation. I was going up that path; maybe the killer was lying in wait for me."

"And, how did he know you were going to be coming along after the explosion? Two hours later."

"How do you know that?"

"Detective Kee relented somewhat in hoarding his secrets. Besides, I heard forensics on the scene say Joe Coffee was killed about an hour before he was discovered by you. The police are speculating thirty minutes to an hour after the stage explosions."

"Discovered by the night maid, not me." I sipped my drink, and placed my head on the table. The piano player had disappeared. For the last hour, I had been listening to an electronic player piano with no pianist clinking at the keyboard. Life no longer real.

"The spear that killed Joe Coffee came from a display in the hotel lobby. What does that tell you?"

My eyes blinked. I remember seeing that spear before. Michael showing the weapon off to tourists, how it was thrown, how it could kill. I would not tell anyone, including my father, that circumstantial tidbit.

"I'm not really feeling in my detecting mode. The killer grabs the spear and kills the old man. That's premeditation."

"Not really. What if something sparked an immediate response? The killer had no time to make his plans, he or she had to improvise. The killer knew where the spear was."

"Spontaneous killing?" My mind sifted through the evening and I reached my guess. "Joe Coffee saw something or knew something that risked exposing the killer's identity. The murderer acted impulsively, not grounds for first degree murder charge, if and when apprehended."

"Very good, my daughter. Joe Coffee could have seen the killer tinkering with the stage, knew that person was not supposed to be there, and when the stage went kerplooie, knew the bomber's identity and assumed the bomber poisoned Oli Palalū."

"Did you ever settle your 'who's on first' game play with Detective Kee, and are you going to get Oli's autopsy results?"

"Detective Kee is swamped with a mad bomber who can chuck a spear, impale a man to a tree; my priorities are not his."

My tipsy mouth yammered.

"Bummer, Dad. I would have thought you could solve all this by now, give me more beach time. Say, after all this, is the Lūʻau Challenge still on for tomorrow?"

"As far as I know. I don't think Manager Cahill has the guts to postpone the event to another date. However, expect a major police presence and explosive sniffing dogs at the front gate."

"I wish I could find Michael. His uncle's death will be hard on him. As much as I think they argued or didn't see eye-to-eye, if you look at all of Uncle Joe's antics, it seemed to always be for Michael's best interest."

"Hard parental love, perhaps. But you could put another spin on it."

"What?"

"Michael becomes enraged that his uncle is trying to disrupt the Memorial, shut down the hotel, ruin Michael's career chances. I heard they had a fight today. A plausible scenario: Michael runs into his uncle near the hotel, confronts him, discovers the old man uses dynamite to fish, probably knew it, becomes incensed, runs and grabs a spear to force the old man to confess, they fight again, and Michael kills him."

"No!" I slurred at my dad.

"Another less desirable scenario is that they fought over a woman."

"A woman?"

"A battle to the death for the woman he loves. Madison Merlot Dayne."

"No!" I fled, stumbling from the accusation. It was not true, or was it? Was a murderer in love with me, I with him? Did I say 'love'? In my room, I passed out, bothered, bewildered ... and maybe frickin' bewitched?

Chapter 31
Innocent But With Doubt

Next morning, the police pieced together a similar scenario following my father's reasoning. The hotel phone *rrringing* woke me, 10:00 a.m. being too early after last night. Ow, my throbbing head felt like two coconuts colliding.

"Is your father around?" Captain Jimmie. I could care less where my father went; I was still mad at him and would be forever.

"Is he still licensed to practice law? As a defense attorney?" I woke up.

"What's going on?"

"They've taken Michael in for questioning. Some crazy notion he had something to do with Uncle Joe's death."

"No! That's ridiculous. Michael was with me; he couldn't have had the opportunity." My muddled mind sought to create a plausible alibi, and failed.

"No, Madison, you're mistaken. Perhaps earlier at the concert, but Michael left with me. He left soon after. Said he had hotel business to attend to and that put him alone in the time frame of Joe Coffee being killed."

Bedcovers were flung aside.

"I'll go find my father; he'll represent Michael. It's all bogus."

"I believe so. Keep me in the loop."

"My father will find the killer. He has some good clues as to who it might be." A simple lie meant to comfort me.

"Good. Let me know if I can help. This island needs to be saved." No, Michael needs to be saved; that's what Captain Jimmie meant.

I found my father in the hotel café going over the judging arrangements with the lūʻau planning committee. When he heard my whispered cries to Michael's plight, he told them all was in order from his perspective, and excused himself. He would see them at 5:00 p.m., the start of the festivities.

Jeffrey borrowed a phone book from the concierge. I drove. He thumbed through the yellow pages.

"Damn. No attorneys named Kee, I was hoping for some help." We both had to laugh, a release valve. Jeffrey had been right to create all possibilities, including Michael's possible involvement. I had let my emotional heart rule my thinking brain.

"Did you ever take a harder look at those photos from your camera?"

"No, I have been a little busy since."

We drove on in silence into Kailua town; as we approached the governmental offices that housed the police, he said, "Look closer at the photos. Look for something out of place, someone where he's not supposed to be. It may not be in the photos, but there's little else to work with."

A kind ploy by my father, his heart in the right place; he hoped to push my mind to consider less stressful diversions.

Even in the humidity, Jeffrey made an entrance into the police station worthy of a star. Pink floral open shirt, a cotton cloth sport jacket. He arched his back with the dignity afforded those at the bar, the legal one, that is.

"I am here representing Michael Ka'aiea. Tell the investigating officers to stop any questioning of him immediately. If I do not see him in the next two minutes…" He left the threat in the imagined world of hellish possibilities. The officer at the front desk looked over my old man and snickered. I could see why; even Jeffrey understood his limited power. He was an off-islander. He might have law and habeas corpus on his side, but not the savoir faire of living on island time at island speed. The officer made a call and a bulky Anglo detective soon made his entrance. Instead of stone-wall tough cop, the officer gave a friendly smile, a disarming hand-shake of two buddies meeting.

"Mr. Dayne, I presume. We received a call to expect your arrival. We're merely conducting a prelim, general questions, not an interrogation."

Who called, I wondered. Captain Jimmie? Did he have such clout to mollify a policeman to an amiable tone. Wealth does create power.

"Then, I am sure Michael would want us present during your 'discussion.'"

"I don't see a problem, since you're saying you're his legal counselor. Of course, the young lady can't be present."

"But, she's his girlfriend, and Michael's devastated at the loss of his uncle." I was flabbergasted at Jeffrey's ploy. It had a nice ring to it. I just wasn't sure of anything, especially this morning after the night under the stage, and thereafter, with another woman in Michael's arms.

"No, she remains. We've some great Hawaiian what-to-see-and-do magazines."

"I don't want to sit bored. I want to see Michael."

"It's okay, Madison, I'll let him know you are here, concerned." They went off and I was left sitting in the police station lobby, I'm sure full of criminal cooties. Like a patient waiting for the doctor's harsh diagnosis, I thumbed through magazines without reading.

Breaking my train of thought that did not exist anyway, Detective Kee walked by, folders under his arm. A familiar face, he recognized me and stopped, all friendly; why are they all so suddenly nice? I jumped him with my fear.

"Didn't you talk to Michael? You knew he had nothing to do with this!"

"I know, but I'm on the outside, like you. I am perceived as a conflict of interest since he is family."

"My father's in there right now, trying to help as an attorney, and you aren't helping us to help Michael."

The detective gave me a side stare of how off my rocker I might be.

"Oli Palalū's autopsy report," I said what I meant.

"I can't release that."

"If I can tell you Jeffrey figured out a substance other than Angel's Trumpet Oli ingested, would you accept Jeffrey needs to view all the facts?"

"And this will help Michael?"

"We both know Michael didn't feed us poisoned poi." Detective Kee scratched behind his ear, befuddled with decisions. As I said before, civilians assisting to solve crimes must not be in any police manual. Contest time.

"Okay, you say a harmful substance in Oli Palalū's system outside of your luncheon food? Guess right and I will see what I can do."

"Marijuana or whatever chemical makes it up," I said, my guess based on a hunch. What did I have to lose? He gave me a dumb expression and walked behind buzzed doors.

Thirty minutes went by and my lethargic magazine thumbing clued me to the best beaches on the island: Honomalino Bay, Ho'okena Beach, Puna Beaches, and at the Captain Cook Monument in Kealakekua Bay. A warning to avoid boogie boarding at Hapuna and Black Sand Beaches. Black Sand rang a memory bell but I could not place it. Had I been there on my last island visit a year ago? All these sandy beach getaways and me with a sinking downer that I'd never run my toes through one of them on this trip.

Michael and Jeffrey appeared from unknown dungeons. Michael's demeanor made me sad. His boyish smile gone, new burdens for youth to carry into manhood. I walked over and gave him a hug. I felt his body lean into me, seeking transference of my strength to him, my tender smile the only medicine I readily had to break his grief.

"You are someone special, a good friend," he said. His eyes were red, bloodshot. Good men may cry without condemnation. I did not want to be just his friend. At this moment I would do anything for him.

I did not realize a car was waiting for him. I remembered them from Michael's meeting in the stone grass amphitheater, the old priests of all the islands. This time there were only four of them. And, one other. I recognized Kukui. Her head bowed, eyes fixated open, like in a trance. She looked as distressed as Michael. I wanted to catch her eye, pass unsaid thoughts to her: *help him*. Michael got into the front passenger seat, two elders in the back on either side of Kukui. I guessed they had the sad task of taking care of the remains of their fellow priest, Joe Pa'ao, the out-of-step purist of all things before civilization found the islands, for better or worse. They departed to their mournful task.

Jeffrey and I were leaving the police station when a clerk came scurrying out after us with a manila folder, sealed.

"Detective Kee said you wanted this list of the best restaurants on the island with the menus he had." I took the bulky envelope and she went back inside.

My father looked disillusioned. "Food? At a time like this? Your boyfriend under a cloud of suspicion?"

I held my prize tight, glad I had the moxie to be of value in what I was deeming the *Case of the Poisoned Poi*. Or, was it the *Case of Stage Fright*?

Or, *Speared to Death*? Whatever, I answered my father's inquiry, gloating. "Food contents and analysis from the stomach of Oli Palalū."

"Let's do lunch," my father suggested, grinning at his Number One and Only Daughter.

Recipe: Pineapple Bomber Cocktail

Ingredients to use:

1 oz Amaretto

3 oz Pineapple Juice

1 oz Southern Comfort

Directions:

To a mixing glass filled with ice, add above ingredients and shake.

Pour into highball glass filled with ice.

Chapter 32
Almost by the Sea

We ate at a place called Quinn's Almost-by-the Sea on Palani Road. I liked it because it was escapism from the gourmet world, and the food was good and not pricey, though I never pick up a check. As they said, near the sea, across the road, but you can't see the whitecaps; a charming hole-in-the-wall, on the street curve, as it is.

No problem with the food, excellent in fact, but I almost lost my lunch when I opened the envelope. I expected the autopsy report to be pages of fine print, clinical medical terms, percentages of defined chemicals. I did not expect color photographs. We stuffed those back in the folder. 'Oli deserved our respect, but not the crime.

Jeffrey, used to reams of jargon data did the scanning; I awaited the pronouncement.

"Well?"

"Datura stramonium."

"Don't do this to me."

"Belladonna alkaloids atropine and scopolamine."

"Talk English, better yet, American."

"Some call it stinkweed, cowboys call it 'locoweed.' On island and elsewhere, we in the legal profession know it as 'Jimson Weed.'

"It's a poison?"

"In heavier doses, lethal, but Oli Palalū did not have a heavy dose in his system."

"Oh, no, not again."

"Let me read you the symptoms: dry mouth, dilated pupils, blurred vision. The psychological effects could include euphoria, confusion, and delirium."

"What I saw in Oli in the garden."

"And one other person with milder symptoms."

Okay, let me think.

"Johnny Rocket. At the beach yelling at me, in the van on the way to the falls."

"And, on stage last night. Euphoric, he was a star in front of his audience, confusion when Michael took it all away from him."

"Let me ask this: was there marijuana in Oli's system?"

"Report says minute quantities, not enough to be a factor. It seems he might have been a recreational smoker, one cigarette in social times, but with his weight, he knew how dangerous it could be."

"How do you know that?"

"Kukui told me that. Said he did not do recreational drugs, except for the occasional puff."

"When did you talk to her?" My feminine nature piqued.

"On the trail at Akaka Falls. I was asking my questions, she was quite pleasant. All of a sudden she got this strange look, stared at the trees, at the stream, and then walked back up the hill."

I said nothing.

"There's one more symptom of Jimson Weed that is intriguing: high temperature." He was testing me. I inhaled all I knew and spewed up the facts.

"Flu. Oli had to cancel several appearances. And when he did, Johnny Rocket took center stage with his brand of Neanderthal rock.

"A drastic opportunity for career advancement?"

"Oli was still required to attract the crowds, to bring in the revenue. If a split were being planned, Johnny Rocket would have to get some lead time exposure."

"But, what killed Oli Palalū? There were only small amounts of all these plant substances in his system and not one could kill him?"

"Ah, my Dear Watson, the combination of Oli's weight and the Angel's Trumpet and the Jimson Weed blended into a toxic milkshake. So says the autopsy summary."

"Why would a killer feed him two different plants, mild dosages, on two separate occasions? And, if the Pāhoehoe Sounds needed Oli, why kill him? Did he outlive his usefulness, even the star he was? Backup group envy?"

"Why only one? Why not two?"

"Only two what?"

"Poisoners, as in plural."

That possibility never crossed my mind.

"You mean, there are two poisoners at large?"

"The poi was meant for us. The poison of your Oli caused his flu symptoms before we arrived. Whoever the Oli poisoner is wants to keep that secret secure because of potential manslaughter charges, but would that person commit murder to do so? Probably not. Maybe a distraction like your push at the falls."

"Okay, answer this: why the stage implosion and Joe Coffee's death?"

"We could have two or up to five separate assailants, one perpetrator more a killer than the rest."

"Good grief."

"Coming to grief seems to be our predicament."

Our lunch proceeded, the food digested, joined with our curdling thoughts. Jeffrey slummed with the common people on fish and chips. The Cajun fish sandwich did the trick for me. Ono (known also as wahoo) central to both dishes. I even got to throw scraps to a scampering mongoose.

I made a bathroom pit stop. On my return, I spotted a familiar face, but not an old friend, sitting at the bar, hunched over an empty drink, another on the way. Weaving, and it was just noontime, this man had great responsibilities on this special day. On our exit, and alerting Jeffrey, we surrounded the inebriated hotel manager.

"Mr. Cahill," I said, enjoying my taunting of a defenseless drunk. "I would have thought you would be at the hotel for the opening of the Lū'au Challenge?"

"Let the Ho'oilina Resort sink into the damn kai."

Not the response I expected.

"Is everything all right, Mr. Cahill?" Jeffrey offered solicitous kindness.

"The Japs sold the hotel this morning, took a loss, just to avoid any more bad publicity. Bombs exploding. Dead bodies." He slurped on his drink.

"The sale should make you happy, new management support to work with."

"The new owners gave me my walking papers same time the news of the sale came out. Gave me sixty days severance and a ticket back to England. Dirty buggers. I leave on the Red Eye tonight. Just like that. And all I did for that hotel." Unemployed and drunk, I pitied the airline attendant who had to deal with this lush on a long flight.

"Who bought the hotel?" Jeffrey questioned, not satisfied he had all the answers from this excuse of a sea slug.

"I don't know. A European company out of Monaco, Corsair Capital; I saw the name on my resignation letter. Damn French frogs, no doubt."

"Are they sending over new management?" My concern was with Michael's future. The new owners might clean house, fire every executive.

"That's the bloody shock. I'm kicked out and the arse they put in my place on a temporary basis hasn't a clue."

"Who's that?" Jeffrey seemed to know the answer, and I wondered why.

"That damn Mike Lake, that's who." The ex-manager of Ho'oilina Resort ordered another drink and we left him to drown such sorrows as failed men might have.

Recipe: Crusted Mahimahi with Crab Bisque

Crab Bisque

4 tablespoons unsalted butter
2 onions, diced
2 tablespoons flour
2 cups heavy (whipping) cream
1 cup coconut milk
2 cups green taro leaves or frozen spinach, chopped
1 1/2 cups fresh lump crabmeat
Salt and freshly ground pepper to taste

In a large saucepan, melt the butter and sauté the onions until translucent,
about 3 minutes. Stir in the flour and blend well.
Add the heavy cream and simmer 5 minutes, stirring frequently.
Stir in the coconut milk, taro or spinach, and crabmeat.
Add salt and pepper.
Reduce the heat to low and cook until the mixture thickens slightly.

Crusted Mahimahi

1 cup panko (Japanese bread crumbs)
1 cup macadamia nuts, finely chopped ½ cup minced fresh parsley
Four 8-ounce mahimahi fillets
Salt and freshly ground pepper to taste
2 eggs, lightly beaten
¼ cup vegetable oil for frying

In a shallow bowl, combine the panko, macadamia nuts, and parsley.
Season the mahimahi with salt and pepper and dust with flour.
Dip each fillet in the eggs,
then the macadamia nut crust mixture, to coat on both sides.
In a large sauté pan or skillet over medium-high heat,
heat the oil and cook the mahimahi for 2 minutes on each side
or until golden brown.

Chapter 33
Lū'au Challenges

The Tenth Annual Lū'au Challenge, a two day event, started as if nothing had happened at the Ho'oilina Kai Grand Hotel Resort. A few worried guests checked out. However, it became apparent Hawaiian tourists don't devour the local news and many tourists were fresh off the airplanes, the newcomers signed on to the promotional package: room and lū'au. The first part of the event included four separate lū'au feasts, sponsored by the final contenders made up of three hotels and one professional caterer of Hawaiian foods. Previous separate island competitions screened the finalists down to these top four. Each entry would field its own brand of lū'au. A whole day of feasting. Another round of competitors vied for the musical awards and would host entertainment venues during the evening hours. On the second night, the finale included an enhanced grand lū'au by the winner and one lavish production highlighted by all performers. Judges, such as my father, presided over the food competition while musical experts would rank and award the best representatives of Island music.

Dutifully lugging the HDTV camera and portable sound system, I followed Jeffrey through the day, judging as he went from table to table performing his tasting duties. For many a tourist, the highlight is the pig prepared in the outside imu the morning of the lū'au, the opening held later at the feast. In the ground a large pit is dug, with kiawe logs placed in the center and river rocks put on top. A fire is built. Hours later the hot rocks and wood coals are spread out. Damp banana stalks are added and banana leaves on which the pig and other foods, like laulau and sweet potatoes are placed, then another covering of ti and banana leaves, and usually, wet burlap bags to hold in the steamy moisture. Dirt is poured over the pit and seven hours later, thereabouts, the famous kalua pig comes forth savory and succulent.

During the afternoon festivities, where I nibbled on more tender oink meat than I should have, I saw nothing of Michael. His new duties must be overwhelming. Desi Cardoza moved among the contestants proclaiming her public relations power. With Michael acting hotel manager, she probably felt her star would be rising. I could see her trying to pull him under his wing, offering her management insight, perhaps hoping, like the band, she could control behind the throne. She did not come our way, avoided Jeffrey, angry still at his bestiality of harming her precious son. Bullshit to that.

The Pāhoehoe Sounds remained officially silent with no press statement about the stage bombing, a calamitous event that could have been milked for a lot of press ink and national television coverage. Jeffrey's opinion had some merit. The band was biding its time. The new and alleged improved Pāhoehoe Sounds, with less Oli influence, had failed at their surprise debut. They were retrenching for the rebound. I had more concerns about Johnny Rocket's response to my dad's fist, fearing the delusional band star might foster some stupid, damaging revenge.

I spotted Paka and Lolo, band members joking and kidding each other, assisting Desi with gofer event tasks, probably picking up extra change, maybe working for free. She did have them dancing by her manipulative stringed fingers.

Considering all that had happened in just a few days, my head seemed in constant jerks, jumpy at any unknown sound, moving away from strangers who approached without warning.

We took a program break around 5:00 p.m. The winners of lūʻau and assorted food dish awards would be announced at the evening entertainment. In my room, I cleansed myself of dust, grime, and imu smoke, and rebuilt my face to a charming glow. This night I would rely on my still camera and save the HDTV for the next night finale. I lay on the bed reviewing my digital shots, several good enough to be included in a Dayne cookbook. Stretching, I turned over and grabbed at the store processed photos. Studying each more carefully, I interpreted the foreground and the background. The front gate mob with Uncle Joe, surrounded by his senior citizen supporters. Three of them I recognized from the car which took Michael from the police station. I laid the photos down in our resort arrival sequence. Our welcome at the hotel's front door with Desi and Manager Cahill. Candids of Michael with luggage. How far he had come in these few days. I felt proud for him: local boy makes good, at least until new management stepped on property. Color snapshots of exotic flowers. Several pics of the ocean and the marina.

Foreground. Background. In scenic shots of panorama, you lose detail seeing the landscape in the larger picture. I snagged my spare camera bag, scrounging for my loop, the magnifier where I could see minutiae.

The marina caught my interest, and more specific the A'Kupu'e Point Tours dock. Grainy, mere pixel dots, but a pony tail; I squinted to see Larry Tutapu standing next to a cooler. The fishing boat was the Raw Tolo Oceans, one of Captain Jimmie's. What was Larry doing? Unloading or loading? I let my suspicions paint a possibility.

I had seen Captain Jimmie with his fish cooler at the beach bar. Larry as First Mate would have access to a ship's portable cooler. He had access to the Angel's Trumpet on the hotel grounds. He would not be out of place bringing the fish catch to the back door of Chef Lorenzo's restaurant. Jeffrey could be wrong. Small acts of sabotage might be a testing ground for a future terrorist pledged to overthrow the U.S. government's hold on the islands. I finished my prep for the evening, threw all the photos in my purse-camera case and went looking for my father. Instead, I found Captain Jimmie and that was okay; he could substantiate some time line.

"How went your day?" Cavalier as usual, dressed in nautical whites.

"The expression 'pigged out' must have been invented at a lū'au." He gave my joke a healthy chuckle. "As you said before, I feel like today was a 'caloric rape.'"

"What?" Mild confusion as if he had forgotten his own joke.

"When you and Dad were talking on your yacht, is what I feel like. Heavenly bloat. At four different lū'aus, munching between takes, I was overwhelmed by a calorie attack." I gave him a teasing smile. He gave me a moment of silence, firm, as if deciding how far he might go, suggestive to a response. Suddenly, to my regret, my mind took over, and I asked, "Remember the day Oli Palalū collapsed and died?"

"No one will forget."

"Do you know what you had Larry Tutapu doing, chores or anything?"

Now, I had his attention.

"Why do you ask?" I pulled out my packet of photos and grabbed the one on top. I brought him over to a desk in the lobby with bright light and pointed out my discovery.

"Did anyone question Larry as to his whereabouts? Two hours earlier I have him at the front gate in protest and there he is acting as if nothing was going on, calmly at work. You know that cooler there could have held the Angel's Trumpet that poisoned Oli. If we could get your permission, without having to secure a court order, search his cabin, check your yacht and boat, I bet a lab could analyze and spectrograph for chemical trace."

"I can't believe Larry would involve himself in that sickening of a crime."

"I'm not saying he is, I just believe the police need to take a closer look."

"Madison, you know I'll cooperate, but Larry has such a bright future, though he's a little radical. Let's wait until the lūʻau competition is over with, not bother the authorities, or interrupt your dad's judging, or even Michael on his special first day.

"Besides, Larry is still out on a fishing charter around the island. I don't expect him back until tomorrow."

"I can wait. I'm just asking questions. My dad is better at the deductive reasoning. I'm on my way to run these photos past him."

"Well, good luck, and be certain before you cast aspersions." He left me, pondering. He had moved from gorgeous sea hunk to lecturing superior. Like my father, sometimes. I didn't like it only because he was right. False accusations could ruin a career; I accepted reluctantly why Captain Jimmie was defensive. He financially supported the underprivileged and probably put more faith in those selected to his special mentoring program to rise above, as Michael had.

Michael. No peep or visual sighting. The absence had not reached the realm of strange; but why couldn't he make a grand appearance, take kudos and applause for his promotion, from good friends, myself included? I guess being vain, still hoping for more.

Jeffrey, the foodie judge, hobnobbed among the various judging committees doing the final comparative analysis. On stage, one musical group performed. The winning lūaʻu would be announced after their act. Should I interrupt? The opportunity arose when a committee of two were calculating up scores; Jeffrey gave me a relieved smile of accomplishment. He looked tired.

"All done; tomorrow let's both escape and find a beach until the evening finale. Drink Mai Tai's and maybe engorge on spam musubi and yellow tail sashimi." He said that, and meant it; thank God, relaxation at last.

"I think Larry Tutapu might be our guilty party."

"Leaping Lizards, Miss Marple, how did you reach such a conclusion? The candlestick in the library? A bloody gaff in the sailor's hammock?"

I let his humor slide. Exhaustion can come about by being too corpulent from food tasting. To match his attempt at cuteness, I told him my joke of caloric rape I had foisted on Captain Jimmie. Jeffrey's expression dead-panned, and he studied me.

"What evidence, Inspector Maigret, have you ascertained against the anarchist Tutapu?"

"The photos you told me to take a second look at." I pulled them out and showed him Larry on the dock. I retold my hypothesis of him going from the front gate to the dock, took him by the restaurant and the hidden grotto. He had time, opportunity, and various motives of revolt yet to be defined.

"Good work, Madison." He took the other photos of the marina, three of them, and glanced through my loop magnifier. He flipped the three together like card shuffling. I had seen him solemn before, this dedication to purpose. A tired man, pondering.

"See if you can locate Detective Kee and tell him I'd like to visit with him after tonight's performance. We'll meet at the beach bar." I saw a twinkle in his eye.

"You know something. It is Larry Tutapu."

"You're jumping at conclusions too fast."

Just like Captain's Jimmie's admonishment.

"No, I'm not."

"One photo does not make a montage." His hands went on my shoulders, not a good sign.

"Madison, we can't play this as a game any longer. People have died, and almost died. I see connections, the vog rising, but it's presently a matter for the police." One of the other judges called him back to go over the final vote. Frustrated, I set out with my instructions to go bring the cavalry to the rescue.

After that everything fell apart. My father was a no-show for the meeting with Detective Kee. And the concierge found me and put into my hands a note on hotel stationery.

Michael wanted to see me, privately.

Recipe: Hearts of Palm and Portuguese Sausage Pistel

Ingredients:
1 sheet of puff pastry cut into 4 squares 2 cups sliced hearts of palm
2 cups diced Portuguese sausage
1 cup diced Maui onion
1 cup shredded smoke provolone cheese 1 cup shredded mozzarella cheese
2 Tb. olive oil
1 egg (for egg wash)

Mango Salsa:
1 ripe mango, diced
1 jalapeno pepper, diced
1 red onion, diced
¼ cup water
2 limes
¼ cup cilantro, chopped ¼ cup mint, chopped

Procedure:
In a medium sauté pan over high heat,
add the oil and cook the onions till tender about 2 minutes,
then add the sausage and cook for 2 more minutes.
Place in a bowl and add the heart of palm, season to taste, then set aside to cool.
Add both cheeses and place on one side of the puff pastry.
Brush edges with egg wash, fold in half and press edges to seal.
To bake place on parchment-lined cookie sheet.
Bake at 400 degrees until puffed and golden brown, approximately 20 minutes.
To make mango salsa, place water, onion, and jalapeno
in a medium pan and cook over high heat till all the water is gone.
Place in a bowl and juice limes over it, let cool,
then add the mango, cilantro, mint and mix well.

Recipe from Devany Vickery-Davidson

Chapter 34
I'm One Dork Chick

The typed note read: 'Sorry I have been so busy. Could you steal away at 8:00 p.m. Meet me at Dock A, the sailboat, *La Chic Dork*. We'll replace under the stage with below deck.' He signed a scrawled signature, 'Michael.'

An invitation with definite outcome, less than an hour away. I made apologies to Detective Kee, tried to mollify him with my Larry Tutapu theory, showed him the photos, went through my spiel of points on why he should be looking more closely at the First Mate. Detective Kee had less patience with my uncorroborated guesses. Facts, he told me, nothing but the facts. His mood was surly from my dad's absence. I made the covering excuse suggesting the foodie star might be delayed with the awards photo shoot since the Grand Wailea over on Maui had won the lūʻau feast competition.

A group of hula dancers from Waikiki's Royal Hawaiian Hotel was performing when I left the happy crowd. The music swayed to my mood. The lighted pathway guided me down to the marina. The harbor boats, anchored silent, mast and mooring lights against the darkness with ever slight wave ripples resembled dancing fireflies. I expected the gate to this dock to be locked like the others, but it wasn't secured, another good sign of expectation.

La Chic Dork, from its stern markings, registered in OR, that is in Cape Lookout, Oregon, bobbed at the end of the dock. No sails unfurled. No festive lights, no Johnny Mathis, no Iz, no Oli drifted melodies from the sailboat. I had this upset feeling that like most executives, Michael's attempt at a romantic rendezvous had been foiled by managerial crisis. I counseled myself to be strong and wait for him. I took a step onto the ship's sides and another step into the stern cockpit. I called out. "Michael." Silence, though I could hear Hawaiian slack key music up near the hotel, the sounds sliding across the harbor's stilled water. I could wait. It would be worth the wait for both of us. I was not a fool to go down below and strip to panties and surprise him. This was his show, his special day, and he would receive a gratifying reward befitting a hotel employee made good.

The rag went over my face, an unseen hand pressing with strength, a smell overpowering. Dizzy stars. My first urge to scream stopped, held in my mind by the split-second thought someone wanted me unconscious, not dead. Not dead, yet. I struggled, gaining an ounce of smarts from deep within. I understood what was happening. Instead of breathing I held what little air in my lungs, the next breath would lead to lights out, kiddo. My swim team training came back; I began counting to what I felt my underwater breath holding record might be, with only a half lung full of clean air. After ten seconds, I faked going limp, hoping, and yes, my attacker lowered me to the ground. I sensed his stare at my stilled body. The pungent gagging rag was removed. My lungs were bursting, and in what I thought an unconscious woman should act like, through clenched teeth I drew in air in slow breaths, not clean air, and felt my stomach lurch toward nausea. I hoped the darkness masked my charade of an incapacitated victim.

I was being dragged by my shoulders through the entryway, I guessed, and felt my feet and legs clomping down the stairs to the below-deck cabin, not exactly what my invitation had suggested. It had been a set up. So eager was I, and why not, a note typed, a signature I would not have recognized anyway. A lamb to the slaughter. God, I hoped not.

Rough and brutish, my hands and feet were tied with hard twists. I was picked up and dumped onto something warm, another body by the contours and light breathing. Another victim! Taking a chance, one eyelid raised to see only darkness, the outside night brighter than the ship's interior. Both eyes opened to adjust, to peer within the black confinement. My attacker had his back to me. A night map reading light weakly illuminated the cabin. I expected a hating Larry Tutapu or a frenzied spiteful Johnny Rocker. I was wrong by a deep 20,000 leagues under the inconceivable.

Captain Jimmie Cooke. He caught me trying to wriggle at my bondage.

"Miss Dayne. I guess I did a poor job at chloroforming. Not an art I've practiced."

"Jimmie, what are you doing?" One of those dumb questions when you are tied up and my father's words, 'this is not a game,' ringing a warning too late.

"I'm afraid I must clean up loose ends caused by you and your father's constant interruptions into my Master Plan."

"You must be crazy." Captain Jimmie was working with his hands on some familiar wiring, and something that looked like cigar-sized tubes… like dynamite sticks. Not a good sign.

Business people may get desperate and become corrupt to increase their wealth; they seldom go mad. Indeed there was a madness to his energy level. I needed some answers, if not being set free.

"How did we mess up this Master Plan? If anything, we were trying to catch a killer." I froze. The meager light caught his snide curl, not a smile of a person who is normal, more as a torturer who knows the punch line to his cruel joke will be a victim.

"Why don't you ask your father?" He pointed. I raised my head to find I had been lying on Jeffrey Dayne's chest. In the dark corner of the cabin floor, I could barely see. His eyes were closed. That must have been a trickle of recently dried blood from his hair down the side of his face.

"Dad!"

"Bumped his head into a sail wrench." I heard him breathing. Was he badly hurt? I nudged my shoulder into him, pushing. I got a low moan through masking tape across his mouth.

"We're going for a short sail," said my kidnapper, my almost boyfriend, certainly ex-boyfriend. "Don't go and play heroine, again. Lie still." He went above deck, and moments later I heard the boat's engine gurgle cough to life. Captain Jimmie moved quickly to throw off the bow and stern lines, and I felt the sailboat bump away from the dock, the propeller hummed as the sailboat glided through the marina harbor.

"Dad." I worked my way up to his face. My teeth pulled off the masking tape from his mouth. He could have suffocated. No one knew that he had allergies, nasal congestion from the island's pollen overdose. He could barely breathe through his nose. My effort was probably just in time. The tape ripping from his mouth brought him back to this irrational world. Eyes fluttered. My own eyes teared up. I gave him a kiss, tasting the tape's icky glue.

"Madison." Sanity returned, thank God. "Jeez. What surfboard hit me?" I could see him trying to comprehend his surroundings.

"Captain Jimmie Cooke kidnapped us. Why I don't know. Where he's taking us I don't know."

Dry-voiced, Jeffrey whispered, "Captain Jimmie wants to kill us?"

"Definitely wants to, but why?" Jeffrey shook his thinking processes awake.

"The noblest of all evil causes: good old-fashioned greed."

"He's rich."

"His wealth is a sickness. Probably psychological father-son image issues, trying to out-achieve the memory of his Wall Street father; he's in turmoil 'cause he'll never match up."

"By killing you? Us?"

"Not at first. His strategy aimed at knocking down the price of the Ho'oilina Kai Resort, forcing the Japanese owners to beg to be bought out."

"The Ho'oilina?"

"Captain Jimmie is Corsair Capital, the new owner of Ho'oilina Kai Resort. He might be hiding behind a dummy Swiss or Monaco shell corporation; and I'm betting he's the sole owner. A true robber baron, a pirate."

"A pirate?" My hands were straining at my knots; I stretched my legs against the bindings. Captain Jimmie could tie a mean sailor's taut-line hitch. Ironic, I considered, Michael had taught him his seafaring.

"When one knows the answer, the clues are too transparent. Corsair is a name for a pirate ship, similar in design to the logo stamped on all his silverware and bar glasses. And what pirate ship do you know personally?"

I stopped the gyrations at my bound predicament and considered. Of course. *Pirates of the Caribbean*. His yacht.

"Somebody might see a parallel; no one would easily draw the conclusion of a joint relationship." Jeffrey started to work on his ropes, the futility at release soon apparent.

"What made you suspect?"

"Two things came together just before I was cudgeled and gagged, all from you."

"Me?"

"You gave the first direction at our killer's identity."

"Yeah, right."

"Take the photos. You saw Larry Tutapu in the photo. He was in all three of your marina shots, correct?"

"Yes." I listened, sensing a new crisis; I needed to use the bathroom.

"But, as I said, 'a picture is not a montage.' I should have told you more, perhaps warned you about the dear captain."

"Let me hear. I'm quite captivated, so to speak."

"Flip all three photos together, and there is a change to one photo's composition. A small silver circle comes into view on deck of the Tolo Raw Oceans. Two photos where it's dark in that space, one where there is a white orb. A reflection from someone else on board as a passing wave raises and lowers the boat."

"A silver circle? You're saying there was a second person on that boat? You think it was Captain Jimmie?" The captain with a reflecting object. No, it couldn't be.

"His telescopic camera. Exactly. He could see the grotto from the boat without having to be anywhere near it."

"And he could see you snapping away at him, hence the break-in at the room."

"Captain Jimmie did that?"

Jeffrey shifted positions, trying to pull himself up, grimacing with the pain of a concussed head.

"Not necessarily. I think you might have been partially right about Larry Tutapu. I think he is a sidekick accomplice, minor in his roles. Captain Jimmie played him, I bet."

"Damn, I showed the photos to Captain Jimmie, basically told him you were going to solve the whole mystery. Made him take the drastic step to conk you on the head." That my actions caused my Dad's capture, our danger, depression overwhelmed me, and I sniffed out emotion through my tear ducts.

"Madison, don't talk like that. You did nothing but trust people. I have the feeling we were already high on his list as being interference."

"He did say, 'cleaning up loose ends'? I don't like the implication."

"We are about to find out. Be strong, Madison. This is a challenge, and let's pray, with escape clauses."

The sailboat idled, the engine stopped. A kerplunk splash, an anchor going overboard. At least, we weren't part of the anchoring process, so far.

Captain Jimmie returned and probably saw our cat-like eyes staring at him.

"Ah, the Daynes, the intrusive epicureans."

"It seems obvious we are on a one-way sail." Why Jeffrey, after being beaten, could find mirth in the macabre, was beyond my perception. Concussion? Did he hold a fatalistic desire to joust with the bad guy who had bested him?

"Right on, old sport."

"But, not immediate dispatch, such as by spear."

A new twist for me. "He killed Joe Coffee?"

"Old Joe probably saw the good captain and his First Mate wiring up the stage."

"Think you know everything, Dayne?" The Captain went back to fiddling with his homemade bombs, creating, as I could see from the cabin floor, some sort of mesh of wires and blasting caps.

"It would be my observation you sabotaged the hotel to push the Japanese into selling. Poison a foodie judge, destroy a stage during a concert. With the hotel in your control and your foundation educating little radicals, I think it is you, and not Larry Tutapu or Michael, who wants to be the power broker on the islands, if there is any political change."

"Michael?" No, it couldn't be true: Michael in league with his uncle's killer? Captain Jimmie provided comfort to my worry, as if it would help the current situation.

"Michael turned out to be a fine boy, incorruptible." There was a proud fatherly lilt in the man's voice. "You don't need to turn a person to gain their trust, to have them unknowingly follow the script of your choosing. If he's flawed, it is with do-good ambition, and that will serve my purpose."

"You arranged his promotion."

"Very good, Miss Dayne. Michael will want to use the hotel, as I do, as a proving ground."

"You providing an indoctrination camp for radicalism," said Jeffrey.

I dove in.

"Your killing Joe Coffee removed a thorn in your plans."

"His death, by whoever's hand, is a boon for the future."

"You're a monster." It was as good as I could give. The ropes held too tight to smash in his face.

"As you might note, if I see opportunity, I adapt and improvise."

"And our murder accomplishes what?" Why did Jeffrey return to this unpleasant subject?

"You perform several functions. Now that the hotel is in new ownership, we have to allay the police suspicions away from Michael, and by your bothersome prying, away from me. You will be blown up in the harbor by the mad bomber who will take the dual rap as Joe Coffee's killer."

"The bomber, that's you? They will be looking for you." I wasn't getting it.

"Who says I'm the bombing type? No, the bomber's exit wraps up, as I said, all the loose ends." With that he walked over to a bunk in the forward steerage, threw off a blanket, and raised the body for us to see. I came as close to fainting for real.

Larry Tutapu. His fixed and clouded eyes stared without life. Captain Jimmie cloaked the dead youth in a life jacket, tied on the wired explosive devices, and dropped the body back down. A future floater adorned with his guilt. A final finesse to fix Larry as the culprit. He took my "lost" digital camera from a drawer and zipped it in Larry's windbreaker pocket.

Loose ends tied up. Shivering, feeling no cold, my body shook in spasms to the horror awaiting us. Jeffrey voiced no such fear, a calmness to our plight, an attitude as if ignoring bound hands he held a smoking pipe and good book, reclining in his favorite leather chair holding forth with pleasant conversation. Instead of going heads-up with a killer.

"Larry had to go," pondered my father. "Why? An accomplice who knew too much?"

"Silly Maoist, a Che Guevera wannabe, thought he would hold me in line, fund his battles with a little blackmail."

"And for my edification, what comes next?"

"This sailboat is wired on timers, sequential like the stage. The boat will blow but not enough. Your bodies will still be identified, depending on how hungry the fish are. Larry kidnapped you both, planned on being a martyr for his cause. He's rumored to dynamite fish, even among the coral reefs. The police will assume his own explosives in wiring the boat misfired by mistake before he had a chance to detonate his vest bomb at the Lūʻau finale. Suicide bombers are the international rage. It's plausible and I think rather a neat package. I, of course, will plead for the memory of misguided youth, set up The Larry Tutapu Scholarship for Hawaiian Studies."

"Your curriculum is not radicalism per se, merely infiltrating the system with those who can benefit you. To what goal, more wealth?"

"Oh, I think Governor has a nice ring to it, U.S. Senator after that, and then who knows? Well, enough of your delaying dialogue. Goodbye. And Madison, for a while it could have been great, but not great enough to be First Lady of the Islands, mine or Michaels."

That hurt; to be dumped before being blown up.

Chapter 35
Fire in the Sky

We heard a whir of a small electric motor, moving off, fading. Captain Jimmie had fled the impending carnage in the sailboat's Zodiac.

My father rolled over on his side and began scooting along the floor.

"Madison, be a dear, and don't just lie there. I think we have only minutes left."

More limber than my father, I took my tied hands and moved them down under my butt and over my feet so they were in front of me. I worked my way to his side and started fiddling with his knots.

"What was this guy, an Eagle Scout?" The various loops and tangles remain secured.

"Try getting to your feet. See if you can open the door." In several maneuvers, I kangaroo bounced and tried the door handle. Rattled but locked.

"Any knives in the galley drawers?" Jeffrey slid up on one of the bunks, his arms still tied behind him.

Hopping over, I found the cabinets bare, even of plates, cooking utensils. It furthered my thoughts that Captain Jimmie might be missing a few spars in his mizzenmast. Had he emptied out the larder, not wanting to waste good dishes and silverware? I noted the sailboat's marine radio missing. Would the police pick up on such details? I doubt there would be much left to raise such suspicions, the plot only to feature Larry T as the deceased killer and us as his last victims.

I moved over to the bunk next to Jeffrey, rolled up and on, and used my feet to turn a latch on a small rectangular porthole. Reversing positions, I yelled, "Help," over and over. No use. My voice carried, though not a great distance, muffled by the lū'au's instrumental drum pounding. Captain Jimmie positioned us in *La Chic Dork* far enough away from the other boats where no rescuer would reach us in time, and not far enough, not beyond the jetty to avoid the outgoing tide, helpful to allow a diving crew to retrieve bodies. Captain Jimmie, for spur of the moment, had planned well.

"What now?" I asked seeking deliverance.

Thump-whoosh!

The back end of the sailboat blowing up was not what I had in mind. The explosion threw me off the bunk onto the floor. Tutapu's body rolled on top of me, and then, the sailboat broke in two, the bow end where we were, shifting up at an angle. As the bay water rushed in the First Mate's body tumbled down into the murky depth. Both Jeffrey and I were perpendicular, he holding onto a bunk cleat and I grasping a galley closet door. The water came up to my waist and then stopped. Our part of the wreckage was buoyant! The night outside through portholes glared orange from the fire consuming the sailboat's stern. People would see the blazing conflagration and rush to search for survivors. We had a chance.

"Madison, dear, any way we could exit immediately?" His voice sounded agitated, lacking his normal confidence, and that scared the hell out of me.

"This part of the sailboat is staying afloat; better to wait for help."

"In other dire cases, perhaps, but not here; remember Captain Jimmie's statement of 'sequential timers.' The first part of that sequential has been met, but when and where is the second sequential?"

Damn, he was right. The madman wanted the boat to sink and knew this might've happened. The bow half of the boat had to be likewise wired. No time to spare.

"We have to dive down, under and back up."

"I don't know if I can swim trussed up like a Thanksgiving turkey."

"Better than as giblets," I told him, positioning myself. "When we surface I can hold onto you." He probably thanked himself for all the swim lessons bought for his precocious, athletic daughter over the years.

Jeffrey, no time to lose, set the example; he turned loose, fell into the liquid abyss and was gone. I followed, feet together, hands close to my side to avoid snagging metal. How far should I swim kicking down before I shoot back up? The fire burning above glazed the water in opaque orange glows. Wreckage floated everywhere. I did not see which way Jeffrey swam.

Shit Almighty! A floating arm appeared in the murkiness, startling the bejezzus out of me. My father did not wear tattoos. I kicked away from the corpse.

I floated upward, cautious against nasty bumps. Night air rushed to my lungs. Like a spinner dolphin running the waves on its tail, I kicked my bound feet, head above water, barely. I swung in all directions searching for my father. In the dark cluttered ocean, I caught a glimpse of him and had to give a laugh to break my fear of what we still faced. He could swim, but not tied up. He lay in the water, floating on his stomach, rolling over as a kayaker is taught, catching a breath with each water roll.

The second explosion ripped the night. I ducked under to avoid raining debris, and needful if not at ease in being alive, I emptied my bladder in sighing relief. So what? We both were still in the shitter.

I butterfly kicked over to my father and caught hold of him, holding with all my might, steadying him, making him lay on his back, telling him to kick out as I did likewise directly below him. Such dogpaddling in place kept us from drowning, moved us nowhere and taxed our strength. Unknown time went by, too long, and I was flagging fast. Hallucinations of wanting to sleep in the deep began to swirl around in my head.

With a lurch, hands went under my armpits and I was yanked upwards and pulled into a boat. I threw up a gallon of salt water. My father lay gasping next to me. Towels were thrown over us as our hands were untied. Thank you. Thank you. Thank you. Thank you.

We were in the launch from the *Pirates of the Caribbean*. The senior steward at the helm, crew members from Captain Jimmie's yacht had saved us. Were they part of his plan, were we going to be loaded up with concrete blocks and tossed overboard? Second time down to Davy Jones's Locker for good measure?

The senior steward recognized us, and stared at my father, shaking his head.

"You stole bad this time. Pissed them off, hey?"

I did not mean to scream...
What had I seen?
They were after me. I was going to die yet tonight...
How the crap could I be so unlucky?

Chapter 36
Fleshing Out the Details

Detective Kee did not believe our story, or more so, gave any credence serious misgivings. My photos of Larry dockside and Captain Jimmie hiding in the shadows were lost in the explosions, though I had the original 640 MB film chip and 35 mm negatives back in my room. I would go get them, I told my father and Kee. The detective said it would be best to search for the body of Larry Tutapu at first light, the alleged killer. Can you believe that? My father went off to make a formal statement to the police, trying to convince them of Captain Jimmie's despicable turn in character. I would join them later for my version.

With purpose, I had begged off, claiming the need for showering, shock, whatever. In my mind, I had to find Michael. He could be in danger. Captain Jimmie was unsound. Delusional. If he knew we had survived, he might believe he had to get rid of all other loose ends. Could Michael be one of them?

Another scenario more tenuous: what if Captain Jimmie showed up and it was his word against ours? What proof did we have to show he was the killer of Uncle Joe Coffee, or for that matter, orchestrating the sail boat and stage explosions? All that could be laid at the feet of the dead First Mate. Michael would know who spoke the truth; he would have faith in me. I chanted as I searched: Michael would know what to do.

The L ū‘au festivities ran their course, the tourists departed, cleanup crews policed the grounds. A few curious spectators at the beach watched the burning embers in the harbor. The executive offices at the hotel were dark and empty. Had they given him an executive cell phone? The front desk had no night number for him. At wits end I began walking up the entry roadway towards the highway, no set course, gathering my thoughts, anguished, realizing that tonight I almost lost my father, forgetting momentarily my own life hung in the balance.

A glow edged over the horizon, away from the hotel, the opposite direction of the golf course, and up from the ocean and the lū‘au grounds. Watching my steps, now off the path, I found myself carefully treading through the maintenance yard, over to where the lava rocks were being pulverized to create pads for future housing units. At a cut in the hillside I saw the bonfire, behind a barbwire fence. Fences had so far not kept me out, or out of trouble.

In a large basin, on a rock pile platform, wood had been piled up and burned furiously, underneath what seemed to be a boiling black kettle. Not coffee pot size, huge, like I had seen in the history books on whaling in the Hawaiian waters, the type of large iron pot they used to boil whale blubber into oil. Around the fire stood about twenty men, naked to the waist, some in grass skirts, others in Hawaiian sarongs, bodies covered with ink scrawls, feathered masks on many, hiding recognition. Religious fervor ruled their chanting emotions; the language, Hawaiian, far from a melodic serenade. A few near the cauldron threw on more wood to stoke the fire, others put stones onto the pyre, against the cauldron. Above them all stood a giant totem, a Tiki god statue, bearing a hideous face, wood carved, flickering grim and sneering, as if alive from the shadow dancing glow of the fanned flames. Was this part of the cooking ceremony of the lū'au that I had missed? A rehearsal for the next night?

The kettle boiled and bubbled. As I stared a hand and arm appeared rising out of the kettle's frothy mix, the fingers black, stiffly pointing to the heavens, and then this "thing" disappeared back into the churning steam.

I did not mean to scream, one that split the night and attracted several of those in on the ceremony's outskirts to look my way. I turned and fled. What had been going on? What had I seen? I caught my breath and took off again when I heard crunching on the lava gravel. They were after me. I was going to die yet tonight! How the crap could I be so unlucky?! They would expect me to run for help toward the hotel. They knew the paths. I would be cornered, and then what? The specter of cannibalism hit me like a lightning bolt. No, it couldn't be. No one did that these days, impossible. Or was it?

I took myself makai, back to the ocean, from whence I had just arisen. The moon hid behind a cloud and my steps became more careful. I paused. The sound of waves against sand. Had I led them astray? It struck me: around the fire, seeing their naked torsos, those were the bodies of old men. They could not catch me if they tried, only someone young and strong...

Arms grasped me. I jumped and screamed again.

"Madison."

Michael. In the dark, I could not see his face, his touch so familiar.

"Oh, Michael, I was looking for you." I threw myself into his arms, smelled the salty sweat of his body. "There are cannibals loose, and Larry's dead, and Captain Jimmie is not your friend, but a killer." I babbled out my speech in lurches of gasps of breath. He led me to a grass bluff above the beach, sat me down, and asked me to start from the beginning.

Michael listened. His questions pertinent and kept me to the facts. I felt assured. He did not doubt my story, too wild to be made-up. The betrayal of Captain Cooke profoundly affected him. His back arched, muscles tightened. His repose broke before my eyes, like watching a dragon birthing from a brittle shell. I had never witnessed a metamorphosis, boy to man, man to what, beast?

"I must go."

"No, no." I clung with my heart.

"I'll take you back to the hotel path and point you in the right direction."

For all I had in me, my mouth searched for his, at first exploding wildly on him, his response hesitant, then a slow response and his arms encased me with protection. His kiss fell away tenderly. The moon crept from around the cloud, moonlight covered the land and I looked into his face, asking without words that he lie me down on the sandy, dune grass bed, and enter me without hesitation.

I froze. His face bore the inked tattoos of the Hawaiians, of those at the fiery cauldron of unknown boiling flesh. He was one of them.

I did not struggle, let him lead, my steps struggling as if in quick sand. When my daze broke, the lighted sign of Ho'oilina Kai Resort was before me. I was alone. As I had known in the events of last evening that I had lost Michael Ka'aiea to unknown forces, tonight, my soul prophesied I had tasted my last kiss of mutual desire. I went to bed in shambles of torn regrets.

Chapter 37
Poolside Interlude

The morning broke to our dismal advantage. Larry Tutapu's body had been recovered with his bomb jacket attached, verifying a significant part of our story. The fishing boat *Raw Tolo Oceans* had disappeared out of the harbor suggesting the flight of Captain Jimmie. Detective Kee and the Hawai'i County police had no choice but to seek a search warrant of his yacht, and put out a broadcast request to detain one James Cooke, as a 'person of interest.'

Whatever else happened seemed of no importance to me as I lay by the hotel swimming pool, hiding behind sunglasses, nursing invisible wounds. I was a big girl, used to the ups and downs of relationships. On one side of the scale, I missed being in Michael's aura. On balance, my expectations had been more superficial, carnal pleasure-seeking. I had failed in not allowing our personalities meet half-way, mine specifically, not grasping until too late a serious relationship had been offered. To my shallowness, playing the good-time girl, I pitted two men's characters against each other, willing to have either man win at a contest of my own selfish creation. In the end, one tried to kill me, the other moved beyond to a higher plane of his own needs. I should respect Michael for his achievements, though I felt short changed, wishing for another chance to prove my worthiness. Time to move on.

"How are you doing?" Michael found the wrong time to show up, just as I had exorcised his voodoo hold on me. He looked like a college student after an all-nighter frat party. So, I told him, "You look like shit."

"The burdens of leadership."

"A goal you sought."

"Yes, too soon, I'm afraid. I don't know if I can cope."

"Of course, you can. If there is destiny, you were made for each other." He sighed and then put a smile to his face. Michael's smile. I would miss such simplistic sincerity in a man's pleasant upturned mouth.

"Considering your close call last night in the harbor, escaping violent death, I assume you had other nightmares." I caught his drift.

"My dreams did get a little wild. If I saw anything unusual last night, I put it down to bad poi I ate at the lūʻau, and a bilge load of sea water I drank in the harbor later that night. No need to bother others with my wandering imagination."

"Poi does not usually sit well with most people from the mainland."

"I was hoping to make it a regular staple, see the islands more. Sadly, Jeffrey Dayne is a man on a quest for insatiable foodie experiences, and I doomed to wander as his sidekick, like Sancho to Don the Q."

Michael's eyes.

"I'm sorry, Madison, that it did not work out between us. For a brief moment…"

"For brief moments, the island became the paradise it's advertised as."

"You know my new job will be all consuming pressure. And there are other responsibilities…"

"It's okay, Michael. You have your chance to succeed; you don't need distractions." We were trying to be magnificent in our joint pained sacrifice. I had to give him the out, bring us back down to certain unsolved elements. So, I asked, "Where do you think Captain Jimmie is?"

Michael gazed at the horizon.

"The police believe he took his fishing boat and skipped out, maybe to Micronesia. The Coast Guard has issued an all-points alert."

I could see in his mannerisms the revelation of his mentor's treachery ached and tore at his feelings. It is hard to respect another when any variation of that emotion is trampled.

"I assume the lūaʻu finale is still on?"

"The show must go on." I laughed at his corporate façade going back into place and he joined in the mirth. Shortly, he departed. We would survive as friends. I could live with that, I guess. I don't know.

Jeffrey found me spraying on my nth layer of sunscreen. I wanted to brown out the bad toxins, not immolate them.

"Two more days and we're out of here."

"Exactly. I've reached my quota on near death experiences. We are finished here."

"Not quite. Captain Cooke tried to poison us, blew up the stage, and then wanted our snooping to stop permanently. I don't think he was the first poisoner of Oli and he probably didn't tip you off the ladder at Akaka Falls."

"We don't have to solve every nuance of a crime spree, do we? Besides, you left out that he murdered Joe Coffee and Larry Tutapu."

"Did he murder Joe Coffee?"

I stopped my lotion slathering. "What are you saying?"

"Nothing, really, except if you recall from his conversation before trying to scuttle us, he never admitted he killed Joe Coffee."

"But he did, no one else had a motive." I knew in an instant that was not true. Michael. Could his turmoil within surface out of control? In a rage to find a weapon, a spear close at hand, he knew where they were. And his motive? Protecting the greater corporate success of Ho'oilina Kai Resort? Protecting someone? I hardly thought so. Definitely not guarding my virtue, as demonstrated by our awkward parting less than an hour ago. I saw my father watching my juvenile mind at work.

"No," I said, affirming what I believed true, not facts, but as I saw it. "No, Captain Jimmie killed old Joe."

"Okay, who fed the Jimson Weed to Oli Palalū?"

Enough already.

"Tomorrow," I said, "let's think about it tomorrow."

"Yes, you need other distractions. Safer ones."

"Yeah, like I've got to concentrate on shooting the last of the HDTV tonight. I'm concentrating on that job right now. Put some lotion on my back, will you." I rolled over, undid my back strap, nestled into the beach towel draped over the chaise lounge, and let all problems outside of five feet from my repose evaporate. I closed my eyes and sought idyllic dreams where they say 'Hawai'i is a state of mind.'

"Slather on the lotion thick," I directed my father, hoping for a native bronze tan, not Ahi-seared tourist burn.

Jeffrey's hands started awkward. He paused a few long seconds, then smoothed out the coconut-aloe basting lotion over my back, onto my legs, in circular motions. He went beyond mere application and returned to begin what I took as a gentle backrub. All senses melted, my eyes shut to the tenderness, right to the tingling sensation when his fingers traced down my back bone, down into my butt crack, down between—!

"Jeffrey!" We had entered a world of erotic child abuse.

"The name's Will. Will Bonney."

"What?" I flipped over, forgetting momentarily my suit top, going European au naturale, modesty quick to cover my breasts. "You!" The leader of the Beautiful People, rubbing me!

"Name's Will. He did wave me over and asked me to put on the lotion."

Jeffrey was nowhere to be seen. Damn prankster that he was.

"I guess it's his practical joke. Hey, like ask me if I could decline? I've seen you around the hotel. Sorry, if I offended you."

I shaded my eyes. Will, whatever his name, uninvited, sat down next to me. He had shaved off his little chin fuzz; either way didn't matter to me, if I cared. Close up inspection, I guessed he might be older than I, but not by much. He towered in his Tommy Bahama bathing trunks, a chest lean more than brawny, good stomach abs. He flashed this childish grin, a full set of teeth, orthodontic perfect. Hazel brown eyes. A slight scar barely visible on his jaw; if self-conscious, a reason for not shaving? Using my Dayne powers of deductive reasoning, highly scientific by how he touched me, I guessed an unattached young man, not gay, definitely cocky and self-assured. His Beautiful People posse nowhere to be seen.

"I thought you and your friends would be out..." I caught myself before he knew I was a first-class snoop.

"Everyone got a break this morning. Some of them are power shopping. After lunch we'll get back together. We're finishing up a group project. Bummer to say, tomorrow is our last day on island." His eyes did linger on mine; was there something said unsaid?

He continued, "Doing a night flight over to Maui."

"Hiding out?"

"What?" Quizzical and startled.

"I mean, what's on Maui to do that you can't do here?" Jeez, did that sound like begging?

"Oh. Some of our group are registered at the Hawai'i Writer's Conference. It starts this week."

"They're writers?" Well, that confirmed my theory they were not empty-headed boobs, except maybe the blonde.

"Two are. One writes political commentary, the other, high tech espionage fiction. Quite good, light years beyond James Bond and his tricked-out Aston Martin. More like Vince Flynn or James Rollins with Matrix high-tech. As for myself, I am going to take a quiet visit to Charles Lindbergh's grave site near Hana." His voice serious below his smile, a bass voice, with light gravel tones, different than Michaels, but slow cadence, strong, commanding, like Michael's. I tried not to compare and jumped into the conversation.

"He's the one who first flew the Atlantic?" I'm no Dumbo; it was once a Jeopardy question. "I didn't know that's where he's buried." I didn't. "For a man who saw from the air the most beautiful places in the world, it says something he chose the Hawaiian Islands to make his final landing." I must have said something right, he actually beamed.

"Exactly."

Freaky. He said 'exactly' like I do.

He continued, "I will stand there for inspiration, pay homage to the ultimate adventurer." He looked at his watch, as did I, almost noon, and his watch very expensive, a Swiss dive watch. "I am sorry, but I have to beg off. Things to do in prep for our final… excursion. By the way, you might not wish to burn that, or I could put help put on sunscreen."

A breast had escaped from my clutched bikini top.

A devilish smile tied to a 'goodbye.' He walked away.

Why did I get this feeling he did not want to go back to his friends? No, only my grasping imagination. Wait, I should be less critical of myself, accept opportunity. One door closes, another opens.

Better yet, where there's a Will there's a way.

After a minute, I followed him unseen into the hotel.

Chapter 38
Serious Games

I thought so. Watching him from behind a hotel pillar, I copied down as he wrote on the flip chart GPS coordinates and a small series of numbers.

N 20 08. 546'   W 155° 48. 077'

N 18 54. 741'   W 20° 05. 022'

N 155 40. 802'   W 155° 29. 335'

AEE-27537

He covered up his clues and started reading through notes, prepping for his meeting and the launch of their last hunt. I raced to my room to change clothes and get a head start. Finally, some fun, verve without danger. I could handle this.

Ignorance made me research this geo-caching, and lo and behold, I had been walking around with my own GPS system, my cell phone. Our hotel courtesy jeep even had a mobile GPS. They were everywhere. At a local sporting goods store I had purchased a mid-range unit and rushed through the basic manual. I hoped I could still get close enough to find at least one of their hidden containers, their cache. To the coordinates, I gathered up three trinkets I would leave behind, if I were successful. Even finding one hiding spot would achieve the surprise I envisioned.

Down the road in the hotel loaner I exceeded the speed limit, one hand looking at my GPS gadget, the other seeing if the direction would take me off the highway.

Surprising, the first coordinate location, not hours away, but just down the road. The tourist map spelled out the area: Black Sand Beach.

Satellites, something like 6 of them whizzing overhead in triangular configuration, gave me guidance to a small shopping center. After walking one way, then the other, checking the different GPS readings, I found the cache, behind a dumpster, under a moldy bag of cut grass clippings. A dark metal container, to me, it seemed like one of those old war ammunition boxes, designed I presumed to be waterproof.

Dramatic pause and sweaty hands like opening a thousand year old tomb of some exotic prince, waiting to be overwhelmed with what little trinkets they had dropped in or a clue to their master treasure.

What the—! —There were three medium-sized ziploc plastic bags of what looked like, was in fact, white powder. The game changed dramatically, if not to a dangerous round of play. It had to be drugs. I dare not open and do a finger taste. What is going on here?

I did not dwell on my discovery, caught up in the intensity of the hunt, addicted to wanting to know what was at the next site. Whether blind to sane reasoning, in turn I wanted to do some of my own serious mind blowing, so I left behind my own trinket gift. Freak on that, Will Bonney.

A mile down the road the next cache almost did me in, mentally. It had been a wicked week of murders and a killer or killers on the loose. And now this: a gun wrapped in black plastic, placed in a buried Tupperware container. Not a real gun and that really confused me. More like a pellet pistol but one I saw with small feathered darts, and a medicine bottle, like those that you stick in to give shots. Clear liquid in the bottle, no markings. I returned the found treasure to its secreted place, under a pile of lava stones, surrounded by white coral rock design, the initials not W.B. but BTK. Meant for one of the Beautiful People, I expect, one of them trained to use the medical silencer. This was getting surreal. Again, I left my teaser gift and ran to the Jeep. Time might be running out. If each team raced to one of these caches, then at the last one, they might already be there. My coordinates, with the added numbers took me down a winding street, towards the ocean, slowing to a guard gate fronting an expensive housing compound. A sign announced: *Black Sand Beach Estates*. Well, that was the end of this hunt. The prize lay beyond that protective barrier and I wasn't about to go and try and lie my way past a guard taking license numbers asking visitors what their business was and their destination.

Hold on, it couldn't be. It was worth a try and I drove up on the owner's roadway side, to the entry pad, just like I owned the place, and punched in: SG 20-9-16 15-6. The gate swung open, the guard wiggled his hand in a shaka hang loose greeting and went back to his paperwork. He did not write down my license plate but I caught sight of the security camera on top of the guard shack that would catalogue my Jeep. Anyone in review would recognize the affixed logo of Ho'olina Kai. Maybe this wasn't such a good idea.

A small street took me among multi-million dollar homes, all in turn, behind their own large protective fences, each with secured gates. I found myself heading into a cul-de-sac, one large castle styled house at the end, above the ocean breakers.

The coordinates stopped me before I would have dead-ended at the fortified gates of the castle. The cache therefore had to be nearby, and I hoped and prayed to the gods, not hidden over a fence, or in someone's yard, someone who might have snarling dogs, exactly the growls I heard close by. Okay, start looking. They tell you to look for worn signs of where people have beaten a footpath to the cache. No past visitors here. This game was a one-timer, and for what purpose I could not fathom. Drugs and a dart gun? Were the other Beautiful People in the medical profession, something to do with, maybe, animals? Maybe these people were kinky, paintball type shoot 'em ups, snorting cocaine, and tranquilizing each other. Nothing seemed to be rationale in explanation. I grew frustrated. I had failed to find the last cache.

To divert suspicion of my search I had raised the Jeep's hood and every once in a while glanced in. Anybody seeing me might believe I had lost an automotive part. Time must have run out. They would drive in and discover me, and what circumstances would occur I dare not start thinking up my imaginary scenarios. I am dealing with reality, crazy as it gets. I raised my eyes to the heavens for divine guidance. Damn. I should have looked up to begin with. There was the last box, well hidden among branches of a bush on the artsy lattice work of a stone wall. The box, in descript, the size of a large soap dish. Inside, what apparently looked like a garage door opener. In fact, it was a garage door opener. Worse than the two previous cache revelations, the thought struck me that over in the Middle East, extremist bombers used cell phone and garage door signals to detonate road side bombs. A bomb? Not again. Three bomb incidents in a single span of island time. Not coincidence but a curse laid on heavy. I now had to think the impossibility as plausible: Will Bonney, the assassin, poised to blow up some famous person or a dignitary? And this is his idea of simple contract hit?

For some time, I held the device in my hand hoping Will Bonney and friends would show up, and I could confront them, and demand an explanation, even on threat of my own life. The street, except for barking dogs, retained a landscaped emptiness. I studied the shrubbery near me and saw no clue to a buried depository of high explosives. Women do this, damn us. I had to know. I climbed back in the Jeep and for protection, ever the stupid-ass, even fastened my seat belt. Ducking down beneath the Jeep's dashboard, holding the opener above my head, I pushed the button.

No explosion. I raised my head and looked around. At the far end of the cul-de-sac, the large metal gate started to swing slowly open. Oh, my gosh. I had the presence of mind, pleased at having avoided being blown up (for the third time), and jumped from the Jeep and stuck my head under the hood. Two armed guards, one with a barking, snapping German Shepherd, came carefully to the open gate, hands on holsters. I kept my head down, faked some sparkplug fiddling, then went back behind the wheel, and after several dramatic exaggerated efforts started my Jeep. As the gate automatically swung slowly closed, they returned inside the compound, inspecting the gate mechanisms for further malfunctions, then resumed their patrol.

With great forethought, I had considered what this last gotcha joke would be. My initial prank was a Ho'oilina Kai room card key; make them go around and try to find the right room and guess why it belonged to a large family staying at the hotel, the card key I found dropped by one of the children. No, I changed my mind. My new idea popped forth; I rummaged through my purse and found what I was looking for. Whatever they were up to, next to a garage door opener to find the business card of Detective Kee of The Big Island Police Department ought to rank as one of the greatest of the 'Okole squeezers.'

Something had gone wrong. When I returned to the hotel, in a hurry to change for the ending festivities of the Lū'au Challenge, there sat the Beautiful People, in cocktail mode, talking quietly. They had not gone off geo-caching. They would not get the shocks of a lifetime. Besides, by the time I entered the lobby, and saw them, my analysis of my own geo-caching discoveries led to the conclusion these people were up to no good. And they might not be as 'beautiful' as they presented themselves to the world. Damn, but if Will Bonney didn't see me and wave, and all the others of his party turned their heads to see where his eyes led, and all smiled as if to extend friendship. Damn them. I fled to my room.

art by Kathy Long

Laka Ka'aiea guides us
Laka Ka'aiea teaches us
Laka Ka'aiea protects
In your light we thrive

Chapter 39
Kingdom Come

The Tenth Annual Lūʻau Challenge ended as no one expected. Desi Cardoza ran around demanding all show participants get back on script, hit their cue marks. Yet, events went beyond her control.

As the sun set, a long war canoe, paddles digging deep, swung around the point, glided in front of Cooke's anchored yacht, and entered the harbor. On the giant screen behind the stage, a television camera with zoom lens brought the canoe into close focus. All rowers were native, dressed in *malo* (tapa loin cloths) and no shirts. I could do little but point my camera at the screen, praying for clarity during editing.

From the stage, a single warrior emerged and blew a conch shell. Hundreds of yards away, another picked up the echo, and another, down to the beach, until the sea trumpet was blown from the bow of the war canoe. On the screen appeared a photo of Oli Palalū in happier times, with his years of life, birth to death, below his name. Only four days ago, his breath gone, life essence extinguished. The tourists all knew the singer had departed this world and the audience gave solemn respect. To the stage walked a Hawaiian chorus and sang with Oli's screen persona. They sang one of his major hits, "Manu ʻŌʻŌ," an old classic that compares a woman to the nearly extinct black honey-eater bird called manu ʻōʻō, whose yellow feathers were valued and used in featherwork. The man refers to himself as the lehua blossoms.

ʻO ka manu ʻōʻō i mālama
A he nani kou hulu ke lei ʻia
Mūkīkī ana ʻoe i ka pua lehua
Kāhea ana ʻoe i ka nui manu
Hoi mai, ʻoni mai
Kō aloha ma Kīhene lehua
N ō Hilo i ka ua kanilehua

Popohi lehua ai Hanakahi
Ho'okahi a'u mea nui aia 'oe
'O kou aloha ua hiki mai.

Precious honey-eater,
Your feathers are beautiful woven into a lei.
You sip lehua flowers
And call other birds.
Come, fly hither
To your beloved
Lehua cluster.
You lehua-sounding rain are
from Hilo,
Shapely lehua at Hanakahi.
The one I love is you
Your lover has come

One of the elders I had seen several times, most recently, I thought, by last night's kettle bonfire, joined the chorus in all his feathered regalia and started chanting. The screen camera again focused live to the large canoe. One costumed native stood and with all reverence, he shell scooped grey powder from a Calabash bowl and flung it into the wind — *La`ama`oma`o, take our brother* — *and upon the ocean waters* — *Swim with him, Ukanipo.* Anyone who was local, anyone who knew, could see Michael chanting and dispersing the ashes of Oli Palalū into the accepting arms of the ancient gods. *Take our brother, Manua, let him wander with Akua-ula and Lakakane and play and sing among the groves of kou trees.*

Through tears, I turned off my camera. A private moment of my own prayer for the departed who sought only to bring his melodic voice to comfort us savage mortals.

The intended program of Hawaiian music and dance resumed its normal scheduling. When Diana Aki sat on a stool playing guitar and singing with her beautiful songbird voice, in the audience a local Hawaiian woman with many orchids in her hair stood up and danced an impromptu hula. Dancers from Na Lei 'O Kaholoku, the Kohala hula troupe led by Nani Lim Yap, sat on lauhala mats and did a vigorous sitting hula in their traditional-style costumes. During another act, tourist children were brought onstage and taught basic hula movements to the delight of the audience, specifically camcording and I-phone video parents.

I sought out Jeffrey who sat with Detective Kee, like old army buddies, chortling over private jokes.

"What did they find on Captain Jimmie's yacht?"

"Vv…ery interest…ing," said the detective laughing at his imitation of an old TV comedy shtick. Very interesting and out of character for the staid police officer. My father held in a giggle.

"Tomorrow, you said, Madison. All will be clear tomorrow." Both men exchanged mischievous grins.

Loud drumbeats stopped me from throwing out a few choice curse words about their anatomy. The crowd grew silent. Once again it seemed the script had been thrown out. Stage lights dimmed to a single string of spots. Drums beat to intensity and stopped. One lone drum began a slow cadence. Conch shells from everywhere, behind the audience, behind stage, blew long drawn-out peals. A procession entered. Priests in flowing robes, followed by spear-bearing warriors; the dancers, all spreading in an arc at the back of the stage. In flowing robes came the priests; I recognized several of them.

"What's going on?" Both men shook their heads in ignorance, but were mesmerized by the pageantry.

Surrounded by other bedecked warriors and carried by the strongest came what I took to be a platform, a paladin, with purple cloth and flowers draped a chair affixed. Sitting in the chair in a yellow and red colored bird plume robe rode Michael Ka'aiea, an expression of seriousness I had never seen. On his head, he wore the mahiole, a feathered war helmet. The carriers lowered their chair and passenger to the stage. A priest stepped up, ignoring the audience, and addressed Michael. The voice boomed loud and reverberated by the speakers. One priest handed Michael a spear, another gave him stalk shoots of a plant. The priest continued to speak Hawaiian in rhythmic cadence. Two of the hula dancers brought him lei, which a priest put around his neck, not the women, I noted. The dancers bowed as they stepped back! I looked around the audience, enthralled at the spectacle. I knew this was not part of the closing ceremonies.

Detective Kee watched open-mouth until he saw my stare. He whispered,

"A lūʻau begins with the introduction of the queen and king. I would've never expected this, not in a million years." He was amazed at his own answer.

"What?" Jeffrey looked to Kee.

"This is a *coronation*."

Yes, I could see the priests invoke spiritual ritual. I thought I saw the circumstances. I whispered back.

"Joe Coffee, Joe Paʻao, died. Michael has been chosen to be the new Kauaʻi clan leader." Then, it struck me. Joe Coffee was removed and Michael moved up in the old society leadership. A motive for murder? My eyes met Jeffrey's and similar thoughts must have been stewing in his cranium. I would not accept the conclusion.

"No, don't you see?" Detective Kee, leaning toward both of us, a few nearby tourists likewise straining for his color commentary.

"This is a coronation for a king. A king for all the Hawaiian islands. The priests are from every island. See the lighter skin torch bearers on the end?" We and a few audience tourists nearby nodded. "They're with the Committee for Economic Independence. And what about the tattoos on those warriors?"

I saw and remembered. "The People's Party. From Larry Tutapu's movement."

"And Larry is conveniently dead." Jeffrey had made his mind up on who the best suspect of all had turned out to be. Island royalty, even if by the proxy of Captain Jimmie.

Something strange happened. Detective Kee stood and slightly bowed his head. I glanced and saw others, some dark skinned, others of Asian descent, not all Polynesian features, standing amongst the crowd, alone, or in small groups. One or two Anglos, local haoles, I guessed. The entire lūʻau food staff at the back of the crowd understood and reacted. Several even fell to their knees, one young man in tattoos, raised a clenched fist.

All paying homage.

A blue stage light followed a young lady to center stage. Another hula dancer. No, different, motions graceful as they were seductive. Instruments played to her rhythm, ancient to us moderns by names called the ipu and ʻiliʻili. Haunting tones. The woman danced, her body swaying, her hands telling a story all so familiar. To me.

Kukui.

No longer pierced and neo-Nazi fashioned. Purged back to her roots, of Ni'ihau. Kuikahi. Someone had saved her spirit from the degradation of her people's honor. She was telling him, all of us, without words. A food server, standing near, also standing in respect, spoke aloud and translated the symbols of Kuikahi's hula.

I hold you in fealty, my life is sworn to you.

You are my alii-nui, King of first rank.

Welcome back to the islands, son of Kumuhonua, son of Pilika`aiea.

As she continued her lilting glide of dance, more for him, than for us, the priest began a devotional Hawaiian chant that those on stage repeated. A voice backstage gave us the English essence.

Laka Ka'aiea guide us. Laka Ka'aiea teach us. Laka Ka'aiea protect us. In your light we thrive.

Michael stood from the chair, from his throne, and she came and knelt down before him, her head pressed to his bare feet. He allowed this tribute and guided her to stand and he kissed both of her cheeks.

Jeffrey let me know what I feared.

"I think we are seeing an ancient form of betrothal."

The newly anointed king returned to his throne and was borne offstage, reborn Kuikahi directly behind in exalted positioning, followed by the rest of the entourage. No one within the cast on stage seemed to have dissented at the ceremony.

The spectacle over, the house lights eased up. The tourists in the audience gave a mixture of polite applause; those who knew local ritual and were more impacted reacted with awe. Detective Kee sat down, exuberant.

"That was really something." He pulled out his cell phone, text messaging the hot news out to the jungle telegraph.

"Something indeed," said Jeffrey Dayne, in contemplation of facts not yet sorted to a logical conclusion.

"This evening sucks," my morose opinion offered, and then changed my mind. Will Bonney from the departing crowd waved, motioning me to meet him halfway. Now, this could be interesting.

Chapter 40
Quite Willing

Good opening line: "Tomorrow, would you like to go for a night scuba dive?" Before my femininity could play offended or demur, my pent-up emotion gushed forth.

"Last night, the boat I was on blew up. I had to dive under the wreck, through a blazing inferno, tread water until I was rescued, holding onto my father, because he was tied up! Yeah, the sea and I get along quite well as bosom buddies."

Will Bonney stared hard into my eyes. Did I see his lip curl in amusement at my ordeal? I'll deck the son-of-a...

"Oh, that was you. I heard about that. All over the resort today. And I thought you were just another attractive girl doing the Island for R&R." His laugh disarming. "You are a force to be reckoned with." The crowd swirling around us bumped me into him too close for casual conversation. Gently, he steadied me away from him.

"No, my offer is sincere. I took a wild guess you might be a diver. If I am wrong..."

"Certified. Dove the Blue Hole in Belize." God, how long ago was that?

"Well, my friends and I —tonight we're packing—tomorrow night is our last night — we catch an 11:00 pm flight over to Maui, so being overachievers we signed up for a night dive, a tour package —and I thought you might want to join us." He rushed his words like a kid pushing all his thoughts into a single breath.

"I don't know. As you might understand I am pretty beat up."

His smile again. "Have you ever dove on a school of manta rays at night, and your diving partners hold the lights for your close-ups as you follow? The dive master and his boat have an underwater video set-up. They produce copies to sell."

Will Bonney, how did he...?

"You know that I am a television producer?" Well, someday, maybe.

"I've seen you around with your camera packs, my ideal of the modern Margaret Bourke-White."

I am impressed. Bourke-White one of my fave heroes, the famed Life Magazine photographer, adventuress to boot. How did he know I considered her an example of career achievement? He held up his hands, palms facing flat.

"No hidden agenda. Two hours max. We head directly to the airport from the tour. It should be fun. As long as your boyfriend doesn't mind?"

"Boyfriend?" That caught me off guard, and recent bittersweet memories started to surface. "No boyfriend." Not now.

"Oh, I thought I saw you with someone. A local, one of the actors in the Lūʻau finale."

"Oh, him. He got engaged…tonight…to someone else."

"These are stories I must hear. Please join us."

We walked to the hotel talking, me doing the most of the babble, a kind of confessional to a stranger. There was ease to his manner, and at any other time, under different circumstances I would find a comfort in his personality. But, not with three mysterious boxes hidden near Black Sand Beach. I focused my tales on the treachery of Captain Jimmie, the murders, the visit to his yacht, a mention of his library, and a not so subtle comment about Captain Jimmie wanting to acquire a book from a gentleman living at (dramatic pause)… Black Sand Beach. I detected a misstep in his stride, maybe not. He said nothing except short questions to keep my adventures unfolding. I glossed over the amorous inclinations with Captain Jimmie and Michael. History and no longer relevant.

He did ask of Captain Jimmie, "Sounds like a real evil person."

"Yes, murderers have that distinction."

When we reached the hotel I realized, as probably he wanted, he knew a lot more about me, than I of him. First lesson of detecting was to ask the questions and not unload one's life story, at least my life of the several days at Hoʻoilina Kai. I should be the one prying.

"You are welcome to join my father and me for a drink in the bar."

"Oh, that's a kind offer. Any other time, but I do have to get ready. I mean, packed."

Turning me down was growing to be a long list. The blonde and he could have hooked up. Or, that Spanish senorita, from the Memorial, the server at Chef Lorenz party. Maybe he's with her. It did not matter, much. After tomorrow night I would never see him again. But there was tomorrow night, and maybe under the right circumstances I could innocently ask questions with subtlety. Unfortunately, subtlety was not my middle name. And with all of my men, if I could say that, those recently met, those whom I had come to know, and not biblically, they all started off with allurement, and ended in danger. And here is William Bonney, a man who hid cocaine and tranquilizer guns, and could open guarded gates. Why should he not fit my current standard of qualification when it came to choosing male companionship?

We were in the hotel to go our separate ways and no suggestion from him of a nightcap in his room. Damn men; can't they follow the script I've written for them? I watched him take the stairs two steps at a time. Agile. Athletic. An unanswered question, one of a thousand, watching him disappear, "And what do you do for a living?" A safe question newly met people might ask without offense. I was afraid I might not want to know the answer, and more particularly whether he would tell me the truth.

Somewhere in the night I traipsed to the bathroom. Out the window, on the horizon, over towards the maintenance sheds, I could see a wavering glow. Too sleepy, I thought I was at intermission to my lengthy list of nightmares. Back in bed, I did pull the sheet over my head, futile protection against the unknown, soon back to my fitful dreams of passion with men without faces, or where my mouth opened to swallow the sea. Before morning, my last vision found me bathing in a boiling cauldron, filled with gurgling lava, my features draining of flesh to boned skeleton. So vivid, I jolted awake to poke my skin and be reassured it still covered a frightened young woman.

Chapter 41
Bracelets of Justice

In the morning, I found Jeffrey on the lobby lanai in a large white wicker chair reading the local newspaper, nibbling a macadamia nut sticky bun, sipping on his mocha Kona latte. The morning held a moist crispness, spreading freshness and aroma from flowers unfolding.

With my father there is security, solid ground to anchor my impetuous behavior, this penchant for getting into trouble. Maybe not.

"Detective Kee and his fellow officers," he said with a twinkle in his eyes, "arrived here a few minutes ago to make an arrest."

My stomach lurched to my throat. *Michael?* No, it couldn't be. I would demand my father stay on the island and defend him. Then, I stopped. No, hold on, there's an entire line-up of suspects to be considered. Had they caught Captain Jimmie? Found him hiding in disguise in a hotel guest room? And what of this Will Bonney? Geo-caching had been a cover, no doubt about that in my mind.

When the police exited the hotel, how totally wrong could I be? They were escorting Desi Cardoza, her hands fashionably wearing handcuff bracelets. Somehow, I felt justified satisfaction, and not even knowing the particulars. As the police car drove off with their criminal apprehended, Detective Kee joined us.

"You look wiped." And he did. With his acceptance I ordered him a straight coffee. He was no enemy. We were on the same side, now with this arrest.

"Pulled an all-nighter. Seems crimes of oddity last night set new records."

I started to pounce on the police investigator with my ton of questions. He saw it coming and jumped in first.

"Your father once again. I don't want him around this island. When he gets back home why don't you and he open up a P.I. shop?" They exchanged buddy bonding smiles. Said the detective, "The Jimson Weed came from a cultivated patch behind Desi Cardoza's house."

"From your socks, along with the marijuana leaf material," said Jeffrey, leaving Detective Kee perplexed at information he had not been privileged to. "I noted several books on Hawaiian medicinal plants with chapters on those that are harmful in Desi's house library."

"This morning we picked up her son for questioning."

"They poisoned Oli?"

"One or both, I'm not sure. We'll interrogate them to see if one gives up the other."

"If a betting man," suggested Jeffrey, "I'd let Johnny Rocket go cold turkey from his druggie use and he'll fink on his Mom. On the other hand, Desi has the mother lion instinct of protection; she'll take the fall, let her son continue with his band career. She's the smart one. Saw the Jimson Weed as an easy way to cause a flu bug and move her son up behind Oli's career and gain some visibility."

"Unless they're both guilty," was my interpretation. "I'd guess Johnny Rocket, just for spite, pushed me at Akaka Falls. In his zonked mind, I would be one less tabloid photographer. Kukui probably saw him leave the group, followed him, and saved my life."

"Speaking of the born-again Kuikahi," Detective Kee added. "She left the Pāhoehoe Sounds. If Johnny Rocket goes away, the band will be no more."

"Oli will live on." I believed that.

"Give her your more interesting news," Jeffrey nudged the policeman, holding back a laugh. Detective Kee hesitated, but relented. He realized father and daughter shared secrets—most of the time.

"Well, last night Burglary was called out on two separate incidents, and they saw some relationship to my cases, and I was brought in." Why was I feeling acid reflux bubbling in my throat?

"Another hotel room break in?"

"Yacht larceny."

"*Pirates of the Caribbean*? Captain Cooke returned?" Alarming fears shot through me.

My father understood my brittle nerves.

"Not likely, Madison. A murderer does not return merely to pilfer his library yet leave cash in his locked desk drawer."

"His library? You mean someone stole musty old books?"

"Very valuable if I recall our tour. A small fortune purloined."

"James Cooke had a state-of-the-art alarm system. Bypassed with finesse. Very similar to the Lorca burglary."

"Lorca? I heard that name before."

"A wealthy Colombian. Feds have had him under investigation for years."

The answer hit me, but I had to ask. "Where does this Lorca live?"

"In a highly protected enclave at Black Sand Beach."

The pieces fell into place.

"How did they get in?" My father urged me on in my interest of playing detective. Little did he know, I hoped.

"They?"

"I assumed more than one. Sounds like a major undertaking."

"Yes, well you're right," said Detective Kee. "More than one, we're pretty positive. Somehow drugged the guards and their dogs."

Tranquilizer gun.

"After climbing the wall?"

"No, somehow they disarmed the front gate and drove in. They could hide the car inside for hours and not be seen."

Entry by gate opener. The whole escapade fit, except for the bags of white powder.

My father likewise seemed to enjoy cops and robbers. "Same M.O. as the yacht break-in? And what did they steal?"

I could guess. "Books."

Kee nodded. "That's what Lorca reported. First Edition Charles Dickens. Complete set of all his writings, including several inscribed copies."

"Kee called me this morning for my take on all this, because, what do you know, one item stolen, of interest, Madison, a manuscript on early Hawaiian cooking: the Andrews collection of native recipes."

"Captain Jimmie mentioned that book specifically. Are you sure it's not him? Breaking in to grab a favorite before skipping out?"

Detective Kee and Father were in mirthful enjoyment of this story telling.

"We don't think so. Why take books when he has equally expensive books on his yacht, left untouched, until last night, by persons unknown. Did we mention the coke?

"Coke? As in cocaine? Fellows, I am getting confused here." *Bags of white powder.* Coming full circle, or like a noose neatly closed tight.

"When the police came back to do a more thorough inventory of Mr. Lorca's losses for insurance purposes (and, don't tell anyone, the return from an anonymous tip), seems like there were small bags of cocaine hidden behind books on his shelves."

My father held disdain for arrogant criminals who thought they possessed any thimbleful of culture. Jeffrey sniffed as the cosmopolitan.

"The gall to hide drugs behind a signed Tom Wolfe's *Electric Kool-Aid Test*. And behind Hunter Thompson's, *Fear and Loathing in Las Vegas*."

"Colombian Pure," affirmed Detective Kee. "Mr. Lorca is swearing police entrapment, that someone planted evidence. That man is up the Waiulu without a paddle."

"But nothing to connect him to Captain Jimmie?"

"No. We're widening the search for the fugitive Captain and the *Raw Tolo Oceans* to include all islands and the mainland. He may have changed the vessel's name, hidden it in a marina on another island, and taken a plane to the four corners of the world. We have changed our bulletin request to 'detain on suspicion of homicide.'"

My turn. I distinctly recalled from yesterday, the guard gate, certainly hidden cameras, the gate of Lorca's mansion opening to the surprise of the guards. The ruse of the broken down jeep. All to be uncovered by any sharp detective like the one who sat next to me.

"It's a coincidence, but I was up near Black Sand Beach yesterday."

"You were?" Here came my father's incredulity, disbelieving in coincidences.

"Somebody told me the beach was a great place to boogie board."

"And did you?" How rude, a father questioning his own daughter.

"No, I got lost and my jeep broke down. Was just gone an hour. About 2 p.m." Okay, alibi in place. I am a forgotten blip to the investigation. Shift back to the other crimes, as I did have a foundational question. "This Lorca fellow, was he an evil person?"

"Drugs definitely says the Interpol report I read," said Kee sipping his coffee for a needed wake-up caffeine fix. "By rumor even death squads. I heard he stole money and jewels from his victims. And, they disappeared forever. No witnesses. He is a persona non grata with the State Department but no one has any evidence he's ever committed a crime, until now. Yes, Miss Dayne, a very evil person."

"And in both robberies, no clues left behind, any suspects?" I could have easily said at this point in the conversation, 'Well, I have a gentleman, yes, a gentleman that requires closer scrutiny of his recent activities.' I said nothing, tantamount to becoming an accomplice, or as my father would offer free counsel, 'you are an un-indicted co-conspirator'. If I had the chance this evening, it was not guilt I would ferret out, but motive.

I did not hear what Detective Kee had been saying.

"Oh, I am sorry, what was that last part?"

"Very odd, but at the Lorca residence, each drug bag had one earring affixed, woman's jewelry, none of them matching. Something very odd about that."

My mind went elsewhere. "On the yacht burglary, did you mention what was stolen there?"

The Detective pulled out a cigarette and lit up. I empathized; his job pressure over unsolved crimes must be overwhelming to drag him back to his nicotine.

"That's another oddity in itself. I had to call your Father early this morning and take him out to the *Pirates of the Caribbean*."

"My father?"

Both men laughed at the private joke. I scowled, tired of their new-found fraternity.

"Hey, Madison, a mystery to me. Seems the Head Steward thought I might have had something to do with the robbery. Can you believe that?"

My eyes rolled to the nearby wall and watched a gecko scamper after a trapped fly. Kee saved me from an inappropriate confession.

"With a crime on board the yacht, we launched a more diligent search of what might have been stolen. Our investigation turned up interesting documents, one a list, with a check-off beside the name of Joe Coffee, a scribbled notation suggesting

Joe Coffee would damage the hotel even with new ownership. Captain Jimmie couldn't have his new investment at risk."

Jeffrey said, "Besides, my only other suspect had an alibi." I knew whom he suspected.

"Okay, who was Michael's alibi? I bet Kuikahi swore blue moons on his innocence?"

"What one might expect from such a virile young man." He enjoyed baiting me. "But no, she wasn't with him. He was with the other band members, trying to calm them down, especially Johnny Rocket, who wanted to fillet me into chum bait."

"And then, there's the rape file your father wanted to see." Detective Kee, like my father, enjoyed teasing an emotionally vulnerable woman. Yeah, wait and see.

"Rape?"

"A Caloric Rapist."

"Yeah, the file on his diet program, on his desk in his office."

"Nothing to do with food," said Detective Kee.

"You know what an anagram is?" Jeffrey again as the patient parental guide.

"Something to do with word jumbles. Shift the letters to get different words."

"Good girl. 'A caloric rapist' becomes 'Corsair Capital.' Seems our captain of the Seven Seas had a penchant for anagram play. It seems when you mentioned that anagram to him, even in jest, not knowing what it meant, he thought I might eventually discover the same. He realized we were expendable, a threat to his, as he said, 'Master Plan.'"

"And what was in this 'rape' file?" They had built me up for this.

"Nothing," they both said simultaneously.

"Captain Cooke must have taken it," I concluded.

"Or the burglar," mused the detective. "Along with the books taken."

I looked to my father, his mind potent in its silence.

"Dad, you have a theory?"

"There could have been two burglars. Two separate crimes."

Chapter 42
The Foundation

This time I said nothing and let Kee speak his disbelief.

"And what leads you to that conclusion?"

"This might require some more pondering on the matter," my father at full Columbo. "I only know that when I first saw the Caloric Rapist file, it was bulky, now it is empty. Yes, Cooke could have taken it, but why, when he left all his other possessions behind, cash and clothes, according to his steward. Cooke, for whatever reason, could have a plan of escape in place, the ability to start over, with part of his wealth secreted away. I am a little confused here, I must admit. But if the file deals with only Hawaiian matters then it is of no use to him."

"But who took the books," asked Kee, offering my father the benefit of his doubts, that he was good at this detecting business.

"A thief of gentle madness, a lover of books; or a burglar of greed with a shopping list. Let me think a while longer. You might as well as tell her about the other file."

"What file?" My mind had been wandering in turmoil, vexed about this Will Bonney character.

"It was the file contents which are extraordinary." Detective Kee sought to be the town crier on the day's surprises. "Corsair Capital was owned by the James Cooke Foundation."

I was trying to follow. "So, the Foundation owns the hotel?"

"Correct. But, when he set up the Foundation in Hawai'i, Cooke added someone he could trust to the Board of Directors to help him select and screen candidates for the scholarship program."

Someone he trusted? You gotta be kidding.

"Michael Kaʻaiea, newly ordained King of Hawaiʻi." That was not a question, instead a bona fide blow me away statement. Both men nodded to my general amazement. I took it from there.

"Michael is not only Manager of the Hoʻoilina Kai Resort, but he controls the hotel."

Jeffrey, the lawyer opined, "Unless Cooke returns or some distant relative of James Cooke appears to contest the foundation's charter and by-laws. In my humble legal opinion any contrary claim would be weak as all the wealth seems to have been first vested in the Foundation and no one coerced Cooke to set it up. No, the foundation by law is inviolate. I would say your former boyfriend is not so much mega rich as he controls wealth, under his direction to do with it as he pleases."

"Do you think he knew he could control the Foundation if something happened to Captain Jimmie, his friend?" I was playing devil's advocate. Detective Kee rose quickly to protect blood kin.

"Cooke could have hidden all the paperwork without Michael knowing. Michael could have thought he was involved just in the paperwork as a 'token' for due diligence on the scholarship program." A weak defense I could let slide.

"Possible," said Jeffrey. For certain he had new ramifications to suspect.

"Well, it's all moot as soon as we have Cooke in custody," reasserted the policeman, back to the official line and he left us on the veranda, both of us, for different reasons, hardly satisfied. I ordered a Bloody Mary.

Chapter 43
Our Own Calorie Hunt

A let down of sorts, back to work. Jeffrey on a schedule to do foodie tasting with two restaurants he had heard about and with me on the camera. We were off.

Driving over to our first destination, the Manago Hotel, along the Mamalahoa Highway, I threw out a nonchalant question, "Oh, I still don't think I heard what books were stolen off the Pirates of the Caribbean?" I held a tight lid to any exuberance at pursuing this line of questioning.

"No rhyme or reason, as far as I can see. Random titles, certainly valuable, but no associated commonality."

"And they were?" Holding my light exasperation in check.

"If I recall, according to the police report, first edition Alexandre Dumas. Another book, I can't recall."

I asked nothing more, only wondering why Will Bonney had taken only these books and not more. If a thief, why not go for the high price ticket items. Should it surprise me when I find my father and I are on the same wavelength?

"If the burglar had taken the *Cook Voyage of Discovery*," he considered, "heavy volumes though they are, that's worth at least $75,000 if not more with the association relationship to William Bligh. The Alexandre Dumas, père, was a signed first edition. Very valuable."

"Dumas?"

"Dumas, the father, authored *The Count of Monte Cristo*. Oh, and the other book, I recall, Robert Louis Stevenson annotated a personal copy of *Treasure Island*.

"And you have no idea why those books?"

He looked at me. "And do you?"

I feigned surprised incredulity. "Who me, of course not, why would I?" Did I deny too quickly? I did suspect the who, but not the why.

"I did not tell Detective Kee, but outside of the books heisted there is another thread of similarity between the Lorca and Cooke break-ins?

"What?" How he pieces together these intangibles is indeed a true wonder.

"Whoever stole these books knows the owners are in no position to take them back. Is it wrong to steal from the vile and corrupt? A moral paradox I find intriguing."

I changed the subject and pointed out we had arrived at the restaurant. And what the hell, I'm being haunted. We stopped in the town of *Captain Cook*.

The Manago Hotel took one back in time, to the early 1900's. Seems it was founded around 1917 by a family who were trying to supplement their income as coffee field laborers. And funky, inside felt exactly 1917. Jeffrey pointed out they were famous for skillet fried pork chops, and thank god, we were only passing by to smell the flavors from the kitchen. What fit my psyche perfectly, there behind the hotel's front registration desk, an appropriate sign: 'In case of tidal wave—1. Remain calm. 2. Pay your bill. 3. Run like hell.' The fact we were on a high bluff and if the tidal wave hit the hotel, the entire island would be obliterated, did not diminish the humorous truism.

Next door, I did buy some sweet potato chips from a store front called Kona Chips, while Jeffrey munched on something called 'furikake shrimp chips', and they weren't half bad either. Now, I see what we are doing and a hit of sadness swept over me. The end of our trip is approaching. We do not have enough time, probably a month would be required, to do sit down tastings of all island varietal menus. The lū'au enough threw a wide net over the Hawaiian cuisine but there is so much more, so little time. Goodbye Mary Teshima and all the wonderful meals you put before us.

Father and daughter hauled down the highway on our fast foodie blitzkrieg with Jeffrey taking notes, asking questions of composition, cooking style, spices used. Quick pit stops included Punalu'u Bake Shop in Na'alehu, near South Point, believe it or not, the southern most part of the United States! Our whirlwind took us past macadamia farms and tasting stops at roadside stands where I found myself addicted to a small fruit called rambutan, sucking away at a dozen, my father laughing when I called them 'rama-lama-ding-dongs'. Even in such a good mood for the day, my mind kept wandering back to the fact I would shortly be facing, once again, something mimicking a date, this time with a man who I knew was a thief.

Recipe: Kona Coffee Rubbed Steaks
with Marsala Wine BBQ Sauce

1/3 cup Kona Coffee, finely ground
2/3 cup brown sugar, finely packed
1 Tablespoon allspice
Hawaiian Salt and Cracked Black Pepper to taste
4 Hawaiian Grass Fed steaks, rib eyes work well with this method

Marsala Wine Sauce
1 cup of your favorite BBQ Sauce
3 Tablespoons soft butter
1/3 cup finely ground Kona coffee ¼ cup Marsala wine

Method for steaks:
Mix rub ingredients together in a small plate and apply to both sides of the steak.
Allow to stand for 4 hours at room temperature. Save drippings and place in sauce.
Mix the sauce ingredients in a large skillet, whisk to combine.
Simmer for a few minutes till all ingredients are incorporated.
Reduce slightly on a low flame. Heat the grill, sear steaks on both sides.
Put them in a sauce pan and pour the sauce over them, heat briefly to incorporate flavors.
Remove the steaks and slice on the diagonal and serve on a platter with the sauce.
This is great with mashed potatoes and a fern salad.

Recipe from Devany Vickery-Davidson

Chapter 44
Shark Bite

By late afternoon when I returned a message light was blinking in my room. Will Bonney, his voice, not as firm in our past meetings, more hesitant.

"Wanted to see if you were still up for a night dive? If so, we are all going to meet in the lobby at 5:00 p.m. The concierge is on call to have the activities shop supply you with any equipment required." He paused. "I would like to see you again." I called his room, but no answer, and left my R.S.V.P. accepting his invitation. As if I'd miss this cat-and-mouse outing, me being the feline.

They had to all be hyper paranoid, waiting for the police to break down their doors. The business card of Kee in the last cache the zinger. I liked the other two trinkets. With the bags of white powder (which held no attached odd pair earrings at my discovery) I placed a swizzle stick with the Ho'olina Kai logo. They could infer somebody was in the bar, observing. They would rack their collective minds trying to focus on one individual. At the cache with the tranquilizer pistol, they would have found a folded candid photograph of them, in group innocence at the airport on their arrival. A quick snapshot with no one the wiser. They would assume that they had been under surveillance from their first day on arrival. By Lorca? A fear of revenge. By the police? Fear for incarceration. Well, one should not go out and steal, and that's what several or all of them had undertaken. Quite successfully, so far, allowing them slight admiration.

I looked at all the angles and could not see any of my practical jokes coming back to me. I didn't think Will for a moment would remember me from the airport. And if so, at the airport he would not have tied me in as a pro photographer. And, I had not been in the hotel bar when they congregated. And our first meeting, Will and I, created spur of the moment by my father. No, they would be looking for greater evil, not for a young woman whose innocent agenda meant only to humble them. No longer the Beautiful People, they were just like myself, insecure. The unanswered question was: would I rat them out?

Knowing my dive muscles were not stretched and pliable I set out on a fast walk around the hotel grounds, stopping every so often for reps of knee-bends and push-ups. Tomorrow night would be my last night on island for my father and me. I wanted to give the place a final look, not so eager to retain any scrapbook memories. In the marina, a salvage vessel hooked in debris from the La Chic Dork of Oregon. In the distance beyond the breakwater, The Pirates of the Caribbean anchored, calm and innocent. Michael would be the ship's new captain, lord over land and sea.

The golf course fairway and green where the Oli Memorial had been sabotaged returned to duffers escaping sand traps. In my exercising trek, at another fairway, I noticed a survey team at work between golf shots. "Excuse me," I had to ask: "What are you doing?"

"We've been asked to redesign and move this Par 3 to the other side of the hill." The surveyor, thinking I must be a V.I.P. guest or future scratch golfer, went on: "I think we can give the new approach a Fazio or Nicklaus bunker look. Like this one, it'll be a tee shot right at the green, the ocean behind the flag pin." Yeah, my handicap is based on miniature golf.

"What's going here? More houses?" I could assume they wanted to increase building density, cram as many housing units with an ocean view, triple their return on capital.

"Not sure, ma'am. There's talk about this being some sort of church." I continued my walk, lopping into a slow jog, feeling upbeat.

Not a white man's church, I wanted to explain to the surveyor, but a hieau. King Michael as Hotel Manager had started his reign. And in a way, I applauded one of his first acts.

My calf muscles ached. Curiosity found me trudging up the road to the maintenance work area. Several resort employees were sorting through the pile of hieau stones with an older man overseeing them. One of the priests. He raised his aged body, wiped perspiration from his brow. When he saw me, he smiled. I returned his confidence with my own sweaty grin. Yes, the Israelites would rebuild the Temple.

From the pathway, my steps slowed as I walked through the crushed lava field, seeking to discover the fire site. There it was, and the black kettle, turned on its side.

Wary, I walked around the large black metal tub. All the rocks I had seen placed on the fire were gone. These I presumed were from the heiau, going through a ritual fire purification, maybe to be the base foundation when it was rebuilt. I glanced inside the kettle. It had been cleansed, the smell of ammonia lingered. I felt the burned wood ashes, warm. Last night, through that misty veil of exhaustion, reality or dreams, was there really another glow in the night sky? Two nights of a burning pyre, burning what, for what purpose? Purging the heiau rocks of their past bulldozer desecration?

Something on the ground caught my eye. I picked it up, turning it over in my hand. Closer to the shoreline would be the skeletal remains of trillions of sea shell fragments, but not out on the lava rock. This was not a sea shell, but what looked to be a tooth, pointed and sharp, a single shark tooth. I looked for others and found none. The old men around the firepit, the priests of the old religion, had been in costume. Perhaps this shark cuspid had broken from one of their ceremonial necklaces.

Chapter 45
Diving for Truth

My scuba gear, rented, sat at the hotel's front door, awaiting our gathering.

Something I had to do. Over at the display of historic war weapons, I saw the empty slot on the wall where the long spear had been taken by a killer, discovered in the body of Joe Pa'oa and now in the police evidence locker. I was there for another reason and reached up and replaced the shark's tooth into the gap of the Shark's Teeth Club. The Lā'au Pālau. It fit perfectly. The club had been washed, a faint hint of cleaning solvent, like ammonia. Brown stains had seeped into the ancient wood to mingle with other violent times back when they recorded history only by dance and chant. Had modern society made any improvements?

I turned to find Will Bonney inspecting me.

"Picking out an implement for a little skull-crushing?"

"If the crime calls for permanent justice."

Our eyes held steady, locked. Smile to smile. Will finally blinked and his smile broadened to cheerfulness. Again, I felt assured my own prankster geo-caching had not been discovered.

"To the car," he said, pointing the way. As we passed through the lobby Detective Kee and another detective stood with the registration desk manager going through print-outs. Sifting for anomalies, seeking out suspicious tourist behavior. Kee looked up and smiled and I waved.

"Buddy of yours?" I slipped my arm around Will's, and gave off an air of dismissive nonchalance.

"Oh, we just met. During the Oli P murder case. Detective Kee of the Big Island Police. I hear he is investigating a string of recent burglaries." I did feel his muscles tighten.

"No jeeps?" Oops, I stumbled in knowing too much, but he did not catch the gaffe.

"Oh, we rented a couple of cars first of the week. Used the hotel Jeeps only for dirt road hill climbs."

No, you didn't, I thought to myself. Not for general rambling. Detective Kee is not going to find you all checking out hotel vehicles the same hour the Lorca caper went down. They had this well planned, like a military operation.

There were five of them, two cars.

Everyone was so cordial, no stuffiness here. I wondered as the guest, or 'date' of their leader, I had passed some litmus test of social acceptance.

Something bothered me.

"Weren't there more of you?" That was said innocent enough.

"Oh, half our group decided to pack up early and head over to Maui."

Fleeing the scene of their crime, most likely. Or were they? This caused me some discomfort. Were they all in cahoots? Maybe some had been invited along to make the geo-caching party halfway legitimate. On the other hand, maybe the illusion of imminent capture I had initiated went too far. Out for my own lark did I have the right to mess with someone else's vacation, even if they were criminals on holiday?

We drove in two cars toward our diving boat at Honokōhau Harbor. The introductions went something like this, if I can recall all the quick exchanges of information. Carson Jackson and Adam Tate, the writers, were in the other car with all equipment. In our car, I sat in the passenger front seat, Will driving. In the back seat sat Cynthia, the blonde bombshell jock. And to my surprise, which I swallowed, masking all emotions, next to Cynthia sat the Spanish-looking girl who had joined their party at the later date. And, where I thought she was a pick-up of one of the guys, Cynthia had her arm around the young woman, Ramona. They held each other's hands. Ramona said nothing the entire trip, and sensing her inbred silence, I did not try to initiate conversation. I was not here to judge; to be floored by the truth of the situation, yes. This led me to a remarkable conclusion: Will Bonney was an open-minded individual, which spoke well of him, and more so, he must have no female encumbrances to deal with. Great, an unattached good-looking man, and leaving town in a few hours. What was I supposed to do? Put my head in his lap?

Cynthia explained she would be staying behind, with Ramona, to train for the upcoming Ironman Triathlon. I could see that, Cynthia for certain. Ramona looked a little more fragile, her eyes sunken, vacant. She kept clutching at a medallion on a gold necklace chain around her neck. For part of the drive I gained from Cynthia an education on the attributes of the island as an athletic proving ground. She could not have been nicer. It dawned on me of all the Beautiful People she alone had strength equal to most of the men, if not beyond, equal to even Will. If I were to parcel out jobs for a dangerous assignment who better to act as the ambivalent seductress, while at the same time breaking a man's neck. No. No, these people were not that cold-blooded. I mean, gut feel, they did seem nice. I revised my suspicions down to believing Cynthia would be the one to climb buildings to gain second floor entry. Lady Rambo. To the group, to the gang, she brought *strength*.

"Carson has published two fictional spy books," explained Will, motioning to the two men in the car in front of us, yet throwing glances in the rear view mirror, as if he expected to find an undercover police car trailing discreetly behind. "Clever plotting."

I said, "Not too clever, I hope. I want the protagonist to triumph and be righteous in the end, not full of tortuous misgivings. I'm tired where the spy or detective is overcoming alcoholism or is in the middle of a bad divorce. No moralizing atonement for me. Tell me a mystery straight and I will solve the crime before the story end." Pushing my luck a little but having a great time at reading faces.

Will giving me a response, another glance to the rearview mirror, not at invisible trailing cars, but at Cynthia.

"Nobility of cause makes the best plotting. Win or lose the action must be justified. All I can say of Carson's work, he's not yet at the top of the best sellers list, but his fan base is growing."

My nimble mind filled in the job descriptions of a gang, this gang, each with a required talent. Cynthia, *brawn*. Will Bonney, *leadership*, even *mastermind*. Carson Jackson, *operational planning*.

"And Mr. Tate, what does he do?"

"Adam works with his father in D.C. A think tank. The Dromedary Group, more of a gentleman's club exchanging data." *Intelligence gathering.*

There they were defined, a most interesting social and larceny club. I left out Ramona, the strange and distant woman. She did not fit any particulars, more ghost-like, her face weighed down by a melancholy.

We had arrived at the harbor marina and as quick boarded our boat, the *"Dive Sage."* Once we stowed our gear the lines were cast off, and with running lights, we bumped and rolled side to side into the incoming waves exiting the harbor's entrance, out into the forever unforgiving Pacific. Only a half hour later, the engine slowed, and stopped, the anchor pitched overboard.

Earlier, we had taken turns below changing into our wetsuits. It was soon apparent Ramona and Carson Jackson were not going to be joining our fun of swimming underwater in wet blackness with slimy, squiggly finny things.

I caught up with Cynthia on the bridge, away from the rest, the dive boat captain oblivious to our woman small talk.

"I have to ask, and I apologize if I am rude, but we Daynes have this cursed curiosity. Ramona seems non-communicative. Is she well?"

Once again, someone was giving me close inspection, a defining moment to see how much I could be trusted. I added, "This goes no further, I promise."

A clearing of Cynthia's throat as if what she was about to tell me had to be yanked guttural from the heart.

"Ramona was raped, savagely, a year ago by soldiers in her home country. Her parents were slaughtered in front of her eyes. Adam, on a government fact finding mission, stumbled across her, lying in a mental clinic, in deep shock. We have all had our roles in her recovery."

I took a gasping breath, my soul ached. I glanced down at Ramona, sitting at the stern of the boat, staring at the waves. Just staring with that nervous tugging at her necklace, like it was a protective talisman, warding off evil spirits, or worse, a cursed reminder of horrific events. Her life was reality not wished on anyone, not a make-up game of plots and scenarios. Not video war games or sweet sixteen parties of idyllic innocence. A cruel world existed out there, evil, inhuman by humans.

Believing I was finding the last pieces to a strange puzzle, I felt I knew the story, and let my next question seem casual, neutral as possible.

"Where's she from?"

"A small town near Bogotá."

Colombia. Lorca.

Chapter 46
The Other Real Captain

"Where are we?"

"Off the Captain Cook Monument." A shiver went up my spine. Will eased closer.

"Are you alright?"

"That name and the darkness reminds me a killer still roams free. Captain Jimmie Cooke. Makes me a little nervous that he might be out there somewhere, nearby, lurking. His insanity might make him believe I am a threat to him."

"Are you?"

"What?"

"A threat?"

"No, I'm not a threat to him…" I started to get this uneasy feeling; did the Beautiful People, at least Will, discover what I had done; did they think I was a threat to their security? What would they do? A diving accident? Cause the bends? I finished my statement trying to re-assert my confidence.

"Captain Jimmie, to pun the expression, made his own berth and now has to lay in it."

"I have a surprise for you."

"What?!" I jumped. Would I be wearing concrete flippers? He motioned to the boat captain who pulled out from a storage box a camera, an underwater camera. And not a tourist store bought instamatic. This was Discovery Channel quality. Here comes Madison, the female Jacques Cousteau. The Food TV Channel Network had to use this footage. I had scored. With the help of this new man in my life, soon leaving.

"Oh, Will, this is fantastic."

"On loan, so be careful. I heard you were a great photographer." We exchanged stone-faced smiles, each waiting for the other to make a slip. I think he sought to define my personality, gauge my reactions to these surprises not so much to believe I was the one who *muggled* the caches, as the geo-cachers would say.

I had wondered about the caches. Why play robbery like a game? As a pulp novel might say, 'they could case the joint' under the cover of being free-spirited rich, spoiled tourists. Devious and methodical planning lay underneath their façade. Someone of their group had scouted their target, meaning Lorca and his cliff-side mansion, and the hidden caches were laid out so no one would be found or caught with the burglary tools prior to their need. And knowing I had this knowledge, certainly the only outsider who knew of their illegal antics, would they wonder if I knew too much?

Already in my wetsuit, I made a grab for my diving gear. Before I flipped over the side, I flat outright told Will Bonney, "I am no threat to anyone." And meant it. I would tell no one what I knew, their secret was safe with me.

"We'll see." His reply did not give me a warm fuzzy feeling of comfort. I found myself sinking into an abyss where the noise of my regulator and my worried thoughts did not comfort.

The water was cold, dark, and deep, and I have miles to go before I sleep. Later, when at the bottom of the eerie tomb-dark ocean, with no one near, he grabbed my ankle. I thought all was over, most particularly my life.

Chapter 47
Treasure Island

"Okay, Madison, here comes Detective Kee. You have held Michael and I in suspense telling us your stories of night diving."

"Don't forget her saying she caught a ride with a sea turtle. Be careful, Madison, State Wildlife doesn't cite you for that." He laughed in good spirits, but I knew Michael wished to be back at the helm of running the hotel. I was no longer a priority in his world.

I had not gotten to the part of the biggest thrill of the night, and that required waiting for Detective Kee's arrival, after all it was a police matter.

Midnight in the closed dining room of the hotel, Michael had them turn on the lights and serve us mango juice, iced. And, now my audience of wise men had gathered. Good, true men.

"What's this about?" Detective Kee to the point, so I threw it back at him.

"I went night diving on a tour boat with a couple I met in Kona. We dove at Captain Cook's Monument." The name made the men flex. The name of Cook, with or without an 'e', had become a pox.

"And I found this." From beside my chair, I hoisted up a green-rusted ammunition box and put it in the middle of the table.

"World War II Army surplus," affirmed my father.

"And this is what you brought me out from town to see?" Detective Kee was close to throwing a fit, so I opened the lid and dumped the jewelry all over the table. Rings, bracelets, necklaces, even a tiara. All real stones from diamonds to rubies and emeralds, a galaxy of dazzle.

From two of them, I gained the expected epitaph of a curse exclamation. Jeffrey only said, "Fascinating."

"They are real aren't they?" But even in asking Michael saw such beauty could not be factory manufactured.

"Anyone want to take a guess on value?" A little fun to bring them back to the enormity of this find. Jeffrey gave his off-the-cuff appraisal.

"A half million, maybe a million at the right auction house. Some of the stone settings look quite old."

"And where did you say you found this... 'treasure'?" Detective Kee had pulled out his ever-faithful notepad, poised to take evidence. I knew I had to get my story right and not fumble the telling. There were a few modified discrepancies to protect the guilty I saw as innocent.

"Better yet, let me show you." In an instant I had Dad's laptop and inserted the disk from the underwater camera. I fast forwarded through murky shots of me getting used to handling the equipment, fast forwarded through the manta ray shots, hundreds of them, back lit from the boat's underwater spot lights. My dad interjected, "Very good, Madison. We can use that."

The camera motion shifted, actually the stop button had been pushed. It was at this moment, unknown to my current audience Will had grabbed my ankle, and I flinched at an anticipated 'accidental' drowning. When the show resumed I was no longer behind the lens, but in front of it. That's what Will had silently sought to signal to me, allowing me the honor of a little stardom. Little did I know at the time, I was being manipulated.

"And that's you," the policeman recognized my curves. "Who's using the camera?"

"The guy's name is William, and his wife's name is Cynthia. I never did get their last names. From Ohio, I think."

Kee made a notation. To give my statement validity, the camera swung over to watch Cynthia effortlessly glide by.

"Nice buoyancy," said my father, gaining snorts from the men, a glare from me. Wait till she wins the Triathlon; quite possible.

"Here I am again. We had been diving out farther, but started going closer to shore. Did you know that Captain Cook was killed on this spot in 1779?" I knew Michael knew, but continued. "Since that time the ocean has risen, and the actual spot of his death is now 10 feet offshore. I had heard there might be a plaque underwater and lined up to the monument on shore and headed that way." Will Bonney had planted the idea aboard ship, and with subtle camera directing led me in the direction he wanted me to go. Gad, so perfect at the subterfuge. Adam Tate swam to the side with another underwater spot light, the undulating temperature in the water currents casting vibrating beams, like looking through jello.

The film sequence shows me kicking in the distant murkiness, at the edge of the light beam's radius. I go over this rock, and then twist around to see what I thought I saw. From the men's perspective I discovered the ammunition box sitting on a large round chunk of coral. In truth, I turned back because it looked like, and I am sure it was, the actual ammunition box, from the geo-caching, the box with the white bags of powder contained within. Could Will see my expression through my face mask, more mortification at what I knew, than surprise? Now, knowing the part I was to play, I slowly opened the military canister, held up a handful of neck-laces, one gold chain, quite similar to the one around Ramona's neck. I even gave off exciting thumbs up to Cynthia and Will. The camera followed as I swam back to the boat, lugging along my own special cache discovery. I liked the game and would miss playing.

I finally understood what the Beautiful People had been up to. This jewelry I had 'discovered' had been stolen and stolen twice. First by a death squad, and later stolen again in retribution, the white bags of powder left behind to exact revenge. Death would be too merciful for Mr. Lorca. Dealing with the American judicial system could equate to a slow, tedious bureaucratic death. With all his money, the evidence would be destructive in the hands of rabid government prosecutors, jail time assured, I hoped, along, as I am sure, were the wishes of the Beautiful People. In truth, as I saw it, the blind woman called Justice is not fair. If I were Ramona I would opt for a surgical knife and be locked in a room with a trussed up Mr. Lorca.

Chapter 48
The Secret Pact

The CD film had run its course. They were amazed. Michael fondling a brace-let, thinking I'm sure of draping it around Kuikahi's wrist. Detective Kee did not catch the stealth of my film work. Filming did not occur on board the boat, no faces seen. My own idea.

"Would you like to hear my theory?" I got immediate nods, and with a dra-matic flourish dropped on the table in front of Detective Kee, two jeweled earrings, not matching. He picked them up as if sacred, as they were.

"The Lorca robbery," said the Detective, shaking his head for comprehension. "They are identical to the ones on the cocaine bags. How did you —?"

I began. "I don't know how or why this 'cache of jewels' ended up at this spot or how I chanced upon it. The location, as I was told, is right at the spot of a very popular snorkeling site. So within a day or so someone else would have stumbled across it." I paused for the effect, for the impact coming.

"Detective Kee, if you confront Lorca he will deny ownership. These I am guessing are the spoils taken from his Death Squad victims in Columbia. There will be no claimants, as probably there are no survivors."

My father, a past legal beagle, thought he saw his daughter as a mercenary, or worse, a corsair, a pirate.

"If no one claims these jewels, then the finder is entitled to a major chunk of the value, after the state takes a tax cut. And you, Madison, are the finder."

The men looked at me in a different light, a callous money-grubbing harpy. Gaining a reward after what I've been through this last week sounded fair trade to me, but not my style.

"No, I don't want any part of this… loot. This is blood money. But I don't think it wise to merely turn it over to the police. Sorry, detective, the police might get a cut of any proceeds for a new police car, then the state's unclaimed property division will tax it into nothingness. Fees, legal bills, false owners, even sticky fingers, all will eat up what we see as value here. I have a better solution." And when I told them, and they debated the merits, in the end, all three agreed. Another group of conspirators I had joined.

I passed the litmus test of the Beautiful People that night. With the ammunition 'treasure' box I knew it had been placed on the coral by one of them; a set up. How easy to drive over to the monument during the day and snorkel out to the hiding spot. On the boat, Will started the ethical battle when he pulled out a handful of the Lorca loot and said, "I think we should divide this up and go our separate ways."

Emphatically, I argued, "No, this goes directly to the police. It is lost or stolen property."

"What if the owner doesn't want it back," jumped in Adam Tate. "What if it turned out to be stolen, the owner has to prove ownership, maybe he can't."

"Finders keepers," said Carson, giving it one last shot in offering complicity. I called their bluff.

"Let's all take it to the police. You can claim a reward for recovery."

I saw Ramona wince and turn away. Perhaps she saw the necklace match to the one her fist clung to, or recognized jewelry belonging to a neighbor.

"Frankly," I said, stamping my foot, playing my indignant role. "I want nothing to do with it. On the spot where Captain Cook was slain, it has to be cursed. No, the police must be brought in."

Which I did, only in a different way. And the Beautiful People acceded to my moral position, and that's what they wanted, to put me to a test. They wanted to be absolutely certain I was honest. An initiation rite? For what reason and purpose, I don't know. Was I now a member of the Beautiful People honorary status society? I don't think so. I did feel a little good, maybe a little bit comfortable with myself. An accomplishment my mother would have been proud of. She had to be smiling.

Still, the lousy part of the evening was the farewell at the airport. Even with the role play to someone else's script it had been a fun evening. Ramona and Cynthia remained with the rental car and would drop me off at the hotel. I waited while Will and his two writer buddies checked in. The old gang, so to speak, was breaking up. Temporarily, I wondered?

This was not to be a mushy-mushy kissy-kissy goodbye. I was exhausted, not feeling urges of romanticism, if any existed. I felt this deep vibe not yet defined and considering my track record with men, I sought the proper soliloquy for his departure. Will voiced the words out of my mouth.

"This could be the beginning of a beautiful friendship."

His touched sincerity made me honestly like him. I tried to respond appropriately as a mature woman, and failed, dammit.

"Yeah, for never seeing you again. Just what is it that you do, Mr. Bonney? We never got around to who you are?" I prepared to steel myself to the letdown that a certified public accountant, or a worse, a small town mortuary owner, might have sparked my interest.

That deep laugh again. "Miss Dayne, you are an adventuress by happenstance born by malevolent intrigues; I am an adventurer by design, a fixer of impossibilities. I believe we are destined to meet again, and not by fate but by calculation. Goodbye."

Gallant to the end, his grin was his farewell, and he departed to his boarding gate. I understood him a little better, too late: *The Count of Monte Cristo* departing from his *Treasure Island*, taking not island postcards, but a suitcase of literary mementos from his most recent escapade.

Would he remember me; but for how long before other females, more attractive and interesting, came into his life? We really didn't get to know each other, never really sat and talked our philosophies, our likes and dislikes. Come to think of it, I don't think he's my type.

"Madison Dayne."

What? I turned into his quick embrace, his kiss to my lips, too brief, moist, unexpected. My eyes closed.

"Your island souvenir," whispered hot in my ear.

My eyes opened. Vanished before my arms could wrap around him, to stop him from leaving. I shook my head at empty space where he had been seconds ago. Damn, he was good. *My Honest Rogue.* A man in control, this fixer of impossibilities. Watch out, Mr. Bonney, I am definitely an impossibility.

I looked back on this last week at my used up quota of near death experiences, or as Will put it, at these 'malevolent intrigues' and the men who so briefly touched my world: A killer, a thief, and a betrothed king. Online dating can't beat this.

Chapter 49
Evening of Few Regrets

I woke to Dad's invitation to dinner for our last night on the island, and I accepted with nothing better to do and wanting to be with my main man.

Tonight, I would be his fairy princess and dressed in my white cotton dress, a light wrap over my shoulders, sandals with pink trim. Thinking back, recalling my childhood when we all would dress up and go to the country club for special dinners, I would try to behave like a grown-up.

Now, only two of us, both growing a little on this trip, dependent on each other's strengths.

I had been certain our last meal would have been with Chef Lorenzo in his restaurant. Instead, we walked to the beach. On the sand, hotel staff had sculpted out a level area and I found a table set, white tablecloth under fine china and Reidel wine glasses. Off to the side a cooking prep table with a burner. My father, Jeffrey Dayne, said to me,

"Tonight will be special. Many great times in the past Elizabeth and I created new dishes and cooked together, it is the proper moment to place those memories in a special place inside the heart, and start building anew."

He handed me a store-bought apron, the label boasting the fabric had been dyed in grey volcanic dirt. Featured on the front was a brightly colored cartoon caricature of a skimpily clad island wahine, eyeing the world with a smoldering, seductive look, while standing at the ocean's edge holding a bubbling tiki cocktail. The apron caption read: *When in doubt, go to the beach!*

"I want you and I," he said, "to fix a dinner that Daniel Thiebaut sent down from his restaurant. A recipe to place in our own special memory book."

The setting sun over a receding tide our backscape; Tiki torches to soften the approaching night's embrace, hinting of a past culture, of those who cooked by fire glow.

I reveled in nature fulfilled: a whale breeched just at the moment of the green flash, and the most special of all: Jeffrey gave me a cooking lesson, my first as a foodie; what a privilege.

"We're going to do Daniel's 'Asian Crab-coated Mon'chong with a Sweet Chili Beurre Blanc."

"Sounds delish. What's a mon-chong?"

"Growing in popularity on the islands. Chefs can do a lot with mon'chong when people are tired of ono and mahimahi preparations. A deep water fish, medium flaky in texture with a high fat content for grilling, as we will do."

"You mean, everything here on the beach?" No problem. The crab crust first, next, grill the fish, and then the sauce."

And we did, father and daughter side by side.

He read out the ingredients.

Recipe: Asian Crab Crust

1/8 cup heavy cream
2 ounces coconut milk
¼ can chicken soup
2 teaspoons corn starch
8 oz. crab meat
4 Shittake mushrooms (which I diced small)
1 Tablespoon red bell pepper (diced small)
1 Tablespoon basil, fresh, chopped
1 Tablespoon cilantro, fresh, chpooed ½ teaspoon ginger, chopped fi-ne
1 Kaffir lime leaf, finely chopped
¼ teaspoon chilli garlic sauce
Juice of ¼ lemon

"Okay, blend cream and coconut milk. Add all ingredients in saucepan, thicken with cornstarch."

"It seems like we are making more than for two."

"Actually a serving for 4." We split tasks. My assignment was to grill the fish on both sides, and set aside. Next I moved over to a wok on the grill to stir fry vegetables and bay bok choy. Jeffrey, in whirl of hand movement created the sauce.

Sweet Chili Beurre Blanc

2 cups of white wine
1 Tablespoon shallots, minced
1 cup of cream
½ cup butter (cut in small pieces)

"Madison, I am going to reduce the wine with shallots by half." The smells began to rise from wok and sauce pans. I sniffed to inhale each dish. "Now, add the cream and we reduce for another 3-4 minutes."

He turned to the fish, coating one side of the fish with 2 table spoons of crab crust mixture, and sprinkled with paprika. We had a small convection oven, where, I don't know how, plugged into some portable power source. He baked the fish at 375 degrees for 3 to 4 minutes.

The vegetables and bok choy first on 2 hot plates (remember though this is a recipe for four). Top with the crab-crusted fish. Just as he was to ready to pour the sauce around the fish, he added a Monte au Beurre, seasoned to taste. 4 Table-spoons of sweet chili (he used the brand May Ploy)—he poured into the butter sauce as he was serving. Garnishes included green onion, diced tomatoes, and ses-ame seeds. Jeffrey added, but optional back mainland, hijiki, calcium-rich seaweed.

Monte au Beurre

Bring 2 Tbsp. water to a simmer in a small saucepan over medium heat.
Reduce heat to medium-low, and gradually whisk in 1 lb. unsalted butter,
1 Tbls. at a time, until water and butter have emulsified.
Keep temperature between 180-190
(if the mixture boils, it will seperate).
Use Monte au Beurre immediately,
or keep it warm in a pan set over a pot of simmering water over medium-low heat.

We sat to dine, satisfied at our creation, anxious to see if our palates agreed.

During dinner, each morsel was tasted with selfish lingering, swimming our palate with a longing desire of more, sad to see the former chewing swallowed, the next bite too soon on our fork. Such debauchery in toying and caressing our food gave us plenty of time to dawdle in our table conversation. Our subject matter remained light and we avoided the tribulations of the last few days, except the latest which my father had to revisit.

"So we all agreed, the four of us, that the jewelry would not be turned over to the authorities. Michael will keep the jewelry secured in the hotel safe. Detective Kee will do his own personal investigation, try to discover any rightful owners, or at least, a list of the victim's families still living."

I finished the bargain struck. "And with time, the jewelry will be sold and through the Cooke Foundation, the residual funds will be distributed to the survivors of Lorca's killings."

"Yes, a nicely tied bundle of a good deed."

"I still worry that Captain Jimmie will suddenly appear and smash everyone's good intentions. Or what if this Lorca asshole beats the drug charges?"

"Michael said he didn't see Captain Jimmie wanting to show his head around here again. By local customs his loss of face makes him a nonperson. Anyway, I thought Detective Kee had a splendid solution: blame all of Lorca's legal problems, including the alleged planting of drug evidence, on Captain Jimmie. Make our fugitive a fink. And as our own official policeman stated: 'If Lorca ever gets out of jail, or has cronies on the outside who still do his bidding, let evil search out evil'."

At dinner's close, how sweet of him, my father gave me a present in wrapping paper with surfboard designs. A new camera to replace mine, drowned in the sailboat sinking, eons ago. This new camera was a beaut.

He handed me another package.

"This came for you this afternoon."

My name in block letters on plain wrapping paper. No postage. No return address. I held it at arm's length.

My father laughed with the knowing.

"I listened. Nothing ticking inside."

A fool for gifts, I ripped it open, found the contents plastic wrapped. A book, no, a manuscript of yellow pages, set in a faded, leather-cracked folder, ink written in an elaborate scrawl. A cookbook of sorts. I passed it over to Jeffrey.

"Good God. *The Andrews Receipt Book*— the first Hawaiian Cookbook. Look here's a date in the margin. 1842. And recipes written in Hawaiian and translated. Amazing. Wonderful. Who sent this to you?" He knew where it had originated from and realized another disturbing connection: Lorca, the burglary, and me.

Above our heads, stars engorged the heavens. "I don't have a clue." But I did.

"Well, we have to get this to Detective Kee. Evidence in that burglary, but I am sure since you started him on stretching the law, he'll find a way to have a museum become conservator. Lorca won't need this back. This is a cultural treasure for the island and the public must see it on display." That word 'treasure' was a word with new meaning.

"Exactly." Whoever sent this gift knew I would do the right thing. I looked to my father, smitten, as he slowly leafed through the manuscript, delicately, ignoring value but seeking the culinary soul of this rediscovered holy relic.

"We will return it, after we copy it," I said. And Jeffrey nodded, happy as the proverbial kid on Christmas morning. With my new camera I captured his elation. Special moments, special person.

As he thumbed the pages, seeking a starting point, a notation in the margin on one page caught my attention, and I asked to view part of the loose-leaf manuscript. The number scribbles were not 200 plus years old in the archaic penmanship of the 1800s author, Lorrin Andrews. No, the writing was more recent, quite modern.

GPS coordinates. N 35° 40. — W 105° 57. — .

My face expelled many expressions, starting with open mouth and wide-eyed, like a slow turning projector reel, from startled to confused, from surprise into enlightenment, more so, wonderment teased with caution.

In that moment, I understood: on that page, a message for only one to decipher.

And I had — an invitation.

My father, perplexed, watched the facial range of my metamorphous.

"Are you alright?"

"Yes, quite."

Later in the evening when we let the night mellow to perfection, he asked, "Where do you want to go next on our foodie travel?"

"New Mexico." My answer, no hesitation, uttered with a single laugh, a smile curling in strange appreciation at someone else's deviousness. The coordinates had to be for a location somewhere in Nevada. Will's T-shirt, the one at the airport, so long ago, had been the GPS location of Nevada. If all things worked out, after New Mexico, maybe we'd pop over to Vegas. I hope, hope. Intuition on my part, if not undefined hope.

I had thought when this question of next destination came up, considering everything that happened this week, I would say 'no,' that this would be my first, and thankfully my last culinary adventure. Yet, by the laws of womanhood, I can change my mind, in fact, several times over. Definitely, the mysterious invitation beckoned, but more important, I did not want to lose the give-take camaraderie I had with my father. What I was feeling now, a full tummy from a meal immensely enjoyed both in the creation and the devouring—plus two glasses of wine. To the conversation I added specifics.

"Santa Fe suits me."

"I was thinking of New Orleans."

"Southwestern cuisine and Navajo-Hopi culture."

"Creole cooking, jazz, and zydeco."

"Insatiable Santa Fe." I thought I had him.

"And, just where does this Will Bonney reside?" He had me.

"Taos."

"Isn't that somewhere near Santa Fe?"

A shooting star arced the night sky, and just before we left the beach, I thought I saw a mermaid pirouette across a wave.

Recipe: Mango Jubilee
(Serves Two)

1 Mango, diced 2oz Brown Sugar 2oz Butter
1oz Kahlua Liquor 1oz Cream
Melt butter in a saute pan. Add Brown Sugar and mix well.
Add diced Mango and Saute for 2 minutes,
flambe with Kahlua Liquor and add Cream.
Place in soup plate with Coconut Ice Cream on top.

Recipe from Daniel Thiebaut and his restaurant in Kamuela

Chapter 50
Closing Ceremonies, Opening Broadsides

Michael Ka'aiea bade us farewell. In fact, the entire front office staff stood formally to mark our island exit with aloha.

"You seem to have shipped them into shape rather quickly." I gave him one of my friendship smiles. This time not dressed in warrior regalia, he looked like a hotel executive should, white slacks, his Hawaiian shirt strong with purple-gold colors.

"With new ownership, a reason to outdo themselves."

"Yes, I heard about the new ownership. I hope it will be used for good intentions."

"If there is a good business plan…"

"Miracles will follow."

We both laughed and then exchanged awkward glances, something more to be said, void of the right words, unsure and inept to the right order.

A hostess handed him a lei of pale ivory flowers. He placed it around my neck, with everyone watching placed pecks on my cheek, quick and official, though the heat of touch lingered. After all, he was the new head honcho of the Ho`oilina Kai Grand Resort and I must be special. Kings don't kiss commoners.

"These flowers are from me to you. Aloha." He wore the same lei, like mine, odd that with each flower the petals were half gone.

Music caught my attention, and I turned as we all did. From the garden amphitheater, a procession stepped its way up toward a flattened hill alongside the main hotel roadway.

In jest, I deadpanned fake disbelief. "Not another ceremony?"

"Dedication of the future convention center. Progress moves forward. Good-bye, Madison. Come back soon. Thank you, Mr. Dayne. You did more than you could ever realize." Jeffrey nodded, shy to the compliment. Two lovely women draped him with orchid lei, followed with customary ritual smooches. I liked mine better.

Michael walked over and joined the multitudes, many dressed in colorful Hawaiian aloha shirts. I saw no segregated groups walking with their own brand of colors. Nor were the people only of Hawaiian descent. *We Are The World* marched.

Jeffrey and I boarded the hotel van. The staff waved at us and returned to usher in the next wave of happy tourists. Our van slowly trailed behind the crowd who had spilled into the roadway, apologetically blocking our way. Not like the protest mob on our arrival.

"The building footprint seems enormous." Flags of nations staked along the four boundaries, two football fields in size. I caught a glimpse of Kukui, blessed as Kuikahi, standing with vestry priests on a small mound of dirt. No longer a hula dancer, she looked more like a... miniature Desi Cardoza... styled less as hotel employee, more... regal? Her presence, her facial expression an air of confidence, maturity the wind tugging at her flowered dress. Is this what a royal consort might look like at a building dedication, or a fiancée to a successful executive?

Jeffrey studied the event in the making. The traffic clogged our vehicle to a halt and we could view the start of the dedication festivities.

"Seems like a few multi-million dollar home sites might have been sacrificed for the tourism convention dollar. That might have been a smart move."

"Michael's?"

"Captain Jimmie Cooke's Master Plan."

"What if he comes back? What if he beats the charges? He'll take it all away from Michael, reap the good that's being done. Look at the people here. The locals usually are angry about something. They're upbeat. A convention center means more jobs. We can't let Captain Jimmie use the hotel to become a stepping stone to the Governorship."

"Captain James Cooke is not coming back. *Ever.*"

"What?"

"Can I tell you a little about when in ancient times they created their heiaus or built royal enclosures?"

"What do you mean he's not coming back? He took off in his boat."

"Did he?" I fell silent. Jeffrey Dayne wanted to put me straight.

"The ancient Hawaiians wanted to secure their structures against evil spirits. They wanted their gods of strength to bless and protect them, so they buried spirit totems who would invoke the proper incantation, to ward off evil spirits, to welcome friendly gods. Look there."

Two warriors, each followed by a priest, entered from opposite sides. The warriors, in native dress, carried two white wooden boxes, like a small steamer trunk … like a child's coffin. My mind started spinning.

"Father," I spoke his name, drawn out in my fear, wanting to hear his story, not wanting to hear. "What's in those boxes?"

"If I were to guess, in one box are the bones of Joe Pa'ao, the priest."

"Father, what's in the other box?"

"Your guess?"

"No way." Disjointed sparks flew together. The shark's tooth from the club, the kettle boiling a sludge viscosity. Two nights in a row.

"Captain Cooke cooked," I said.

No one else was in the van, the driver outside waiting for the crowds to move out of the roadway, observing the unfolding spectacle.

"In 1779," my father continued, "when the Hawaiians killed Captain Cook they put him in a fire, burned off all the soft issue, and divided his bones among all the lesser chiefs. It was a special honor to have the bones of this mighty chief, the god Lono they had originally thought. The British sailors had to go around and trade to gain back enough bones so explorer Cook could be interred in England. Were all bones acquired? Perhaps certain bones remained on this island and were passed down through the generations. Perhaps the bone that one priest is waving above the boxes is a talisman of the first European. Such a holy relic could conjure up a lot of serious mojo."

"What are they going to do?"

"Not the expert, I would say Ying and Yang, Hawaiian feng shui. Opposite forces to bring all unsettled issues, past and future, into spiritual balance. It looks like the bones will be buried at the two corner posts of the entry door to the convention center. The bones of a kahuna, Joe Pa'ao, will sanctify goodness, bless this place. Cooke's bones, not as evil, but bones of a great enemy will warn off the evil spirits: see what can happen if you try to come in here and cause trouble."

"But why not at the heiau? That would be important in revitalizing the ancient religion."

"I don't know. Michael told me the convention center was special."

"You talked to Michael? When?"

"This morning. I asked him if he had sent that package, the cookbook, to you, and he said 'no.' Also, I told him my theory on how Hawaiian truths become Island legends."

The van finally headed out to the highway, to the airport, where as we drove, I looked over the lava fields with their winsome tuffs of grass, growing out of the rock, brittle life clinging in a harsh climate. As I listened to Jeffrey's theory, I tried to read all the graffiti of white sea coral as we whizzed by, hoping to spot a message left for me. *Mad 2 LVE* came the closest.

"Michael said the night of our sailboat mishap…"

Still very vivid in my nightmares. "You mean almost blown up and nearly drowned?"

"He heard about the evil Captain Cooke."

"I found him and told him."

Jeffrey knew I would always be his bothersome nettle. He continued.

"This is somewhat my conjecture. Michael gathered up members of his court, the priests and warriors from the lū'au." Or, as I now knew, they got together after boiling up old Joe Coffee into wax and bones. I should tell my father, the cook, boiled human flesh has a distinct odor.

"Their guess is that Jimmie, having believed we were at the bottom of the lagoon, retreated to his yacht. After my statement to the police I was up most of the night restless, sitting out on my room deck, watching shooting stars, reviewing all we had faced. I saw the old war canoe, like a shadow, move across the harbor.

The Hawaiians rowed out and confronted Joe Coffee's killer and exacted revenge equal to the crime."

I could see this. A smug Captain Jimmie looking up to see feathered and masked warriors enter his office. A weapon raised.

"Conked with a shark's teeth war club, the lāʻau pā lau."

My surprise tidbit exasperated his story telling.

"How do you know that!? Did Michael tell you that?"

"No, conjecture on my part." Jeffrey knew otherwise.

"The police found feathers around the deck they couldn't explain. Costume feathers if they feel further investigation warranted. Probably not. They're looking for an escaped killer, not a floating crime scene."

"Captain Cooke ends up in a box, put there by religious paniola vigilantes." Island cowboys. "But what about this 'Master Plan?'"

"The file of Corsair Capital…"

"A caloric rapist." I could tease as well as receive.

"Yes, Madison. When Detective Kee showed me the file, empty from what I had seen on the captain's ship-office desk. "

"Ah, Sherlock, a Master Plan to power, purloined by suspects unknown."

"Not unknown. There were two separate thefts, the first was the file, taken after Captain Cooke was fatally confronted by Michael and the elders. Michael probably knew what the file contained, perhaps even helped in researching in its creation."

Michael. I would find it hard to reconcile Michael's involvement in another man's death, even if it was revenge on his uncle's killing. An idea struck me to the serious side. "Not a Master Plan but a 'Business Plan'."

"A good choice of words. I told Michael, speaking vaguely, suggesting that whoever took those papers, and if they could control the foundation, could do good for the island people, or could be subverted by the same greed that poisoned Captain Jimmie's sense of decency, his quest for personal glory. On the other hand, I told him, Captain Jimmie could be half way to Tahiti by now."

"And the boat is missing."

"That cabin cruiser probably sleeps with the fishes, deep-sixed in a thousand fathoms. To the police and public Captain Jimmie will be on the run forever, his only fame as an outlaw legend."

"When in fact, he's a Jimmy Hoffa foundation footer for a convention door."

We had arrived at the airport's passenger departure and began the process of security screening to our gate. "What was Michael's response to your tale of current Hawaiian history?"

"Did you not take note of our great send-off ? As head chief he will be glad when the great iron bird takes flight to LAX."

Chapter 51
New Positioning

Jeffrey went off to buy a local newspaper. I browsed the gift shop, making no purchases. My Hawaiian trinkets of remembrances would have to be mixed memories. In refrigerated coolers, I spied the lei for tourist sales. Selling them was a venerable, wrinkled Hawaiian woman in her mu'umu'u, who sat stringing dendrobium orchids. I politely interrupted her concentration to ask if there was any significance to the white flower lei I wore.

"They don't seem to be orchids," I queried, politely. "Half the petals are missing."

The old woman gave a strange, faraway look. Her eyes closed and her lips moved in murmurs. Heavy seconds passed.

"Hawaiian give this to you?"

"Yes."

"Naupaka, the flower of separated lovers, when royalty cannot marry commoner. Kapu. Torn in parting sorrow, Naupaka took a flower from her ear and tore it in half and gave the other to Kaui, one lover to the mountains, the other to the beach, never to be together. Plants were so sad they began to grow like Naupaka's flower with only half their petals. Hawaiian give this to you, means heavens will cry soon. That he is crying."

My father had been standing behind me, listening.

My fingers played with a flower petal, my sadness too obvious.

"You know he did like you, maybe even more than the word 'like.'"

"I don't know." I walked with him, the lei maker watching our departure, certainly wondering what spells we haoles had cast on one of their own.

"As he tries to succeed, king or businessman, Michael has to bear his own personal demon, the responsibility of tradition."

"He has Kuikahi by his side."

"Perhaps, but did you really analyze the ceremony, observe the stilted motions of a script written by the old priests? Tradition. Ancient rules void of flexibility to modern sensibilities."

Jeffrey put his arm around me with a supportive hug.

"Madison, if it's a future marriage, it's an arranged one, and I believe not his first choice. Heavy the shoulders of he who wears the Naupaka lei. He had to sacrifice the woman he wished to love to help the people he loved."

I walked to the outdoor waiting area, wanting to leave as soon as possible, tears in my eyes. I watched the airplanes land and take off, people escaping to, escaping from. The weather was changing. Dark storm clouds hugged by rain squalls moved on the horizon toward the island of Hawai'i.

"The Master Plan is a masterstroke."

My father showed me the local paper, the front page headline. "Public to Vote on Casinos." I read the lead paragraph. A State Senator introduced a bill in the Hawai'i legislature calling for a statewide referendum legalizing casino gambling. Jeffrey encapsulated the news:

"The story goes on to say that the casino can only be owned or controlled by those local citizens with twenty-five percent or more of Hawaiian blood ancestry. Note: they did not say 100% Hawaiian blood. And one casino will be designated on only one island for a ten-year monopoly to test the viability, and then, voters will decide if they want casinos on other islands. Guess which island is the test case?"

The Master Plan, a business plan, initiated to run a fated course.

"This island."

"What building do you know on this island will be big enough to accommodate gaming tourists from mainland and Asia?

"The future Ho'oilina Kai Grand Resort Convention Center."

"Paragraph three of the story; notice who introduced the legislation," I read aloud.

"State Senator Raymond Kee of O'ahu." In my mind, I saw a Banyan family tree with multi-dangling roots.

Little impressed Jeffrey; here, he smiled.

"The Master Plan is moving beyond one single grab at power. There may not need to be political insurrection to replace democracy with monarchy. A casino will create a vast pool of wealth. The empowered meek will not inherit the earth; they will buy it, beginning with an island."

Our flight called, we waited our turn to walk to the plane. Feather moist gusts stirred the air, wind blowing me away, as it had blown me here. I watched a private jet pull up to the terminal a hundred yards away, next to another, both having arrived within minutes of each other. I drew Jeffrey's attention to the side-by-side jets, sleek, expensive.

We let other passengers walk past us and paused at the bottom of our jet's boarding steps. I pointed.

"That logo on the plane tail looks familiar."

"Yes. Four Aces is their symbol. The first, or is it the second, largest casino corporation in the world. The land sharks smell fresh dollars to munch on and are circling."

Poor Michael. Did he know what he must face: lobbyist pressures, the political infighting? I watched a gaggle of dark-suited men, no one greeting them with aloha, totally out of Island synch, march to a waiting cherry red Escalade chariot.

Our flight attendant called down to us; we were the last boarding. As I climbed the steps, the door of the second private jet sprung open, steps extended. Two young Asian men, impeccably dressed, came off the jet, each carrying a fluffy Toy Pekinese dog. A woman, head erect, looking to be in her late sixties, using an ornate cane as her guide with firm stabs at the ground walked with purpose to her chauffeured opal white limousine. I knew.

"The Queen Mother returneth."

Jeffrey concurred.

"Tsin Kee, the estranged mother, to claim the rightful place near her son." I truly felt sorry for Kuikahi and the coming battle of feminine wills.

I looked to the departing vehicles and spoke more to myself, "Arriving arrogant like past seafaring conquerors." I saw a sun ray pierce the approaching storm, splitting the color spectrum into a misty rainbow.

"This time it will be different. They haven't yet met King Michael Laka Ka'aiea the First and his Anuenue people."

Raindrops kissed my face.

Insatiable Jeffrey Dayne shut one mental menu and opened another. Before entering the cabin to search out our seats in scrunched cattle-car humanity, my father teased, jokester that he is, "I wonder who makes the best tequila-lime carnitas tacos in Santa Fe?"

"Santa Fe? Isn't that close to Taos?" asked I, his stalwart daughter, Madison Merlot Dayne.

Acknowledgments

This is the 10th Anniversary Edition. And again, I wish to thank the original cast of friends and supporters who brought this foodie travel mystery to life.

In my library I hold precious the first edition of *A Dictionary of the Hawaiian Language* by Lorrin Andrews, 1865, printed by Henry M. Whitney of Honolulu. The first Hawaiian dictionary was a 30 year labor of love by Mr. Andrews and contains approximately 15,500 words.

Achieving the proper island nuances and spellings were painstakingly overseen by Leslie Lang (leslielang.com), an accomplished freelance writer. Her husband, photographer Macario, and daughter, Emma Rose, provided a view into comfortable Hilo home life. Thanks for the farm fresh eggs, tangerines, and avocados. [Since this book was first published Macario passed away, and my total sympathy of the loss of a creative artist]

Appreciation to photographer Barrett Adams and his wife, seahorse enthusiast Christy Adams and to Chef Amy Ferguson (www.CaterHawaii. com) who gave the behind-the-scene culinary tour.

Artists, who provide rich island interpretations, interpretations, several works which are displayed in my home, need to receive accolades and require a visit to their portfolios. Kathy Long (KathyLong.com), Brad Parker who painted the art used on the cover (tikishark.com), last art in the book, 'King K' by the late Herb Kawainui Kane — "A Living Treasure of Hawai'i" (HerbKaneStudio.com), and Cindy Coats (www.CindyCoats.com), Joanna Carolan of Kaua'i and the late master, John Kelly.

Ancient rock art depicted throughout book from "Petroglyphs of Hawaii" by L.R. McBride (1969, The Petroglyph Press, Hilo). Updated copies of this book are available.

And always, to wife Pamela, who enjoys the Big Island and all its best features, from culinary to whale watching. Visit her Facebook site: Kitchen a'stir.

'King K' by artist Herb Kawainui Kane

Quest Mystery

Following the mid 2020 republication of the first Quest Mystery, *Vegas Die*, the updated *Captain Cooked* reflects the impact of Covid 19 and the pandemic on treasure hunters. Meaning that in 2020-2021 readers (including the author) can't easily travel to Hawai'i and hide and search for clues to a treasure. As such, the cash prize treasure in this book is hidden somewhere in the 9th Island, Las Vegas, Nevada. More information, rules & regs, perhaps more clues, can be found at the author's website: www.spgrogan.com

Recipe: Madison's Apartment Kalua Pig Out

I call it this for those who have tasted imu cooked pig
and want to try this at home, inexpensively.

1 pork butt
1 tablespoon Hawaiian or Kosher salt
1 tablespoon liquid smoke

Place the pork in a roaster pan on a rack (this will drain off extra fat).
Season the pork with salt and liquid smoke.
If you can find ti leaves, cover the pork with the leaves. Cover with foil.
Do use the foil even if you can't find Ti leaves.
Roast in the oven at 325 degrees for 4 hours. When cooled, shred the meat.

[Still won't be as good as the Kalua Pig & Cabbage entree
I discovered at Bamboo Restaurant up in Hāw'i.]

Aloha Brunch Bread Pudding

2 tablespoons butter
1 cup diced Maui onion
½ cup chopped red and yellow bell pepper
1 Hawaiian chile very finely chopped (omit this if your guests are wimps)
¾ teaspoon sea salt
¼ teaspoon black pepper
2 teaspoons minced garlic
1 tablespoon chopped parsley
1 tablespoon chopped cilantro
1 tablespoon fresh chopped thyme
¼ cup dark Hana Bay Rum
1 teaspoon vanilla
1 cup diced Portuguese sausage
6 slices of bacon, cooked and crumbled
8 eggs
3 cups whole milk
1 cup heavy cream
8 cups stale Portugese Sweet Bread (such as King's Hawaiian)
2 cups Gruyere or Swiss cheese, shredded
Paprika

Preheat oven to 350 degree.
Lightly grease a 9 X 13 inch baking dish with 2 tbs. of butter.
Heat 2 T of butter in a sauté pan at med to high heat and add the onions,
peppers and garlic until soft. Add the parsley, cilantro and thyme.
Add Rum and reduce slightly. Remove from heat.
In another pan, cook the sausage and cook until brown & remove from heat.
In a large bowl, combine the milk, cream, eggs, vanilla salt and pepper.
Add the onion mixture, the sausage, bacon and the cheese to the cream mixture and combine.
Add the bread to the baking dish and pour the mixture over the top and let it all soak in.
Sprinkle with paprika. Bake for 1 hour until completely set.
Serve with a fruit salad.

Recipe from Devany Vickery-Davidson

Recipe: Liliko'i Bars

Preheat oven to 350°F.
Lightly spray 9 x 13 pan with butter flavored non-stick spray. Set aside.

Crust:
2 c flour
1/2 c sugar
1 c butter

Optional: up to 1 c finely chopped nuts (I use a hand-crank nut grinder)
Mix flour and sugar together. Cut butter into flour mixture until it looks like cornmeal.
Pour into pan and just level evenly on bottom of pan. Try not to press down on it.
Bake in oven for 20-30 minutes until almost nut brown. Prepare filling while crust is baking.

Filling:
3/4 c pure liliko'i juice
2 Tbsp. lemon juice (Optional)
1 1/4 c sugar
4 eggs
1/4 c flour
1/2 tsp. baking powder

Put all ingredients except baking powder into blender or food processor
and blend/process until smooth. Just before crust comes out of the oven,
add baking powder and blend/process until fully mixed in with rest of liquid.
Remove pan from oven, pour filling over hot crust and return to oven. Bake for 10 minutes.
Turn oven OFF and leave pan in oven another 12 minutes.
Remove pan and let cool. Serve at room temperature or chill in 'fridge.

Baker's notes:
After much experimentation, I've learned that if you don't press the crust mixture
down in the pan it will come out easier when you go to serve it.
The nuts add a little more crunch to the overall texture which is not necessarily
to everyone's liking. The lemon juice in the filling
is to cut some of the cloying aftertaste of the liliko'i, which can be quite strong.
I like a softer, more custardy filling and so the residual heat of the oven cooling slightly
towards the end of the baking time produces that result.

Created by Big Island caterer Francine Morales-McCully

Recipe: Mauna Kea Chevre and Mango Quiche
(Serving for 16)

Ingredients:
4 Whole Eggs
4 Egg Yolks
1/2 Qt. Cream
Salt & Pepper (to taste)
4 Mangoes (peeled & sliced)
Directions:
Bring cream to boil.
Temper eggs.

Pour into pie shell and then top with mango.
Top with sauteed Maui onion & Mauna Kea Chevre (goat cheese).
Bake at 325 degrees for approximately 45 minutes.
Remove from oven and let cool before serving.

from Merriman's Chef Neil Murphy

Wasabi Cream Sauce

Ingredients:
2 tablespoons shallots, minced
½ cup dry white wine
½ cup fish stock
¾ cup heavy cream
1 tablespoon fresh, grated wasabi
1 tablespoon water
2 teaspoons cornstarch
+ 2 teaspoons cold water, to thicken sauce

To Prepare:
Put the wine and shallots in a large sauce pan
and cook over medium heat until most of the wine has evaporated.
Add the fish stock, heavy cream, and wasabi.
Bring the sauce to a boil, then lower the heat to medium-low.
Add the cornstarch slurry and stir.
The sauce should thicken nicely; whisk to combine and remove any lumps.
This sauce would go good with the crusted mahimahi found on page 173 in lieu of the crab bisque.
Put the sauce on the plate first and cooked fish on top. Garnish with parsley.

from Chef Colin Nakagawa, The Seaside Restaurant a & Aqua Farm - Hilo

Recipe: O's Bistro's Ahi Loco Moco,
Veggie Fried Rice and Lemon Ginger Shoyu Butter

2 5-oz Ahi Steaks (your choice to season, sear or grill)
4 Large Organic Eggs ... your style, poached, fried, scrambled

Veggie Fried Rice
2 c. Leftover Rice (your choice)
1 tsp. Sesame Oil
1/2 Tbsp. Vegetable Oil
1 Tbsp. Shoyu (preferably Raw)

1-1/2 c. Mix of garlic, mushrooms, onion,
spinach, etc (veggies) Green Onion and cilantro to taste and for garnish
First rub the rice with the oils and sesame for a uniform flavor and color.
Saute your choice of veggies, except the spinach, in a very small amount of oil
until al dente. Add seasoning by adding more shoyu or salt.

Lemon Ginger Shoyu Butter Sauce
1 lg peeled and minced shallot
2 cloves Garlic, peeled and minced
1 knuckle peeled and grated fresh with ginger root
1/2 c. White Wine
Juice of 1/2 sm. Lemon (or to taste)
1/4 lb. Unsalted Butter

Shoyu to taste and Salt if needed to balance taste.
In a small sauce pan simmer the shallot, garlic and ginger
in the wine with lemon juice reducing liquid by half to two-thirds.
Then add cold cubes of butter to the reduction,
whisking quickly to emulsify the sauce ... Adjust the seasoning to taste.
Arrange in either an udon or pasta bowl:
A mound of Rice, seared or grilled Fish then the eggs...
spoon a small amount of the butter sauce over the eggs and fish.
Garnish with Sprigs of Cilantro and Julienne Green Onion...
a small dish of sauce accompanying the dish is favored.

recipe from Chef Amy Ferguson, CaterHawaii.com

Join the Quest

Recipe Table of Contents

Addison & Highsmith

**Other fine works of fiction
from Addison & Highsmith Publishers,
a division of Histria Books:**

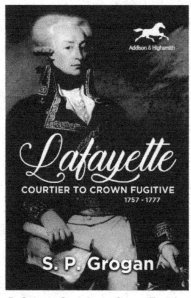

*Lafayette: Courtier to Crown Fugitive,
1757-1777 by S.P. Grogan*

*Vegas Die: A Quest Murder Mystery
by S.P. Grogan*

Visit

HistriaBooks.com